There's something between us, you can't deny it.

Melisande growled low with frustration. *I don't want you, Feral. I don't want your voice in my head. I don't want anything to do with you. And that isn't ever going to change.*

For a moment he was silent. Then the fox paused and swung his head back, watching her. *Is your antipathy toward me or toward all Ferals?*

Does it matter?

You wound me, pet. My heart may never heal. Once again, the fox paused to look back at her. Then his mouth snapped closed and he eyed her with an intensity that told her he hadn't given up. Not at all.

He wouldn't succeed. But he scared her all the same. Because he stirred things inside her that had lain dormant for so long she'd thought them gone forever.

Things that could, if she wasn't careful, destroy her.

Praise for the
FERAL WARRIORS

"The Feral Warriors are hot."
New York Times bestselling author Rachel Vincent

"Magic and passion run wild in this steamy paranormal series . . . Palmer piles on the searing kisses and passionate interludes as she sets up an intriguing world."

Publishers Weekly

"Fans of out-of-the-ordinary paranormal romance are going to add Pamela Palmer's Feral Warrior series to their keeper list!"
New York Times bestselling author Maggie Shayne

By Pamela Palmer

Vamp City Novels
A BLOOD SEDUCTION

Feral Warriors Novels
A LOVE UNTAMED
ECSTASY UNTAMED
HUNGER UNTAMED
RAPTURE UNTAMED
PASSION UNTAMED
OBSESSION UNTAMED
DESIRE UNTAMED

PAMELA PALMER

A LOVE UNTAMED

A FERAL WARRIORS NOVEL

AVON

An Imprint of HarperCollinsPublishers

AVON BOOKS
An Imprint of HarperCollins*Publishers*
10 East 53rd Street
New York, New York 10022-5299

Copyright © 2013 by Pamela Palmer
ISBN 978-0-06-210751-0
www.avonromance.com

First Avon Books mass market printing: January 2013

Avon Trademark Reg. U.S. Pat. Off. and in Other Countries, Marca Registrada, Hecho en U.S.A.
HarperCollins® is a registered trademark of HarperCollins Publishers.

Printed in the U.S.A.

10 9 8 7 6 5 4 3 2 1

To my father, Stew Palmer, one of the finest men
I've ever known. Thanks, Dad, for everything.

Acknowledgments

A huge thanks to Laurin Wittig and Anne Shaw Moran for love, laughter, support, and sisterhood, and for your help in raising the book babies.

Thanks also to May Chen, Robin Rue, Pamela Spengler-Jaffee, Jessie Edwards, Chelsey Emmelhainz, Sara Schwager, Kim Castillo, Tom Egner, and all the wonderful people at Avon Books who've played a critical part in getting my books on the shelves and into the hands of readers. You're a dream to work with.

Most especially, thanks to my wonderful readers. I adore you, every one.

And to my family, as always, my love and gratitude.

A LOVE UNTAMED

Chapter One

Eight days ago

Kieran twisted, avoiding the male's kick, then swung out with his own, slamming his opponent to the hardwood floor.

"Good, try!" Kieran said, holding his hand out to the male and helping him up. "Again."

The male groaned but nodded, shoving a sweaty lock of hair out of his eyes. The gym, on the outskirts of Dublin, was unairconditioned and hot despite the late-spring temperatures outside, smelling of sweat and hard work. Inside, more than forty new recruits sparred.

As the two men circled, Kieran called to the larger group, "Watch your opponent's hands. Always know where they are. Hands are a Mage's most dangerous weapons." He didn't have to add that a Mage could enthrall a Therian with a single touch, rendering him a puppet to be turned on his fellows. Or to be captured or killed. The Therians had been at war with the Mage for millennia and his recruits knew it all too well.

Fortunately, Therians had the advantage of muscle mass few Mage possessed. Once they'd had far more advantage than that. At one time, all Therians had been shape-shifters, able to shift into their animals at will. But those days ended five millennia ago when, for a brief period of time, the Mage and Therians banded together, mortgaging the bulk of their power to defeat the Daemons, who were terrorizing the Earth. They'd succeeded. The Daemons had been locked in a mystical blade from which they'd never escaped. But the power the two races had mortgaged never returned. When the dust had settled, only one Therian of each of the animal lines had retained the power of his or her animal, and the ability to shift. Those few had banded together, the strongest and finest of the race, and become known as the Feral Warriors.

The rest of the Therians, Kieran included, shifted only in their dreams, fighting their enemies the human way. With their fists and knives.

His opponent leaped at him, too high, and Kieran

easily flipped him over his shoulder. "Keep your center of gravity low, boyo. Try it again."

The male looked thirty but could be anywhere from twenty-five to a thousand or more, as all immortals ceased to age once they were fully grown. The man hunched over for a moment, catching his breath. "Any word on the new fox?"

The fox Feral Warrior had died last month in a Mage attack of some sort. The Feral Warriors tended to be a tight-knit and tight-lipped bunch, and the details had never been leaked to the greater Therian community. But the death itself had not been kept a secret. When one Feral died, the animal spirit flew to the next in the line, the strongest Therian with that animal's shifter DNA, marking him to take the dead shifter's place. The marking could take weeks, even months, but ultimately, another would be marked. And the entire Therian world was abuzz with excitement, each of them wondering if he . . . or she . . . might be the one.

Kieran shook his head. "No word." A flicker of hope danced in his chest because the truth was, it *could* be him. Unlike most Therians, he *knew* he possessed fox-shifter DNA. After five millennia, most Therians no longer knew their ancestral makeup. But Kieran's father was old, born only a few hundred years after the Sacrifice. And his father's mother had been born a fox shifter.

Both had been talented intuitives, often knowing

things before they happened. Kieran had inherited that ability to a lesser degree. To a fairly useless degree, unfortunately. His own gut offered him truths that were generally so vague as to be worse than nothing.

He could be the one marked this time if the animal spirit deemed him the strongest and finest of those who possessed the fox-shifter DNA. The thought filled him both with a wild excitement and mixed emotions. Being chosen would be a tremendous honor. And being able to shape-shift as his ancestors had? *Incredible*. But being chosen to become a Feral Warrior was a life's commitment. There was no turning it down and no going back. All Feral Warriors lived together with the Radiant, the one woman marked by the goddess to pull the energies from the earth that empowered the Ferals. The new fox would have to move to Great Falls, Virginia, and live at Feral House with the other shifters. He would become part of a greater whole, one of the warriors on the front lines of the battle to protect the world from the threat of the Daemons' return.

Kieran looked up at the wooden rafters above, his mind across the Atlantic. All things considered, would he choose to be the new fox shifter if the choice were his?

With a low chuckle, he nodded to himself. Hell, yes.

"Switch partners!" he called, and three female recruits rushed him at once, all with that look in their eyes that told him they'd be happy to partner with him in any way he wished. With a grin that encompassed all three, he motioned one to approach him and the other two to face one another. All three laughed. The one he'd chosen to work with gave him a beaming smile that quickly turned to surprise as he swept her feet out from under her. She slammed onto her back on the wood floor with a sharp cry of pain.

He refused to train his recruits on mats. Therians were immortal and indestructible. They might break something in the fall, but they'd heal within a minute. It was better if they learned to deal with the pain right from the start. If they weren't suited to the Therian Guard, he wanted to know it now.

"Keep your mind on the fight, pet," he told the woman, helping her up.

She threw him a look that was part wary smile, part feminine speculation. "You've got good moves, Kieran."

He laughed. "Aye, I do. But the only moves I'm showing you here, pet, are the ones that might keep you alive if the Daemons return. Come now," he said, crouching low and beginning to circle her. "Let's see what you can do."

Fifteen minutes later, he took a break, letting one of his subordinates lead the training as he grabbed his towel and wiped the sweat from his brow and the back of his neck. Jill, one of his lieutenants, joined him, her long legs encased in black fighting pants, her smile as warm and inviting as an Irish pub on a cold winter's night as she handed him a cup of water.

"I've never seen so many female Therians wanting to learn to fight," she murmured. "Most of them have no business here."

Kieran shrugged. "They want to learn how to defend themselves."

Jill snorted. "What they want is a chance at your bed. You're a legend, you know."

Aye, he did, though he was well used to it.

He glanced around the room and found nearly two-thirds of the class paying more attention to his movements than to their opponents'. No coincidence, two-thirds of the class was female. He'd been blessed or cursed—he often couldn't decide which—with the ability to draw females like bees to honey whether he wanted to or not. They watched him with eyes full of invitation, the bolder ones offering themselves freely.

"When the call went out to the Therian enclaves to get their people in fighting shape, every female in the British Isles chose our group to train with. I wonder why," Jill added dryly.

Kieran took a long swig of the cool water and smiled. "You jealous, pet?"

Her expression turned serious. "I could be, Kieran. If I thought I could ever truly win your heart."

Inside, he squirmed. This was the discussion he

loathed, for he truly hated the thought of hurting her. Of hurting any of them.

"I've no heart to give you, Jill," he said quietly, regretfully.

"So you've told me many a time, but you're wrong, Kieran. You've a big heart in that finely hewn chest. You just haven't met the right female, yet. And as much as I wish otherwise, I'm not the one."

No, she wasn't. No woman was, as he tried to tell them all. He'd watched one woman whom he'd loved more than his own life die. It didn't matter that she'd been his sister, not his lover. Over the centuries, he'd watched good friends take mates in a ritual that bound one to the other body and soul, and watched as one died and the one left behind suffered untold agony, unable to fully live again. Mating bonds between the immortals was far more than a simple promise to love and cherish. They could not be severed. No, he would never take a mate. If losing his sister could hurt so much, how much more would losing a wife? He'd long ago decided that love of any kind led to heartache and nothing more. He was better off without it.

He hooked his arm around Jill's neck and placed a kiss on her cheek. "You're a fine thing, pet. And I love you in my way, you know that."

"Aye, I know it, Kieran. I know it."

Releasing Jill, he turned his attention back to the

class, ignoring the females, too many of whom were still paying him more mind than they were their opponents. Two of the males caught his attention, one of the smaller men whom Kieran had already pegged as a future leader, and a beefy Welshman with a look in his eye that Kieran didn't like—a hard gleam Kieran suspected revealed a mean streak. Either the attitude or the male were going to have to go.

As Kieran watched, the Welshman's opponent, quick and tough, managed to throw the bigger man. A flash caught Kieran's eye, light reflecting on metal, as the Welshman, still on his arse, swung out. A knife, dammit. The blade sliced through the smaller man's thigh in a spray of blood.

Feck.

Kieran reached him in a dozen angry strides, slammed his fist through the wanker's face as he ripped the knife from his hand, then threw the blade hard, burying it deep in one of the wood ceiling beams.

"What did I tell you on the first day of training?" he shouted. "No knives! No. Knives."

The Welshman leaped to his feet, fury in his eyes. And suddenly those eyes began to change to animal eyes as only a true shifter's ever would.

Bloody hell.

As Kieran stared, fangs dropped from the blackguard's mouth, and the wanker began to laugh. Though he'd yet to shift, and wouldn't until he'd been brought into his animal during a ritual performed by the rest of the Feral Warriors, it was clear the fox shifter had been chosen. Even the newly marked could pull fangs and claws—what the shifters called *going feral*.

He stared at the wanker. The *finest* in the fox shifter line? Well, bloody fecking hell.

The new Feral Warrior swung, for once catching Kieran off guard. Too late, Kieran realized that the hand coming for him was now filled with sharp claws. He felt those claws rip down his face, from temple to jaw, removing skin and muscle, showering him in his own warm blood.

Pain burned through his face as he healed. Fury roared through his mind at the fact that this asshole had been chosen to defend the race. Over *him*.

With a growl, Kieran threw a punch, intending to show the bastard he could still take him, but his hand didn't . . . *wouldn't* . . . close and he wound up scratching the Welshman instead. No, not scratching . . . *clawing*. He stared at the flesh now hanging from the man's shocked face. And at the bloody claws where a moment ago his own fingernails had been.

What the feck? Had he turned into a bloody monster?

His tongue snagged on the teeth suddenly crowding his mouth. No, not teeth. *Fangs*. Like the Welshman, he'd gone feral.

But . . . *two* new Feral Warriors? Impossible . . . unless another had died without them knowing.

Dismay, shock, and elation all warred within him, all trying to find purchase.

People crowded around them, gaping, silent. It wasn't every day a Therian got to see a Feral Warrior. Kieran himself had never laid eyes on one, not in the entirety of his over three hundred years. Now, apparently, he was one.

The others all started talking at once.

"I thought only the fox had died."

"Maybe the Ferals were attacked again, and we didn't know."

"You have to call Feral House."

Kieran met the Welshman's gaze, glad to see the male's eyes were once more human, his fangs and claws retracted. Kieran's own slid away as well.

Jill joined him, her eyes wide in her face, drenched in dismay. "You're leaving, then. To join the Ferals."

"Aye." The thought sent a thrill through his body.

"It's a dangerous business," she said, her voice uneven. "They're on the front line of the battle. Two are dead."

But the front line was exactly where he wanted to be. Fighting back evil, making a difference. He met the Welshman's gaze and saw again that look in his eyes that he didn't like. Maybe the male was one of those who didn't take well to authority, in any form. Or maybe he was just an asshole. Either way, apparently they were now brothers. For the rest of their immortal lives.

As he pulled out his phone to call his enclave and get the number for Feral House, goose bumps rose on his arms, the telltale sign that his intuition was kicking in with some tidbit of knowledge that would likely be of little use.

Wrong.

Wrong? And what in the hell did that mean? That he was wrong in thinking his "gift" would be of little use? Wrong in trying to call Feral House right now? The time in Washington, D.C., was . . . about 7:30 A.M. Too early?

Or was his gut trying to tell him something more profound?

Who knew? There was no use worrying about it. What was done was done. He'd been marked to join the exclusive ranks of the Feral Warriors, and there was no turning it down. Nor did he want to.

All his life, he'd dreamed that this moment might someday be his, and he was damned well going to celebrate it. Even if his gut continued to whisper that one word over and over.

Wrong.

Three days ago

Just before dawn on a cloudless night, Kieran strode through the woods that hung high above the rocky falls of the Potomac River in Great Falls, Virginia, surrounded by Feral Warriors, both old and new. He'd thought that the fact that he and the Welshman had both been marked meant two of the Feral Warriors had died, but that wasn't the case, thank the goddess.

For millennia, there had been twenty-six Feral Warriors, twenty-six animal shape-shifters left in the world, each of whom shifted into a different, unique animal. Then, six centuries ago, seventeen of them fell into a spirit trap, never to return. The spirit trap had separated the men from their animal spirits, killing the men and holding the animal spirits so they could never mark another. For six hundred years, the Feral Warriors had numbered only nine.

Then a week ago, the first of the seventeen lost animal spirits had returned. Word hadn't reached Dublin, but the Ferals had believed their new fox shifter had arrived. Instead, the new Feral had shifted into a saber-toothed cat, one of the seventeen lost animals. As the Ferals rejoiced, eight more had been marked and made their way to Feral House including Kieran and the Welshman. Tonight was their Renascence, the ritual that would bring them into their animals for the first time, revealing which animal had chosen each.

Kieran strode down to the cliffs beside Jag, one of the original Ferals, and Ewan, another of the newly marked, one he'd fought beside on both sides of the Atlantic, on and off for decades. A good man, thank the goddess. If they'd all been like the Welshman,

Kieran might have begun to wonder if the animal spirits truly marked the best in the line, as had always been claimed. The new Ferals were, by and large, an unruly lot, but the originals showed every sign of living up to the legend. From what Kieran had seen, they were a good, honorable bunch and a true brotherhood.

"How does this work?" Kieran asked Jag, as the band of more than a dozen immortal males strode, shirtless and barefoot, along the rocks. Lyon, Chief of the Ferals, brought up the rear with his mate, Kara, their Radiant.

"We'll call a mystic circle upon the goddess stone in order to hide what goes on from any humans who happen by. Then it's ritual time, pretty boy." Jag grinned. "I don't want to spoil the surprise."

A hard thrill coursed through Kieran. He was about to shift into an animal for the very first time. How many times had he done so in his dreams? How many times had he wondered what it must have been like in those ancient days, when all Therians shifted? Too many to count.

As he climbed down the rocks, he wondered which of the animal spirits had marked him. He hoped the fox, for that was the ancestry he knew. His mother had possessed no knowledge of her own Therian heritage. Few Therians ever mated, and virtually none were monogamous unless they did. His mother had never known who her father was, let alone his deep animal

DNA. Which meant, Kieran could potentially have been marked by any of the seventeen animal spirits as well as the fox.

He'd find out soon enough.

As the original Ferals gathered around Kara, Lyon turned to the newcomers. "Stay back until we come for you. If you touch Kara when she's radiant, without an armband, she'll kill you."

"You should see her when she glows," Ewan said quietly, leaning close. "It's a sight you won't forget."

Kieran grinned. "It's a sight we'll become well used to."

Ewan chuckled, his excitement matching Kieran's own. "That we will."

As Kieran watched, Kara lifted her arms and literally began to glow as if she'd swallowed a small piece of the sun. She was such a sweet thing, pretty and quite young, not even a true thirty yet. She wore a slinky ritual gown and flip-flops, her hair in a ponytail. And he liked her immensely.

Lyon watched his mate with the devotion of a truly besotted mate, at once fiercely protective and tenderly in love.

Ritual words were spoken, blood was let, and suddenly Kieran felt a blast of energy power through his body in a euphoric rush. Lights sparkled all around him, and he found himself standing at knee level, on all fours, his snout protruding from his face. Excitement burst within him, then joy as he turned his head, eyeing his red fur, bushy tail, and very foxlike body.

He was now surrounded by a polar bear where Ewan had stood, a crocodile in place of the Welshman, a grizzly, snow leopard, white tiger, lynx, and even an eagle.

"Shift back," Kougar told them.

Kieran imagined himself once more standing on two feet, and in another shower of sparkling lights, in another euphoric rush, he found himself a man once more.

"Henceforth, you will be known as . . ." Kougar's straight arm came down, pointing from one new Feral to the next, starting with him. "Fox, Grizz, Polaris, Lepard, Witt, Eigle, Lynks, Croc."

Ewan slapped him on the back. "What do you say, Fox?" He laughed heartily. "The ladies will love that."

Kieran . . . no, he was Fox now . . . grinned and slapped the polar bear shifter on the back in return. "I'd say it's a fine night, Polaris. A fine night indeed."

As Ewan turned to congratulate the others, Jag approached, slapping forearms with Kieran in the traditional Feral greeting. "Welcome to the pack, Fox-man."

"Kara!"

At Lyon's alarmed tone, Kieran and Jag whirled, watching as Lyon swept a fainting Kara into his arms. None of the other new Ferals seemed to notice, but the originals and Fox all gathered close.

"What's the matter with her?" Fox asked.

Kara, rousing, curled her arm around Lyon's neck. "I'm okay. It's just . . . the rituals. It's like they're sucking me dry."

Nine collective breaths released at once.

Lyon tipped his head against the Radiant's. "You scared me."

Smiling softly, Kara pressed her hand to her mate's cheek. "I love you."

"My heart."

Kieran . . . Fox . . . watched them, wondering at the courage . . . and foolishness . . . it took to care so much, to love so deeply. A mistake he refused to ever make himself.

Chapter Two

Two days ago

Fox strode through Feral House, his boots clicking on the hardwood floor, the golden fox-head armband that had appeared during his first shift tight around his upper arm, his mind in turmoil. For days his gut had continued to whisper that same fecking word. *Wrong.*

And now he thought he knew why. Hell, everything was wrong. The situation at Feral House could not be worse.

Last night, the new Ferals, those who'd been marked by the lost animal spirits, had risen up against the rest of them, attempting to slaughter them. Jag and Paenther had been badly injured, badly enough that all had feared for their lives, but they were pulling through. One of the new Ferals, Eigle, was dead. And the rest were gone. Even Ewan . . . Polaris.

It was all too clear that the evil Mage were behind this. Somehow, the Mage had freed the trapped animal spirits and infected them with some kind of dark magic that had not only kept them from marking the best of the line but had somehow managed to control the resulting Ferals, turning them into their own evil Feral army.

The good Feral Warriors were in a hell of a mess.

Thank the goddess he'd been marked by the fox and not one of the seventeen lost spirits. As he strode down the hallway, he saw Kougar coming out of the media room.

"Any news?" Fox asked. Kougar was a cold-eyed warrior with a mustache and goatee that made him look more than a little unapproachable. But he'd welcomed Fox warmly and given him no reason to think he wouldn't share whatever he knew.

"Jag and Paenther will be returning soon. And we may be able to cure the new Ferals of that dark infection."

"That's brilliant. Then the Mage plot will have failed."

Kougar plucked at his goatee. "Not entirely. Not all those marked were the best of their line. Perhaps none of them were."

While Fox had the highest respect for Ewan and

hated that his friend had been caught up in this mess, he could only feel relief that the asshole Welshman wasn't actually meant to be marked. His faith in the Feral Warriors as a whole, and his pride in being one of them, had been restored.

"The Shaman believes that my mate, Ariana, may have the solution buried inside the wealth of knowledge in her head," Kougar continued.

"That's a bloody intriguing comment."

Kougar looked at him. "Are you aware that she's Ilina? The queen of the Ilinas?"

Fox nodded. "I heard. Which is another bloody intriguing comment. For a thousand years, the world thought the Ilinas extinct." He cocked his head at the far-more-senior Feral. "You knew the truth."

"No. I only learned the truth recently."

"Where have they been all this time?"

"Most of them in the Crystal Realm, their castle in the clouds."

Fox knew he meant that literally.

"Ariana will be arriving momentarily."

Even as Kougar said the words, Fox smelled a whiff of pine, then watched, awestruck, as two petite beauties materialized out of thin air.

Ilinas.

The one was a pretty brunette dressed in jeans and boots and leather jacket. The way she looked at Kougar, with a lover's smile, told him she must be Ariana.

But it was the other one who caught Fox's attention and clamped her pretty little fist tight around it. Her hair as light as her companion's was dark, she was dressed in a timeless outfit that marked her a warrior—leggings and tunic that skimmed graceful curves, a knife hanging from the belt at her slender waist, golden hair falling in a thick braid down her back. She appeared as delicate as a doll—her head small and lovely, her nose pert, her mouth a pretty, petal pink.

But when she glanced his way, sapphire eyes pinned him, eyes as hard as blue diamonds, and, suddenly, she didn't seem delicate at all.

As their gazes held, his heart went still, then began beating like a herd of spooked cattle. Fire leaped into her eyes, but not the kind of fire he was used to. There was no warmth in those sapphire eyes, no desire. Only a bright, cutting heat that promised to flay the flesh from his bones.

The beauty jerked her gaze from his, turning toward Kougar and his mate.

Hawke and Faith joined Fox. He hadn't even seen them enter the hallway.

"Amazing that they still exist, isn't it?" Fox murmured to the pair, unable to tear his gaze away from the Ilina. She was like a little spitfire, eyes snapping with anger, that pretty mouth twisted with annoyance. Still . . . "She's a fine thing, the blonde."

"That's Melisande," Hawke said quietly beside him.

Melisande. A lovely name for an intriguing woman.

"Apparently she tried to kill Lyon a couple of weeks ago," Hawke continued.

Fox glanced at him with surprise. "And he let her live?" His gaze returned to the female with a new appreciation. So she knew how to use that sword. No, not delicate at all.

"That was my reaction the first time I heard. It was something of a misunderstanding, and they've called a truce of sorts. But the woman apparently has a chip on her shoulder the size of the South Pole when it comes to Ferals. That one's trouble with a capital T."

Sapphire eyes cut to him, then away again, without an ounce of interest. Without a modicum of warmth. "Chips can be knocked off."

Faith snorted beside him. "So can heads."

Fox chuckled. "She hasn't met the right Feral yet, is all."

Hawke clasped him on the shoulder. "You'd have more luck taming a tornado."

Kougar turned to them. "Fox, Faith, I'd like you to meet Ariana, Queen of the Ilinas and my mate. And her second, Melisande."

The blonde scowled, and he wondered if she was really as cold as she pretended to be. If he'd seen only her, he might wonder if that were typical of her race, but Ariana's eyes radiated warmth and love along with strength.

Melisande interested him mightily. His gaze dropped to her mouth, a paradox if ever there was one. At once hard enough to flay a man alive and yet shaped like a lover's dream—the bottom lip plump and kissable, the top sculpted in pale pink perfection.

Ariana strode forward and introductions were made. Then she turned back toward Kougar. "Where's the Shaman? I understand we have work to do."

As Ariana started back to the doorway, where Melisande and Kougar waited, Fox followed, eyeing Melisande, turning on the charm. Could such a cold woman be charmed? The thought made him smile. It had been too long since any female had presented a challenge.

With each step he took, the woman grew more beautiful. Her skin was a flawless cream, as soft, he was certain, as her eyes were hard. Her lashes, a darker gold than her hair, perfectly framed those magnificent eyes. Her body, though small, was perfectly proportioned, her curves neither too slender nor too round. And his hands itched to clutch her waist and pull her against him.

As he drew close, her scent, of wild heather, teased his nose, nearly drowning him in pleasure.

"Melisande, is it?" he asked, drawing on the full force of his Irish upbringing. "A beautiful name for a beautiful woman."

Sapphire eyes snapped at him with disbelief, cer-

tainly not the usual reaction to his attention, but he
played the game the way he knew how. He held out
his hand to her, uncertain whether she would meet him
halfway and suspecting that if she did, it would be with
a huff or a roll of pretty blue eyes. Either would be fine
as long as he got to touch her.

"I'm Fox, Melisande. It's a pleasure to meet you."

"That's what you think." Her voice was music laced
with acid. She ignored his outstretched hand, her eyes
narrowing as she smiled at him, but there was nothing
pleasant about that smile. Hawke's words came back to
him, that he'd have more luck taming a tornado, and it
occurred to him that he might finally have come across
a female who was immune to his charms.

"Mel," Ariana warned.

The petite blonde flung her empty hand toward him
as if it were not empty at all, as if she meant to toss a
fireball in his face.

Instead, exquisite sexual pleasure rushed through his
body on a blast so strong, so pure, that he nearly came
right there in the middle of the hallway. On a groan,
he arched his back, his eyes dropping closed as the
pleasure roared through him, wave after wave of pure
ecstasy.

When he could move again, his eyes snapped open,
and he straightened to find the most fascinating woman
he'd ever met staring at him in wide-eyed disbelief, her
mouth forming a horrified O.

A grin spread slowly across his face, his gaze locking with hers. The next time he felt that kind of rapture in her presence, he'd be deep inside of her, and she'd be screaming her release right along with him.

Go to hell shimmered in Melisande's eyes as if she'd heard his silent promise, her mouth snapping closed, once more tightening into a hard line. With a low growl of fury, the beauty disappeared, misting away.

Fox began to laugh.

"What did you do to her?" Kougar asked, clearly puzzled.

Fox shook his head. "I've no bloody idea."

"Watch your step," Ariana warned softly. "Melisande is a good person, but she has a violent and justified hatred of Therians. While she's obligated to honor my alliance with the Ferals, she's unpredictable. She won't try to kill you. But that's about all I can guarantee. And if you hurt her, even that's off the table."

"Point taken." But the grin hovered at the edges of his mouth, the pleasure still coursing through his body. He had no intention of hurting her. Not at all. What he had in mind would have her arching with as much pleasure as she'd just given him. And more. Far more.

As Ariana left to speak to the Shaman, Lyon and Kara strode down the hallway toward them. Lyon caressed his mate's hair. "Are you up to it?"

"Of course." Kara smiled, gazing up at her mate with adoration. In the short time he'd been at Feral House,

Fox had come to realize that the love between the Ferals' chief and their Radiant was the beating heart of the house and the bedrock that held them all together regardless of what crisis they found themselves in. And they'd faced one crisis after another since his arrival.

Kara turned front again, catching Fox watching them. She smiled at him sweetly, a woman impossible not to adore. In her jeans and bare feet, she exuded a girl-next-door wholesomeness at odds with her role as the most powerful of the nonshifting Therians. In some ways, she was more powerful even than the shifters, for without her, within a couple of months, they'd begin to lose the power of their animals.

"Radiance," Lyon said, squeezing his mate's shoulder gently.

Though it wasn't necessary to take a shot of radiance directly from the source—Kara empowered them through proximity—none of them ever turned down an invitation for that pure energy rush.

As Kara held her hands out at her sides, Kougar stepped forward and curled his fingers around one slender wrist, a smile for her in his eyes. Hawke tugged on her ponytail like a fond older brother, then wrapped his hand around her other wrist. As Lyon slid his hand beneath Kara's ponytail, pressing his palm against the back of her neck in a gesture at once possessive and tender, Fox stepped forward to kneel at her feet, slipping his hand around one bare ankle.

"Little Radiant," Lyon said softly, and, a moment later, Kara lit up, her skin glowing brightly enough to light a darkened room. *Going radiant,* they called it.

Warm, lush energy rushed through Fox's body—the Earth's energy, the lifeblood of a Feral Warrior, channeled through the golden armband that had appeared during his first shift.

But it was the rush of a different energy, one of pure rapture that he couldn't get out of his mind. Nor could he think of anything but the sapphire-eyed beauty who'd delivered it. And how he was going to coax her into his bed.

Melisande stormed down the Grand Corridor of the Ilinas palace in the Crystal Realm, grabbing an ancient vase off its pedestal and smashing it on the emerald floor with a roar of fury that set the chandeliers to swaying, the torches on the crystal walls to flickering, and the few Ilina sisters who'd been keeping a wary eye on her fleeing in mist.

"Dammit!"

Even now, far from Feral House, that shifter's face swam in her mind.

Fox.

She'd noticed him the moment she'd misted into Feral House at Ariana's side, though what female with eyes in her head wouldn't have? The male was appallingly good-looking, a Greek god with golden waves of hair falling to broad shoulders framing a face of true perfection—high cheekbones, a straight patrician nose, a strong, chiseled jaw, and eyes the blue of a summer sky. Dressed in black military pants and an army green tee, he'd looked like the warrior he undoubtedly was. And, oh, that T-shirt had fit him well, pulling snuggly across his chest and arms, setting off his muscular form to true perfection. Around one thick biceps had curled the golden Feral armband with the head of a fox.

She'd found herself staring at him, unable to look away. That she'd noticed him annoyed her. That he'd caught her staring at him infuriated her. But the worst . . . the very worst . . . was that when their gazes met, she'd felt awareness . . . *awareness* . . . for the first time in *forever*. Her cheeks had heated, her breath had scattered, her pulse had raced and had yet to calm.

The remnants of a Ming vase crunched under her heels as she paced, fury vibrating through every pore of her body, making her hands clench and unclench at her sides.

The damned Feral had noticed her reaction to him and acted upon it, flirting with her like she was a normal, sex-starved Ilina. She'd meant to show him exactly what she thought of him. He should have felt pain. *Pain*. Instead, he'd felt pleasure, arching as if he were in the throes of orgasm.

The breath caught in her lungs, and she sank back against the nearest wall, one hand curved protectively around her stomach, the other palming her forehead. She was still there moments later, her mind reeling, when her queen and friend materialized at her side.

Ariana touched her shoulder. "What happened down there, Mel?" she asked worriedly.

Melisande glared at her. "I'm going to kill him." At Ariana's raised eyebrow, Melisande rolled her eyes. "I'm *not* going to kill him. But I want to. You have no idea how much I want to."

Ariana studied her. "He's the one, isn't he? The one you can't intentionally harm. The one suited to be your mate."

Melisande started to laugh, then choked instead, pushing away from the wall. "*Never.* I want no male. Especially not a shifter." She'd hated the shifters for so long, both the Feral Warriors who were able to access the power of their animals and the nonshifting Therians. They were all shifters to her. All equally vile.

Well, maybe not vile. Not all of them. As much as she hated to admit it, the current batch of Ferals appeared to be honorable enough. The nine originals, at least. Ariana certainly thought so. And she couldn't deny they were fighting to keep Satanan and his Daemon horde from rising again, which any creature of the world appreciated.

But that didn't alter the fact that her history with shifters was a bad one. She'd spent most of her life hating them. Now, her traitorous body wanted one of them. She dug her fingers into her scalp and met Ariana's sympathetic gaze.

"I don't want to feel this way."

Ariana's eyes widened. "You want him."

"No. *Yes.*" *Heaven help her.* For centuries, thanks to a traitorous shifter and his horrid clan, she'd been unable to bear a man's touch. The thought of it still filled her with dread. But her body had somehow awakened again despite that. And it *wanted*.

She shook her head, eyeing her friend helplessly. "When I blasted Fox . . . the pleasure he felt . . . *I felt it, too.*" Not like he had, not . . . *orgasmic*. But even now, tendrils of heat swam through her blood, dampening her in secret places.

"I don't want this!" she shouted at the top of her lungs, gripping her head because, even as her body ached, her mind reeled with horror at the thought of lying with a man again. Memories she'd locked down for so long were beginning to stir, memories of soul-destroying betrayal, and of soul-stealing pain.

"Why now?" she cried. "Why a shifter? Why *him*?"

"Mel . . . I'm sorry."

None of this would have happened if Ariana hadn't found Kougar again, if she hadn't married him, forcing the Ilinas and the Feral Warriors into this unholy alliance, and the thought hung thickly in the air between them, unspoken.

"Is there anything I can do?" Ariana asked quietly.

Melisande met her friend's gaze. "Leave Kougar and forbid us from ever going near the Ferals again."

A glint of dark humor gleamed in Ariana's eyes. "Other than that." Ariana stepped closer, her eyes soft and serious. "Mel, if you need to step down from your post for a while, I completely understand."

"No." The word shot from Melisande's mouth before her brain fully processed the ramifications of Ariana's offer.

"Think about it," Ariana said kindly, then misted away, leaving Melisande standing among the wreckage of the shattered vase and the remnants of her own hard-won equilibrium.

With a groan, she leaned back against the nearest wall, closing her eyes, forcing herself to consider her options. Because stepping down from her post as Ariana's second-in-command would mean no longer having to go anywhere near Feral House. Or the far-too-disturbing Fox.

But there was no real choice, she knew that. She was by far the strongest of Ariana's warriors, by far the best able to protect her queen and her race. Ironically, the only one she trusted as much was Kougar. He would give up his life for his mate and had nearly done so not long ago.

But with the Mage determined to free the Daemons back into the world, none of them could be too careful. Melisande sighed. She had no choice, not really. Dodging Feral House, and Fox, meant dodging her responsibilities, and that was something she would never do.

Perhaps if she ignored the too-handsome shifter, he'd go away. She snorted. After she'd nearly driven him to sexual release with a flick of her hand? Not likely. He knew she hadn't meant for that to happen. Worse, he knew she'd been affected as well. The knowledge had gleamed plain as day in the predatory look in his eyes.

No, he wasn't likely to lose interest anytime soon. The male was bent on seduction. And her defenses were badly shaken.

One day ago

Kara sat on the floor of Skye and Paenther's bedroom, playing with Skye's pets, smiling at the antics of the black miniature schnauzer, Lady, and the tabby kitten, Tramp, as they simultaneously attacked a vicious chew toy. She was glad for the distraction.

Skye stood at the window, worry drifting off her in waves, a worry Kara shared, though not to the same razor-sharp degree. Skye's mate, Paenther, was in Poland, having led the team sent to battle the evil Ferals and to stop the ritual they'd begun that appeared designed to empower the High Daemon Satanan. Lyon remained at Feral House with a handful of men and all the Ferals' mates. Feral House had to be protected. But those left behind paced. And worried.

Skye gasped. "Kara . . ."

"What's the matter?" Dear God, if Skye had felt her mating bond break . . .

"Come here. Quick."

Kara jumped up and ran to join Skye at the window. Peering out, she saw movement beyond the trees. Vehicles. Men leaping out in dark clothing.

"Police," Kara gasped. "A SWAT team by the looks of it. Oh, this can't be good." She raced for the door, flung it open, and ran. "Lyon!"

Her mate was halfway up the first flight of stairs before she reached the top step. He was so beautiful, her Lyon, so powerful and regal and sweet. "Cops. A SWAT team. I think they're coming here."

"Foyer, now!" he shouted. The Ferals all possessed far stronger hearing than humans, or even the nonshifting Therians. But if his nearby warriors didn't respond right away, he could contact them in an instant by shifting into his lion and calling to them telepathically.

Lyon held out his hand for her as she raced down the stairs to join him. But when she reached him, he pulled her close, kissed her hair, then said, "Stay here." As he strode into the living room to peer out the front window, Skye joined her.

Not ten seconds later, Tighe, Jag, and Jag's mate, Olivia, came running. Lynks appeared at the top of the stairs and started down at a more sedate pace. One of the two new Ferals who'd been cleared of the dark magic, Lynks was now a full-fledged member of the Feral team even if Lyon had admitted to her in private that the man was too soft to have ever been the one meant to be marked.

"We have trouble," Lyon told them, striding from the living room. "There's a human SWAT team surrounding the house."

In an instant, in a spray of colored lights, Tighe shifted into a fifteen-foot Bengal tiger, undoubtedly to speak to his pregnant mate, Delaney, who was napping upstairs. Ex-FBI, she was believed dead by her human colleagues. It wouldn't do for them to find her alive and well . . . and immortal. Nor could they find Xavier, their cook's assistant for whom the humans had been searching for weeks, or their cook, Pink, who could never pass for human.

Lyon's thoughts were clearly running parallel to Kara's own. His gaze caressed her with that uberprotectiveness that both warmed her and sometimes drove her nuts. "Get the wives, Pink, and Xavier to the deep basement, my heart." His gaze swung to Olivia. "You'll accompany me outside, pretend to be my wife. If the situation gets out of hand, weaken them."

Olivia was not only a warrior who'd fought with the Therian Guard for centuries, but she possessed the rare ability of being able to suck the life force from others.

And she had the control to drain just enough of an opponent's energy to weaken and not kill.

"I'll attempt to cloud the mind of the leader." Lyon's gaze swung to his three warriors even as he began plucking knives from his boots and shoving them in the drawer of the hall table. If they frisked him, he clearly didn't want them finding his weapons. "If they get inside, knock them out and cloud their minds. No deaths."

The last thing they needed was to become a target for the humans. Kara might not be a warrior, but she could certainly understand the ramifications of the humans' believing that the Ferals posed a danger. They'd have to leave Feral House, perhaps battle their way out, likely revealing their immortality. A disaster in every possible way.

Delaney came running down the stairs, a gun strapped to her still slender waist. Less than two months pregnant, she had yet to start showing.

"I'll get Xavier and Pink," Delaney said.

Skye hurried after her, then glanced back at Kara.

Kara nodded. "I'll join you in a minute." Her heart was pounding at the thought of Lyon's walking outside where all those humans would be training guns on him. While the immortals didn't age and healed most wounds almost instantly, none of them were truly immortal. They could die. And the thought of losing Lyon terrified her.

She glanced at Jag, saw the hard granite of his jaw, and knew he was just as worried about Olivia. But he was a warrior first, and what was more, so was Olivia, and he knew it. Olivia was the best woman for this job, and Jag would keep his mouth shut even if it killed him. By the clench of his fists, Kara suspected it just might.

"Police! Come out with your hands up!"

Lyon eyed Olivia and took a deep breath. "Are you ready, wife?" he said, reminding her of her role.

The redhead gave him a decisive nod. "Ready, husband."

"Lynks, cover the back of the house," Tighe called. "Everyone else, out of the foyer." If the cops saw several more large males, it would make it impossible for Lyon to convince them Feral House was merely an innocuous, if huge, family home.

Kara slipped into the hallway that led to both the back of the house and the basement, Lynks following. As he brushed past her, she paused. She knew she should go downstairs. That's what Lyon wanted her to do. But she couldn't make her feet move. Not when Lyon could die out there. Through the now-open front door, she heard him.

"What's the problem, Officer?" Lyon asked.

"Get on the ground. Facedown!"

"There's no need for that," Lyon replied calmly.

Kara wished she could see what was happening. Was he clouding their minds, pushing suggestions into them? He was trying, she knew that much.

"We have a report of gunshots and screaming coming from this house," another cop said.

Kara clenched her teeth against the lie. The house was fully warded against sound. Not even standing on the front doorstep would anyone hear the roar of the animals inside. The "report" was bogus and had probably come from the Mage just to cause them trouble.

"Kara."

Lynks startled her, squeezing her shoulder. "They're going to overrun this place. You've got to hide."

She looked at the new shifter, meeting his nervous gaze. She agreed with Lyon's assessment, that Lynks was not the one meant to be marked. He had the mien of a teacher or an accountant, not a warrior. If the humans got inside, it would be up to Jag and Tighe to contain them. She seriously doubted Lynks would be of much help.

"Okay." Pressing her fist against her tense stomach, she turned and strode to the basement door, slipping inside, surprised when Lynks followed her down instead of closing it behind her.

"I'm just going to check on the others," he said.

Which would leave the back door unprotected. Coward or not, was the man stupid? "Lynks . . ."

But as she turned to urge him to cover his post, he gripped her shoulder, too tight. A hard look leaped into his eyes, alarming her.

"I'm sorry, Kara."

Before she could open her mouth to call for help, he jammed his thumb beneath her ear.

Her world went dark.

Lyon kept his arms in the air, his gaze locked with the human's in front of him. "There's nothing wrong here, Officer. We had the television on, and the windows open."

"I told you it was too loud," Olivia added tartly. She turned to the officer. "He insists on being able to hear the TV anywhere in the house."

Lyon's gaze moved to another of the officers, then another still, catching their gazes, trying to calm them, to steal their wariness. If he could touch them, it would be far easier. But that wasn't a possibility at the moment. He had to get them out of here without incident. Because there were too damn many cop cars. In the distance, gathering along the street, he could see neighbors watching the goings-on with avid eyes. If Feral House were overrun, the cops disappearing inside, he feared there would be no end to this. There were only so many defensive positions the Ferals could take before they were forced to reveal themselves. And that was the one thing they could never do. Once the humans realized shape-shifters and magic-wielders lived among them, the immortals would be forever on the run, hunted to extinction.

"This is all a misunderstanding," Lyon said quietly to

the man in front of him, his gaze once more locked on his. "There's nothing the matter here."

"What's he saying?" one of the others asked a companion on the other side of the driveway. They might be speaking far too quietly for a human to overhear at this distance, but not a Feral. "Why the hell doesn't Jim have him on the ground?"

"Beats me. He's one big motherfucker, isn't he?" The cop yawned. "Damn I'm tired. And I finally got a good night's sleep last night."

The man in front of him yawned as well. Lyon refrained from glancing at Olivia, but he was certain now that she'd begun draining them.

Finally, the tension broke. The officer lowered his gun with a nod. "This was clearly a misunderstanding. I apologize."

Lyon lowered his hands slowly in as nonthreatening a manner as possible. "Apology accepted, Officer."

Lyon held out his hand to Olivia and together they turned and made their way back to the house. He wouldn't breathe easily until the humans piled into their cars and left. The Ferals would have to watch that they didn't return.

"It had to have been the Mage," Olivia said quietly beside him, as they climbed the brick steps to the front door. "But why?"

"That's what we have to find out."

Closing the front door behind them, Lyon met Tighe's

and Jag's gazes, then the three took up posts at the various windows, watching until the cops retreated.

"Where's Lynks?" Lyon asked.

"Keeping an eye out back."

"Good."

Finally, the cops were gone. Tighe pushed away from the window. "I'll get Delaney and the others." Three minutes later, he returned. "Roar, where's Kara?"

Lyon turned from the window with a jerk, a vise clamping around his heart even as he turned inward and found her. He always knew where she was. "She's on the basement stairs," he replied even as he started for the basement himself because, *good goddess,* Tighe had just come that way. And if he hadn't seen her . . .

Lyon broke into a run, nearly tearing the basement door off his hinges in his need to find his mate.

Ice formed at the edges of his thoughts, sweat broke out on the back of his neck. There was a logical explanation. There had to be. But his warrior's instinct said otherwise.

He followed his Finder's sense straight to the closed cellar door in front of which sat Kara's bright green flip-flops.

No. *Goddess, no!* He picked up the shoes, his breath leaving his body as if he'd been slammed in the gut with a battering ram. *"No!"* he roared, and tore open the cellar doors, racing up into the sunshine, Kara's flip-flops clenched in his hands.

"Kara!"

He couldn't see her. He couldn't *sense* her except in the flip-flops now held within his claws. He began to run, listening, searching, his heart battering the walls of his chest.

"Roar." Tighe grabbed his arm. "Get back in your skin. You've gone feral. The cops could still be watching."

Lyon struggled against the raging need to rip apart everything and anything in his path. The ice spreading across his thoughts made it nearly impossible to think. "They've taken her," he growled. "They've taken my mate! My life."

Tighe growled low in agreement. "The cops were the distraction."

Kara.

His head pounded, his mind screamed. His heart broke.

Kara!

He would stop at nothing . . . *nothing* . . . until she was once more safely in his arms.

Chapter
Three

Today

Fox followed Kougar into the huge, formally decorated dining room of Feral House through the back
door, his T-shirt plastered with sweat, his sense of
frustration and helplessness mounting by the hour until
he felt as if he were going to leap out of his skin. For
twenty-four hours, they'd searched every square inch of
the surrounding area and found no sign of Kara and no
clue who'd taken her and Lynks. Unless Lynks was the
one at fault, which made no sense. He'd been cleared of
the darkness. But they just didn't know.

The trail ended a quarter of a mile from the house,

where Kara had undoubtedly been shoved into a vehicle. There were no clues beyond that. None.

In all likelihood, the Mage leader, Inir, had ordered
her snatched for his evil Ferals, who would need her
radiance every bit as much as the nine.

Fox strode to the dining-room table where it sat in
front of the wide bank of windows overlooking the
sunlit, wooded backyard. It was laden with pitchers
of water and lemonade and heaping platters of food—
everything from sandwiches and cookies to thick slabs
of ham and roast beef. Meals had become a thing of
the past as they searched for Kara. They ate when they
could, now.

Jag and Lyon were already there, Jag downing a large
glass of water, Lyon trying to stab a slice of ham with
his fork, but the fork buckled under the clench of his
fist, and he tossed it aside onto a growing pile of crumpled silverware, and tried again.

The Chief of the Ferals was holding on to control,
barely, and it was costing him. His mouth was brack-
eted by lines of strain, his jaw tight enough that Fox
wasn't sure he'd be able to chew the meat if he ever got
it to his mouth. Fox ached for the male. They all did.

Lyon barely looked up as they entered, his eyes without a glimmer of hope that they'd found any sign of
Kara. If anyone had, they'd all know. Their best hope
was Hawke and Falkyn, who'd returned from Poland
about two hours after the rest of them. They'd taken to

the skies and had yet to return. The worst of it was, after twenty-four hours, the nearby searching was useless, and they all knew it. Kara was far from Feral House by now and had been from the moment they'd realized she was missing. The kidnappers had used a vehicle, and the Ferals not only had no idea what it looked like, but no clue where it was going. Searches on foot and by air weren't going to help, but they had to do something other than sit on their asses.

Rage burned through Fox's blood. Frustration tried to claw its way out of his flesh.

Instead, they were forced to await word from their allies, Mage and Therian alike, for a list of Mage strongholds and any sign of recent activity at any of them. But so far, no one had come up with a single fecking clue.

Fox grabbed a glass, filled it with water, and downed it in one chug.

The Ferals should have been able to sense which direction Kara had gone through their natural ability to follow radiance. In the old days, it was the only way a newly marked Feral ever found his way to Feral House, which moved often. But that sense, too, had been blocked. If not for Lyon's mating bond, which remained strong and unbroken, they might fear Kara dead.

She still lived, thank the goddess, but she was too far away to strengthen them. And in time, that would become a problem. After a couple of months without proximity to radiance, the Ferals would begin to lose their ability to shift. After two years, they'd all be dead.

If only his own useless fecking intuition would jump in and help for once. But his useless *fecking* gut had been useless fecking *silent*.

Lyon tossed yet another twisted fork onto the table.

Fox refilled his glass with water, but as he lifted it to his mouth, his hand clenched too tight, shattering the glass, spraying him with water. The frustration boiling inside of him erupted, breaking the surface with his fangs and claws.

Growling, he swung toward the others, none of whom were paying him much attention. Goddess, he'd never felt so out of control.

"Where the feck is she?"

Without warning, Jag leaped at him, ripping the flesh off his shoulder with his own suddenly sprouted claws, knocking him to the ground. "You want a fight, pretty boy?" he growled around his fangs as they began beating the crap out of one another. "Me, too."

A moment later, Lyon joined the fray. Claws ripped flesh, fangs dripped with blood.

Adrenaline roared through Fox's body, the pain drowned out by the excitement. He growled and fought and nearly laughed out loud at the sheer pleasure of releasing the pent-up frustration that had been tearing him apart.

He caught the same excited gleam in Jag's eyes. But not Lyon's. The Chief of the Ferals' anguish ran far too deep.

Lyon swung away first, turning his back on them, his shoulders hunched, his hands fisted, his claws slicing up his palms until blood ran in a steady trickle onto the floor. Without another word, he stalked out of the dining room. The rest of them watched him go.

Fox suddenly felt like shite. "My apologies," he told the other two, his fangs and claws receding.

"No apologies necessary," Kougar said evenly, picking up a sandwich. "New Ferals are notorious for losing control like that. I've been waiting for it to happen."

"I'm usually even-tempered."

"Which is why it hasn't happened sooner. *Going feral* helps us get the frustration out of our systems. Lyon's suffering goes too deep. But this was good for him. He needed an outlet."

Jag clapped Fox on his now-healed shoulder. "You fight like a natural, pretty boy."

Fox acknowledged the compliment with a nod. "If only we had someone to fight other than each other." He looked at Kougar. "Is there anything the Ilinas can do to help?" Just the word *Ilinas* had his pulse lifting as thoughts of Melisande rushed through his head. Despite everything that had happened, he'd been unable to forget her for even a moment, however much he'd tried.

"Unfortunately, no. They can find one another, or their mates, but otherwise, they can only follow maps and directions, like the rest of us. Lyon's asked them to help out here. Ariana should be arriving shortly to discuss the plans with him." His mouth tightened. "Or with Paenther." Lyon's second.

Would Melisande accompany her queen? At the thought, Fox's pulse quickened.

The sound of shouts outside had all three of them slamming down glasses, tossing aside sandwiches, and racing for the hallway. They reached the foyer just as Paenther wrenched open the front door.

"You killed my daughter, you whoreson! You killed her!" The furious voice carried from the front drive.

Paenther strode outside, Fox and the others hard on his heels.

In the wide circular drive in front of Feral House, Tighe and Vhyper, two of the original nine Ferals, stood beside Tighe's white Land Rover, arms crossed as they watched a furious man Fox didn't know pound the shit out of Grizz, another of the seventeen who, like Lynks, had presumably been cleared of the dark magic.

As Paenther and Fox strode down the brick walk, Tighe circled the combatants to meet them.

"What's going on?" Paenther demanded, his strong Native American heritage evident in the tone of his skin, the slash of high cheekbones, and the jet-black hair.

"Your guess is as good as mine," Tighe replied. "Vhyper and I just picked up Rikkert from the airport. Grizz was crossing the driveway, heading toward the house, when we drove up. Rikkert leaped from the Rover and attacked him."

Fox had heard that several more newly marked Ferals, more of the seventeen, had made contact and were making their way to Feral House. Rikkert must be one of them.

They watched the fight with disbelief, but none bothered to step in. Over seven feet of hard, bad-tempered bear in either form, Grizz didn't need defending, especially since a Feral who'd come into his animal power, as Grizz had, could defeat any nonshifted Therian, marked or unmarked. If Grizz wanted to end the fight, he'd end it. In a heartbeat. Fox suspected he wasn't the only one who'd like to know why the male didn't. He was taking one hell of a beating.

"That's enough," Paenther said quietly. "We don't need anyone calling the cops again." There were no houses bumping up against Feral House, and the vehicles blocked the sight of those on the other side of the shallow woods. But sound carried outside.

With a fist covered in tattooed eagle feathers, Rikkert continued to punch Grizz in the face, over and over, the crack of bone making Fox's stomach hurt. Rikkert had tats everywhere, covering nearly every inch of his exposed skin. Most appeared to be depictions of animals, including a snake that curled around his neck, battling a stallion. A tusk, or horn of some kind, curled out from beneath one of his ears, cutting across his cheek, its point coming to rest just beneath his eye.

Tighe and Jag waded into the fight and hauled the enraged Rikkert off the downed man.

Paenther nodded toward the house. "Get him inside." As the two Ferals led the newest member of the team away, Paenther moved to stand over Grizz, who remained on the ground, one hand pressing against his forehead in a pose that spoke more of a pain of the heart than of the flesh. "What in the hell was that all about?"

"None of your fucking business." Grizz rolled over and pushed himself to his seven-foot-plus height, his face still bloody, but already fully healed, and strode toward the woods that separated Feral House from the rocky cliffs that overhung the Potomac River.

As the rest of them watched him go, Paenther let out a frustrated sound. "We need a break. Just one fucking break." He turned back to the house, and Fox and the others followed.

As they stepped into the foyer, Fox caught the scent of pine. His pulse leaped. A moment later, two women materialized at the base of the stairs. Ariana.

And Melisande.

Fox's heart skipped a beat, a sensual energy dancing over his skin as he struggled not to stare at the woman who'd been haunting his every thought for the past two days. She was dressed the same as before, in leggings and a tunic, though today's tunic was more copper in color than true brown and set off her slender curves and flawless complexion to perfection. Her mouth was flat, as if Feral House was the last place she wanted to be, her chin stubborn and hard. But her eyes found him as if she felt his presence as keenly as he felt hers. Their gazes caught. Her ripe lips parted on a shallow breath, color blooming in ivory cheeks even as those sapphire eyes filled with dismay. And frustration.

She tore her gaze away, leaving him breathless, his heart hammering in his chest. As tempted as he was to stop, to just stand near her, he forced himself to keep going, to continue across the foyer to the hallway leading to the dining room. Melisande and Ariana were here for Lyon, not for him.

He nodded as he passed the two beauties, then headed back toward the dining room and his lunch. He needed food. And a cold beer. Maybe several. But as he reached the hallway, he glanced back, unable to resist one last glimpse, and found Melisande staring after him with a hard mouth and eyes filled with confusion . . . and desire.

It was all he could do to keep going when his feet wanted to turn back and close the distance between them. Now wasn't the time to pursue the woman, he knew that. Not with Kara missing. Not with half of the new Ferals turning against them. But, *goddess,* what she did to him.

Sooner or later, she was going to be his.

Melisande tore her gaze away from the now-empty threshold, shaking her head, stifling a groan, *hating* that she kept reacting to that male. Her pulse was pounding, her body flushed and damp, and all from merely looking at him. But, heaven help her, even with his shirt ripped and blood everywhere, he was a sight to behold with those piercing blue eyes and that fine, fine chest. At least this time he hadn't tried to flirt with her, though for a moment, his eyes had flared with heat, and she knew he was as affected by her as she was by him. Dammit.

She tried to force her attention back to the foyer and to Paenther as he spoke to Ariana, beside her, but she found herself shifting restlessly from one foot to the other, too aware of the feel of her soft tunic where it touched her skin, skimming now-taut nipples, caressing her arms and back and shoulders. What would it feel like to have Fox's hands on her instead?

The question popped unbidden into her mind, and she shoved it away with a scowl. *By the mist.*

"I want Ilina eyes on Feral House at all times," Paenther was saying. "If anyone comes near—anyone other than those who live here—I want to know about it immediately."

Ariana nodded. "Tell me how many warriors you need, Paenther, and they'll be at your disposal."

"Half a dozen, preferably in mist form so they won't be seen by passing humans. Is that possible?"

Ariana nodded. "Yes, if they're careful."

"Good."

The front door opened, sunshine pouring into the foyer as Hawke and Faith strolled in. No, she was Falkyn now, the first female Feral in centuries. Exhaustion and defeat lined both of their faces. The hopeful tension that had risen in the foyer at their appearance released in despair.

"Any news?" Hawke asked, closing the door behind him.

"None." Paenther's voice was hard as stone.

Melisande didn't envy the Mage who'd taken the Ferals' Radiant. They wouldn't survive the Ferals' retribution. And if there was one thing she understood very, very well, it was the need for vengeance. Castin was still out there somewhere, the shifter who'd betrayed her all those years ago, leading her and seven of her Ilina sisters into a trap that would see her friends dead and her damaged beyond repair. He still lived, she could feel it in her bones, and someday their paths would cross again. And on that day, she would cut out his heart.

A trip of sensual energy danced over Melisande's flesh, making her gasp, pulling her gaze to the threshold where Fox had disappeared a short time ago. He stood there again, some twenty feet away, one shoulder propped against the doorframe, a bottle of beer dangling from his fingers. That sky blue gaze caught hers, snaring her in a velvet grip, accelerating her heart rate. The barest of smiles lifted his mouth, a smile that stirred the traitorous attraction. A softness entered his eyes, wrapping around her, stroking over her flesh like a warm, gentle touch, igniting a longing she didn't understand.

And didn't want.

She wrenched her gaze away, once more breathless and unsettled, perspiring in a room gone suddenly too warm. Damn him!

"We'll be going," Ariana said beside her, then shared a brief, tender kiss with Kougar, her mate.

Melisande ignored the mated pair, struggling to get her traitorous pulse under control even as she fought to keep from looking at the man who'd set it to flight in the first place. *Stars in heaven,* it had been so long since she'd felt anything like this, since she'd felt virtually anything at all. And she didn't want to be feeling now.

She liked who she was, *what* she was—a warrior capable of doing what must be done to protect her queen and her race. Some called her cold, even heartless, but she was fine with that. Better than fine. It was exactly what she wanted.

Feelings made a warrior soft, made her lose her edge. And that was something Melisande refused to allow.

Fox watched Melisande disappear, misting out of the crowded Feral House foyer, leaving him feeling solar-plexed. Every time he came anywhere near her, he felt a buzz of desire unlike anything he'd ever experienced, a shadow of the pleasure she'd blasted him with the first time, perhaps, but incredible, all the same.

He'd been attracted to her from the moment he first saw her. She was so small, so . . . perfect. And he had to admit, that hard-ass attitude of hers turned him on, probably because no other woman had ever shoved such blatant stop signs in his face. She was a challenge, without a doubt. But she was more than that.

Each time their gazes met, he felt as if he were being sucked into a whirlpool. And he wondered if perhaps she felt the same, if some of her anger wasn't simply a determination to resist.

And just how long would she be able to resist? The question tantalized.

"Where are the new Ferals?" Hawke asked, hooking his arm around Falkyn's shoulders, pulling her close against his side, a look on his face that had all of them straightening. Tensing.

"Lepard is down in the gym with some of the others," Paenther replied. "Grizz took off on foot into the woods a while ago." He glanced at Tighe. "Rikkert?"

"Vhyper took him back to the dining room to settle him down."

Hawke nodded. "We need to talk."

"Lyon's office." Paenther turned and started down the hall, Hawke, Falkyn, Kougar, and Tighe close behind. When Jag stepped forward, Fox hesitated. Technically, he was one of the new ones, if not one of the seventeen.

Jag glanced at him. "Come on, Foxylocks."

Fox flipped him off, grinned, and followed. It was odd, and sometimes awkward, to be straddling the two camps. He might be a new Feral, but the animal spirit who'd marked him had been one of the nine never lost, never infected.

As they started back to Lyon's office, a shiver stole through him from out of nowhere. An odd shiver more of the mind than the body. A moment later two words formed in his head.

West Virginia.

Had his gut offered up a truth at last? Though what kind of truth West Virginia presented, he had no idea. Usually goose bumps preceded his intuitions, but he knew the nature of gifts tended to change after one was marked by the animal.

So, was his gut telling him to go to West Virginia? Was that where the Mage had taken Kara? The thought teased him, lifting his pulse with excitement, then dropping it just as fast. His intuition more often than not offered up relatively useless information. For all he knew, his gut was trying to tell him that West Virginia was the current location of his next car.

Hell, he didn't even know *where* in West Virginia.

Lyon, standing by the window rigid as stone, turned when they entered.

"Hawke has information."

At the flare of hope in Lyon's eyes, Hawke held up his hand. "Not about Kara, Roar. I'm sorry."

The Chief of the Ferals nodded, his body turning once more to marble.

When all eight were pressed into Lyon's office, Paenther closed the door and turned to Hawke expectantly.

The hawk shifter lifted one steepled brow. "We've been acting under the assumption that the new Ferals were marked by accident, that the dark magic hampered the animal spirits' abilities to mark the best of the line, leaving the ones marked a random selection. We were wrong."

Grunts and groans peppered the small room.

"The dark magic," Hawke continued, "was designed to force the spirits to choose the morally weakest— the most evil—of each animal line. The falcon spirit fought hard against that dictate and managed to choose the one she wanted. Others probably did, too. But we already know Maxim was pure evil, so some of the animal spirits failed. Bottom line, there were no accidental markings. The new Ferals are each either the best or worst of their respective animal lines."

"How do we know which is which?" Lyon demanded.

Hawke shook his head. "We don't know." He glanced at Jag. "As we've seen, you can't always judge a man's soul by his actions."

Jag gave a rueful shrug. From what Fox had been able to piece together, Jag had been the resident bad boy, driving his Feral brothers to murderous intent on a regular basis, until he met Olivia.

"Then we have no choice." Kougar's voice was cool as ice. "We collect all seventeen in the prisons."

Hawke's hold on his mate tightened.

Kougar's gaze slid to the female Feral, a cutie with dark, blue-tipped hair and a killer smile. "Sixteen. Not Falkyn." Though Falkyn was one of the newly marked seventeen, she was soon to be Hawke's mate, and there was no doubt in any of their minds that she was the one meant to be marked.

Kougar turned to the others, meeting each man's gaze, one after the other, ending with his chief's. "Then we start over."

Start over. *Kill them.*

Falkyn wrenched free of Hawke's protective hold. "Grizz fought the darkness to help you. You voted to trust him."

Jag grunted. "That was before Rikkert accused him of murder."

Three heads jerked toward Jag, then Paenther as he explained the altercation in front of the house a short time ago and how Grizz hadn't lifted a hand against his attacker.

Hawke frowned. "What makes a man take a beating like that without defending himself?"

"Guilt," Jag, Fox, and Kougar said simultaneously.

Hawke nodded. "The evil don't feel guilt. Not like that. Only those with a fully functioning conscience. We've seen his anger-management issues. It's probably no surprise that he's caused trouble before. But we've seen evidence of honor in the male."

"Are you willing to stake her life on it?" Kougar's gaze flicked to Falkyn. "And ours. Because if we make one mistake, if we allow one evil Feral to remain within our ranks, we're compromised. Inir will find a way to use him to destroy us. And if we go down, the Daemons rise, and the world as we know it will be over. Everything we've fought for will be lost."

Lyon lifted his hand, drawing all attention back to him. "We can't start over until all seventeen are accounted for."

Jag snorted. "As soon as word gets out that the new Ferals are all dead men, none will come near this place, good or bad."

"Then word can't get out," Lyon said.

Not for the first time, Fox thanked the goddess that he wasn't one of the seventeen. The return of the lost animal spirits should have been a godsend. Instead, thanks to the Mage, it was turning into a nightmare.

Fox opened his mouth to tell him about his gut instinct, but Lyon began to lay out a plan, and Fox remained silent. What good was *West Virginia*? The last thing they needed right now was a wild-goose chase courtesy of the newbie. If only his gut would offer him something useful.   •

"**W**here's Lyon?" Grizz demanded as he strode into the foyer, eyeing one of the Ferals' brides. Tall and attractive with a gun strapped at her waist, her name began with a D. Delaney.

"His office, I think," she said. "I heard voices in there a moment ago."

With a brief nod, Grizz headed toward the closed office door. After the run-in with Rikkert, he'd started toward the rocky falls, then forced himself to return to Feral House. The situation was fucking impossible now. He'd lay it all out for Lyon, let the Feral chief decide how he wanted to handle it.

It was too fucking bad that there was no unmarking a Feral Warrior once he was marked because he'd do it in a pig's breath. He wasn't a team player and never had been. He didn't want this fucking job.

As he reached for the knob to Lyon's closed office door, voices carried to him, low but audible. His hand froze.

"Rikkert will be easy to take down. He hasn't come into his animal. Grizz is going to be the problem. How in the hell are we supposed to get a monster grizzly into the prison without losing limbs? He's not about to go willingly."

What the fuck? Grizz pulled his hand away from the knob, his head beginning to pound. He was *not* hearing this.

"He won't go easily, that's for damn sure. Lepard might. He allowed himself to be captured once. He might again."

A grunt. "Not if he figures out he won't come out of the prisons alive."

Grizz's blood ran cold.

"He might. They're all the best or the worst of their lines. If we can just figure out how to identify those who were meant to be marked, we won't have to kill them. Not the good ones."

The best or . . . *the worst?* And what was he? Not the best. Definitely not the best. But the worst? Hells balls.

"You do realize that it could be months before we can round up . . . or at least account for . . . all seventeen."

"What choice do we have?"

"We'll have to lure Grizz down there first. He can't be warned. If he shifts, we're grizzly food."

"When?"

"Tonight."

Grizz had heard enough. He turned away from the door and strode down the hall to the foyer, his footfalls silent despite his size, his head pounding. The fuckers were going to kill the new Ferals! Wipe them all out. And dammit to hell, he'd been afraid of this because it was exactly what he'd do in their position. Kill the infected ones and hope the next lot were the ones meant to be marked. Especially now when they'd figured out that some were the worst of their line and might be true evil.

He entered the foyer and headed for the door, veering at the last minute toward the hall table and the wooden bowl where he'd seen some of the Ferals drop their car keys. He'd get nowhere on foot, not with Hawke and Falkyn hunting him from the air.

He grabbed a set of keys with a tag marked FORD ESCAPE and was five strides from the front door when a sound caught his ear and he turned to find Lepard coming out of the basement, his face flushed with sweat, his short, newly white hair plastered to his scalp. Another of the newly marked seventeen, Lepard had been ensnared in the dark magic and had followed the evil Feral, Maxim, to Poland where he'd been forced to help in some kind of ritual to aid Satanan and his Daemon horde's efforts to rise. But he'd fought the darkness, allowing the good Ferals to capture him. He wasn't the worst of his line, Grizz would bet money on it. Would he bet his life on it? Yeah, maybe he would.

"Come with me," he told the snow leopard.

Lepard looked at him with confusion. "Where are you going?"

"I said . . . come." He'd grab Rikkert, too, if he thought there was any chance the male would come with him willingly without trying to kill him. There wasn't.

Lepard glanced down at himself. "I'm a little . . ."

Grizz said nothing, just stared at the man, conveying . . . hell, he didn't know what he was conveying, but Lepard seemed to hear it anyway.

"I guess I could use some air."

Yeah. Air. And survival. Something the snow leopard might not get if he stayed. Grizz led the way out the front door, spying the Ford in the wide, circular drive amid the impressive collection of other, far more expensive, vehicles.

Where he was going or what he was going to do, he had no idea. Something. Overheard words replayed in his head. *If we can just figure out how to identify those who were meant to be marked . . .*

That was the key. Even if he knew he wasn't one of them.

Maybe, just maybe, something good could come out of his fucked-up life. Even if it turned out to be the last thing he did.

When the meeting ended, as they left Lyon's office, Fox caught up with Paenther. "May I have a word?"

The black-haired male nodded, led him into the empty war room, and closed the door.

"This is probably as useless as a chocolate teapot," Fox began. "But I've always been a bit of an intuitive, and my gut's offered me a truth."

Paenther's eyes sharpened, making Fox feel pressure to give him a gem. If only he had one. "West Virginia," he blurted. "That's it. Nothing more specific."

The male stared at him, his eyes narrowing. "The Cub, your predecessor, had almost the same intuition, only with him it was the mountains of western Virginia. He led me straight into Mage captivity."

Feck.

"He also led me straight to Vhyper, whom we'd been searching for."

"The fox line has always been intuitive."

Paenther nodded. "Sly's intuition was sporadic, but when it was on, it was dead right."

"Another of my predecessors?"

"The one before the Cub." Paenther eyed Fox shrewdly. "Do you think Kara's in West Virginia?"

"I've no idea. Maybe it's a West Virginia license plate we should be looking for. Or it might be the home of my next girlfriend." He shrugged. "It's likely nothing useful at all, but I thought I should let someone know."

Paenther eyed him shrewdly. "And not create chaos." Which would surely happen if Lyon thought there was a chance that he knew where Kara was. "I'll have our allies focus their attention on West Virginia."

"Paenther . . ." He didn't want to make too much of this.

Lyon's second clasped Fox on the shoulder. "At least for now. It's something, Fox, when we've had nothing at all."

And if it turned out to be the useless fluff it probably was?

They wouldn't be any closer to finding Kara.

Chapter
Four

Three hours later, after an intense workout in the gym beneath the house, Fox strode toward the stairs, sweat soaking his hair, his T-shirt plastered to his chest. Jag and Tighe had been working with him on his shifting, which he still didn't have under control. He could shift into his fox without much trouble or concentration, but the size he ended up was the problem. While many of the cat Ferals could downsize their animals, making it possible for them to pass themselves off as house-cats, Fox tended to shift straight to supersize. A fox the size of a Great Dane wasn't necessarily a bad thing in battle, but it was a bit problematic if he had to shift any-where near humans. The bottom line was, he needed to be able to control the shift, to be able to move in and out of his animal form smoothly, in the size he needed, without thought or effort. Especially with them on the verge of war.

And right now he couldn't.

Wulfe strode in the front door, looking as exhausted as he probably felt. "Any news?" Wulfe was one of the biggest of the Ferals, second only to Grizz, his face a mask of scars.

"Nothing." Fox wasn't about to mention West Virginia. "You've been searching?"

"Tracking with my nose, yes. I was hoping to pick up a familiar scent, even just a Mage scent, but I found nothing. Lots of humans. I couldn't even scent the Mage who must have dragged Kara and Lynks into the vehicle."

"Makes you wonder how much Lynks struggled, doesn't it?"

Wulfe nodded. "Makes me wonder if he's the one who took her."

Fox frowned. "Maybe he was." He told Wulfe about Hawke's revelation, that the new Ferals were all the best or the worst. "So even if he was cleared of the dark magic, if he had a black soul . . ."

"Dammit to hell," Wulfe muttered. "Unfortunately, this doesn't change anything. It doesn't help us find her."

The scent of pine wafted through the foyer, and a

moment later, two Ilinas materialized not six feet away. Fox's wayward pulse lifted, then settled again when he saw that neither was Melisande.

The taller of the two caught sight of Wulfe and gasped, her eyes widening with something akin to revulsion. Wulfe scowled, turned, and started up the stairs.

"Cressida!" the other one hissed.

"Sorry, Phylicia!" Cressida grimaced. "He startled me. How does he have scars like that? Is he not immortal?"

"He's immortal," Fox assured them, though he'd wondered the same about Wulfe. He turned on his charmer's smile. "And what can I do for you lovely ladies?" He'd seen Phylicia in the prisons a couple of mornings ago. Kougar had called her to attempt to clear Grizz of the darkness in the traditional, carnal, way. It had failed, though the attempt had steamed up the underground chambers.

Phylicia had watched Fox hungrily then, as she was now. Sex sirens, Kougar called them. Some, not all. As Fox eyed Phylicia's sleeveless tunic, which revealed more lush, lovely curves than it hid, he believed it. With her raven hair falling to her waist and her eyes the inhumanly bright blue of most Ilinas, she was a beauty, to be sure.

But it was another Ilina he longed to see. A blonde with sapphire eyes.

Phylicia met his smile with a sultry one of her own and sidled up to him. "I was hoping I'd run into you." She slid her hand up his damp chest, the invitation in her eyes neon bright.

"Were you now?" He grinned, in his element. "And did you come just to see me, lovely one?"

"We've come to relieve the watch," Cressida explained. "But we're early." She eyed him as hungrily as Phylicia did, moving to his other side. "Phyl said you were delicious."

"Are you busy, warrior?" Phylicia purred, running a finger just inside the waistband of his pants. Perfume burst around him, like a garden in full summer glory. The famed Ilina mating scent? Intoxicating. And yet . . .

"I was just heading up to take a shower."

Their laughter enveloped him, sliding over him like soft hands. "We'll join you."

Every masculine instinct he possessed urged him to agree. They were absolutely lovely and hungry for sex. But for a reason he didn't understand, he was not. Now, if one of them had been Melisande . . .

Paenther strolled into the foyer, his gaze slamming into Fox's as a smile lit the dark warrior's eyes. "That gut of yours is gold."

Fox looked at him in surprise.

Paenther nodded with a gleam of excitement. "We've got our first good lead. War room in fifteen minutes."

As Paenther continued through the foyer, Fox gave

the lovelies each a brief squeeze, then stepped away from them. "I'm sorry, ladies. Perhaps later."

Without a backward glance, he turned and took the stairs two at a time, his mood buoyant. As he strode down the hallway toward his bedroom, relief flowed through him warmly, pride straightening his spine. He'd given them their first lead in finding Kara. And a good one. Hot damn.

He stripped as he crossed his bedroom, then stepped into the shower in the adjoining private bathroom before the water switched from cold to warm, not about to be late for that meeting.

As he dunked his head under the cool spray, he let the grin loose. Maybe he and his gut could make a difference after all. But as he reached for the soap, his brain exploded, his vision going black. *Feck!* He reached out blindly, his palm slapping against the tile wall to keep himself from going down.

And just as suddenly, he could see again. Except . . . what he was seeing wasn't real. At least it sure as hell wasn't in his shower. It wasn't even clear, more like watching an old photograph come to life. A movie in sepia tones. A movie he was part of.

He was chained standing up, the rock rough against his bare back, the steel manacles cold against his wrists and ankles. Inside, he felt a deep, pounding . . . *misery*. A misery that turned to fury as a man walked into the unfinished, stone room.

The male was dressed in the blood red robe of the Mage elemental. *Good goddess,* was this the famed Inir? The man hardly looked the part of one of the most dangerous immortals on the planet, not with his unimpressive stature and round face, not until Fox looked into his eyes, eyes of pure copper. Eyes that gleamed with cold, soulless malice.

"The fox shifter," the Mage said, his voice as cold as his eyes. "We meet at last. I've been hunting you for some time, did you know that?" He smiled a smile of pure evil. "Now you're mine. And soon . . ."

The sound dissipated moments before the vision faded to black. Fox found himself once more staring at the water running in rivulets down the shower tile.

His heart pounded. *Holy hell.* He'd never experienced anything like that in his life. Never. Then again, he'd been warned that new Ferals often acquired new abilities.

He dunked his head under the now-warm water. A premonition? Was that what that was? Had he just intuited his own captivity? *Mage* captivity?

Bloody fecking hell.

This was one foresight he had to make damn sure did not come true.

Fox strode downstairs, still shaken from his premonition in the shower, to find a tense, tight little gathering in the foyer.

"It was at least a couple of hours ago," Delaney said. Tighe stood beside her, his arm around her shoulders, as Jag, Hawke, and Kougar listened close. "Grizz wanted to know where Lyon was, and I told him I'd heard voices in his office."

Oh feck.

Jag groaned. "If he overheard our plan . . ."

Tighe glanced at Fox as he joined them and filled him in. "Grizz and Lepard are missing, along with the Ford Escape."

Fox grimaced. "We don't need those two on the loose with that kind of knowledge."

"Do we just let them go?" Jag asked.

Kougar nodded. "For now." He turned to Jag. "Rikkert is in his room. Escort him downstairs and lock him up, then meet us in the war room."

"I'll give you a hand," Tighe said. He kissed his mate and started up the stairs after Jag.

Kougar's gaze moved between the two remaining warriors. "We've got another new Feral flying in tonight. Two others are past due. When they arrive, take their phones and escort them downstairs."

"Not much of a welcome," Hawke muttered.

Kougar shook his head. "No, it's not."

The doorbell rang. Kougar and Fox exchanged a wary look, but Hawke's face lit up. "That'll be Zeeland. He called to say he and Julianne would be stopping by."

"Yeah?" Fox was pleased. One of the nonshifting

Therians, Zeeland was a member of the British Therian Guard, of which Fox had been a part for decades.

Hawke opened the door, and Fox's old friend stepped into the foyer, accompanied by a small, attractive brunette with turquoise eyes almost as bright as an Ilina's.

Zeeland said hello to Hawke, then spotted Fox. "Kieran!" The two men greeted one another warmly. "Or is it Fox, now?"

"It's Fox, though it's hard to change names after three hundred years."

Pleasure lit Zeeland's eyes. "I always thought you should have been one of the Ferals. I'm glad the goddess got it right."

"I've always thought the same about you, Zee. Though I have to admit, I'm kind of glad you haven't been marked. You heard about Ewan?" Ewan had also fought with them.

Zeeland frowned. "I hear the Mage have their claws in him. Has he really gone to the dark side?"

Fox frowned, nodding. "He's under the thrall of the dark magic that infected all of the seventeen." Ewan was one of the seventeen who Fox felt utterly certain was the one meant to be marked. But how did you prove something like that? "Unfortunately, we have to catch him before we can cure him."

"I hope you do it soon." Zee curved his arm around the woman's shoulders and pulled her close. "I'd like you to meet my mate, Julianne."

Fox smiled. He'd heard Zee had taken a mate, a young beauty from one of the Washington, D.C. area enclaves.

Above, Tighe and Jag started down the stairs, Rikkert between them. Since Rikkert was accompanying them calmly, he clearly didn't have any idea why he was being led to the basement. It was just as well.

As the trio reached the foyer, Tighe clasped Rikkert on the shoulder. "We'll make introductions later, during the welcome reception. But right now, we have work to do downstairs, and you're going to help."

Of course, there wouldn't be a welcome reception, not for Rikkert. He wouldn't be coming out of that basement anytime soon. If ever. Fox felt bad for him. How rotten to be marked to be one of the elite Feral Warriors only to discover it meant imprisonment? Maybe even death.

Fox turned his attention back to Zeeland and his bride. "So this is Julianne." He took the woman's hand and lifted it to his lips in a gallant, old-world gesture, enjoying the freedom to charm, knowing he'd never turn her head. Mating bonds were solid.

"Did Zeeland mention me?" Julianne's smile was at once surprised, shy, and delighted, charming him in return.

"Only when he was in his cups, and then he droned on and on about the beauteous Julianne, his sunshine, too young, etc., etc." He winked at her. "I take it you are no longer too young."

"I'm not." She cut Zee a smile laced with exasperation. "I haven't been for five years."

"Five years?" Fox's gaze went from one to the other. "He didn't tell me that."

"I was an idiot," Zeeland said, pulling Julianne closer. "But she's mine now, and I'm never leaving her again." The look that passed between the pair was filled with such a depth of tenderness that Fox almost felt compelled to look away. Another fool risking all for love.

"So," Fox said, breaking the spell. "What brings you here?"

Both Zee's and Julianne's expressions changed, rippling with a tension that surprised him.

"Julianne is here to meet Ariana."

Fox cocked his head, suspicion leaping. "You have the look of an Ilina," he murmured.

Julianne blanched.

Fox watched her, mortified. "I said the wrong thing."

Zeeland pulled his mate closer, but he shook his head. "No. It's the truth and no longer the secret it once was. Julianne is one-quarter Ilina."

Fox started with surprise. "I didn't know they . . . had babies." The legends claimed that the all-female race reproduced through magic, their maidens born fully grown and ready to take their place in Ilina society.

"They don't, usually. It's very, very rare for an Ilina to conceive. Rarer still for one to give birth." Zeeland's mouth hardened. "When Julianne was nine, her parents were killed in cold blood, leaving her an orphan. A few months ago, the same Ilina tried to drag us into the Crystal Realm to suffer the same fate."

Fox stared at him, his brows drawing down. *"Why?"*

"Because everyone still thought them extinct, and we learned the truth. They killed to keep their secret."

Fox tried to imagine one of those petite, pretty mist warriors taking life in cold blood. The sweet Cressida. The sultry Phylicia. The cold-eyed Melisande . . .

A chill of understanding skated over his scalp. It was Melisande.

Julianne's mouth compressed. "Kougar says that Ariana didn't sanction the killing of my parents. She didn't even know about it until very recently. She's been asking to meet me." She frowned prettily. "I need to understand my heritage. I need to know who I am."

"I'm not sure how much time Ariana will have today," Hawke said. "We've just received our first good lead on Kara. I'm sure we'll be heading out soon."

"Then perhaps my arrival is timely," Zeeland said. "If the Ferals need backup, I'm available."

Kougar stepped forward. "We could use you, Zeeland." He greeted Zee with his usual reserve, then surprised Fox by leaning down to give Julianne a kiss on the cheek. "You have nothing to fear, Julianne. Ariana is as nervous about meeting you as you are her. Your introduction to your heritage was a poor one."

"You could say that," Zeeland said darkly. "I'm not leaving her side."

"Ariana would never harm one of her own." Kougar turned to Julianne. "You're one of hers, now, whether or not you choose to acknowledge the connection."

"It's not Ariana I'm worried about," Zee muttered.

Kougar nodded toward the other hallway. "We're meeting in the war room. I'm afraid it's a closed meeting, but you're welcome to await Ariana in the dining room. Pink will be happy to serve you refreshments."

Before Zeeland had a chance to reply, half a dozen Ilinas materialized in the foyer, Ariana among them, along with Phylicia, Cressida, and Melisande.

Fox's gaze found her in an instant, energy and desire sliding over his skin like the soft caress of feminine fingers, sending his pulse into overdrive and the blood flowing hotly through his veins. Even with that hard warrior's expression, she was inexpressibly lovely, her features even and pure, her jaw proud, her body lithe and lovely.

Her gaze zeroed in on him, that same mix of anger, confusion, and desire swirling in sapphire eyes. But as she jerked her gaze away from his, turning it to the others, she froze. Her eyes narrowed, her hand flying to the hilt of her sword as her body tensed, as if for battle.

Fox took a step forward, driven by an inexplicable need to protect her. But Hawke put a hand on his arm, holding him back as Kougar placed himself squarely between Melisande and Zeeland.

His old friend had shoved Julianne behind him and was drawing his own knife, a low sound of fury rumbling from his throat.

Bloody hell. He'd been right about Melisande's being the one responsible for the deaths of Julianne's parents. And Kougar had clearly anticipated the confrontation.

"Put the knife away, Zeeland," Kougar said calmly.

"You defend her?" Zeeland demanded.

Melisande stepped to the side, where she could see Zeeland, no remorse in her expression. Instead, she wore a hard look that said, *bring it on*. But as Fox watched her, something happened. Chaos flared in the cold depths of her eyes, and she swayed ever so slightly, her skin turning pale as new snow. With a hard breath, she seemed to gather her wits, her shields slamming down until nothing showed but that cold warrior's façade.

It all happened so quickly, he wondered if he'd imagined it. But she was still pale. And if he were to touch her, if she were ever to allow that, he knew he'd feel tremors rippling through her slender form.

As Ariana stepped close to Melisande's side, Kougar crossed his arms and faced Zeeland fully. "Melisande is no danger to you or your mate, Zeeland. Unless you attack her. And then, if you survive, you'll answer to me."

Zeeland's disappointment in Kougar's position was patently obvious, but he was a soldier first. He sheathed his knife, but his expression made it clear that Melisande had better keep her distance, or he would happily cut out her heart.

At Ariana's touch of her arm, Melisande slowly sheathed her own blade and didn't look any happier about doing so than Zeeland had. As Fox watched her, she glanced at him, and in those glorious, sapphire eyes, for the breadth of a heartbeat, emotion flared once more. Accusation. Disbelief. Fear.

Why?

The woman baffled him. It was as if she wanted the world to think her a cold-blooded killer. But the fact that Kougar defended her told him it was just a façade. There was more to the story, more to *her*. Much more.

Every time he saw her, he became more intrigued. She stirred his most basic instincts—to possess, to protect. And he became more and more convinced it would take a concerted effort to break through those walls of hers. But he had all the time in the world.

He hoped.

Melisande strode down the hallway to the war room beside Ariana. Her chin was high, her back straight even if she could feel Zeeland's gaze like a dagger in her spine.

She was shaking.

Stars in heaven. As she'd faced Zeeland's fury, as she'd met the hatred in Julianne's eyes, for one horrible moment, emotions she'd thought long dead rushed up, threatening to strangle her. Sorrow, regret. She'd fought them back, and they'd slunk away as quickly as they'd appeared, but they had not closed the door behind them. Even now, she could feel them swirling inside her like sharks beneath the ice. Awakening. And it could not be borne.

The stirrings of desire for the Greek god were bad enough. But she would not feel remorse for something she had no reason to regret. She refused. For centuries, she'd kept her eye on Julianne's mother, the only half-Ilina in existence, hoping she'd never turn to mist and learn of her true nature. But she had, and Melisande had revealed herself to her, warning her never to tell another soul. Ever. The survival of the entire Ilina race depended upon it. But the woman had ignored her, spilling her secret to a lover. And Melisande had had no choice but to silence them both.

Like mother, like daughter, Julianne had done the same, revealing her secret to Zeeland. If not for Kougar's interference, they too would have lived out their last few days in the Crystal Realm.

She refused to feel guilt for that. *Refused.*

And she wouldn't feel guilt, she wouldn't feel *anything* if not for Fox, damn him. If only she hadn't tried to blast him. Something had happened when the pleasure she'd inadvertently thrown at him rebounded on her. The part of her that had been locked so firmly away for centuries was beginning to push free again. Her breath caught, a sick knot forming in her stomach as everything she'd worked for, everything she was, threatened to slip through her fingers.

She would not let it happen.

It was all the fault of that damned golden shifter. Even now, even without looking, she knew exactly where he was. As the small procession strode to the war room, he followed behind Kougar, Wulfe at his side. She felt him, his energy like a beacon, calling to her.

They filed into the war room, the Ferals with wives taking seats at the table beside their mates, the others standing against the walls of the room. Melisande stood at the back of the room with three of her sisters, her arms crossed tight against her chest in an effort to still the faint trembling that wouldn't stop.

The room filled quickly, the scent of hard male bodies teasing her nose, reminding her of the carnal longings that had once been a constant part of her life. Now it was only one male who claimed her attention. Her gaze slid to where Fox stood against the adjoining wall beside Wulfe. And Phylicia.

An unexpected burst of anger flared inside of her, startling her as much as it dismayed. *Jealousy.* This was a day for lows. And Phylicia didn't deserve it. One of the youngest of her sisters, Phylicia had spent most of her life hiding in the Crystal Realm, forbidden the pleasures of males and sex for fear the truth of their extinction . . . or lack thereof . . . would leak to the Mage who were trying to destroy them.

Melisande crossed her arms tighter, setting her jaw as she reminded herself that she should encourage Phylicia to bed Fox. With the shifter's attention turned elsewhere, perhaps this unholy connection between them would finally break. All would go back to the way it was before.

Which was all she wanted. *All* she wanted.

Paenther began to speak, drawing all eyes toward the front of the room. "We have a lead, thanks to Fox and his intuition."

The Greek God smiled faintly and gave a nod. But his gaze slid to her as if, in this crowded room, she was the only one he saw. Not Phylicia fawning beside him, not his brothers or their wives. Her.

As their gazes locked, her pulse tripped, heat flushing her cheeks. She tried to pull her gaze away and couldn't.

"Fox suggested we investigate a link with West Virginia," Paenther continued, drawing the gazes front again, including Fox's.

With a trembling breath, Melisande looked toward the windows and tried to rally her defenses. Maybe she really was going to have to give up her role as Ariana's second and put as much distance between her and that shifter as she could manage. Every time she was near him . . .

She felt them, the whispers of the emotions of the others, startling her and chilling her to the bone. Her eyes widened.

No, no, no.

Frustration, desperation, hope slid around her like swirls of smoke. Not her emotion. Theirs.

Something she'd not felt in centuries, not since Castin's treachery. Long ago, she'd been a different person, gifted with the ability to sense the emotions of others and ease their torment. A Ceraph, they'd called her, touched by the grace of the goddess herself. She'd been no warrior then, gentle and kind, unable and unwilling to kill. But Castin had changed all that, changed her, when he betrayed her, handing her over to his clan to be raped and tortured mercilessly in a bid for a power she'd had no ability to give them. They'd all but destroyed her, taking everything she was, leaving a cold-hearted, vengeance-driven warrior in her place.

And now another shifter, Fox, was threatening to shatter that woman, too.

Paenther's voice filled the room. "In following up on our two missing new Ferals, I discovered that one of them, Estevan, called home last night. We've traced the cell signal to West Virginia, not far from Elkins. I called my Mage contact and learned that it's long been rumored that Inir once had a stronghold in the Allegheny Mountains near Elkins. Twenty minutes ago, one of his men stumbled upon an abandoned pickup with Canadian tags on the mountain where the stronghold is rumored to have been. We've run the tags. The truck belongs to the second of our missing Ferals and is only five miles from where Estevan made that call."

Silence hung over the room as all absorbed the information.

Kougar stroked his goatee. "If the new Ferals are being drawn to that mountain, Inir is there. And probably Kara. Inir will demand she bring the new Ferals into their animals."

The Ferals exchanged angry, worried glances as Paenther continued. "My Mage contact warned me that if this is indeed Inir's stronghold, we'll be up against powerful magic. We've seen strong warding before, the kind that will confuse and confound until the trespasser doesn't know where he is, let alone where the Mage stronghold lies. The warding on this mountain may be a hundred times worse, especially if it contains Daemon magic. There are rumors of people . . . Mage . . . disappearing, never to be seen again. We have to be prepared for anything."

"We're getting Kara back," Jag growled.

Rough sounds of agreement peppered the room.

Melisande felt the flare of their resolve, and her own. Theirs to find their Radiant, hers to get as far away from Fox and the destruction he would wreak on her life as quickly as possible. Ariana was going to have to choose another second.

The thought of losing her position, her place, was like a blow. But the prospect of losing herself was far, far worse.

"We'll be sending three teams out there ASAP," Paenther said. "Hawke and Falkyn, you'll do aerial reconnaissance and grid the search to try to minimize the warding's confusion. Jag, you'll lead the second team, with Fox and Olivia. Lyon will lead the third, with Kougar and Wulfe."

"Where is the king of the beasts?" Jag asked. "Shouldn't he be here?"

Paenther shook his head. "He's already out there. The moment I told him what I'd learned, he called for Ilina transport and was gone."

Wulfe grunted. "He could walk into a trap."

"I sent four maidens with him," Ariana told them. "If there's trouble, they'll get him out of there quickly, whether he wants to leave or not."

Paenther turned to Ariana. "I'd like for two of your mist warriors to remain with each of the ground teams."

"Of course." Ariana's gaze caught Melisande's. "Mel will oversee the troop assignments."

Melisande nodded. Oversee the assignments, yes. Accompany the Ferals? Not a chance.

"Hawke."

At Paenther's prompt, Hawke opened the laptop in front of him and began tapping the keys.

Phylicia disappeared from Fox's side, misting beside Melisande a moment later, bending close to her ear. "Put me with Fox's team."

Out of the corner of her eye, Melisande caught a glimpse of photographs filling the screen.

"These are our two missing Ferals," Paenther told them.

"I want him," Phylicia whispered.

Melisande's jaw tightened, but she nodded, glancing at Phylicia. "All right."

"The one on the left is Estevan," Paenther continued. "The other is Castin."

Melisande jerked at the name, one she hadn't heard in centuries. Her gaze swung to the front, and she saw the pictures fully. Time stopped as she stared at the dark-haired visage of her betrayer. The air froze in her lungs. Her vision began to waver.

Castin. Hatred flared up, a blazing inferno that ripped across the surface of her mind. Her head pounded, her face turned hot then cold as she remembered that night as if it were hours ago and not centuries. *Castin.* The only one she'd never found, the only one she'd never made pay for what he'd done to her and her sisters.

"Are you all right?" Phylicia asked quietly.

Stars in heaven. She fought to breathe, to corral her reaction. "Yes." But echoes of ancient screams tore through her head until she could barely hear herself think.

One thought broke through, crystal clear. This was the answer she'd been searching for, the certain means of locking away her emotions and her awakening softer self once and for all. Secure the vengeance she'd sought for so very long.

Castin must die, and before his first shift, because once he acquired the power of his animal, he'd be almost impossible to kill. She had to find him before the Feral teams searching for him did. Which meant she was going to have to accompany them.

"I know Castin," Fox said. "I worked with him briefly, years ago. He's a fine warrior."

Melisande's gaze wasn't the only one to snap to the Greek god.

"Then your team will track him." Paenther turned to Kougar. "Yours will follow Estevan. If our guess is right, you'll converge on Inir's stronghold."

Melisande's head began to throb. The last thing she wanted was to accompany Fox and his team, to be forced to spend long hours in that shifter's company. Especially with Phylicia trying to maneuver him into her bed . . . or her body.

But as badly as she wanted to stay away from Fox, she wanted . . . *needed* . . . her vengeance more.

Melisande deposited Jag on the pine-needle-strewn ground beneath the trees, took form, and stepped back, watching as the two Feral males and Jag's mate, Olivia, dropped to their knees dizzily, spilling their lunches onto the dirt.

Phylicia and Marguerite, who'd transported the others, came to stand beside her.

"Marguerite, you'll return to the Crystal Realm. I'll be accompanying this group."

Both Ilinas looked at Melisande with surprise, but neither questioned her. With a quick nod, Marguerite misted away.

Phylicia grasped her hand with an excited grin. "I'm

glad you're coming with us, Mel. This is going to be so much fun!"

Melisande didn't return the woman's smile and wouldn't have even if she could. Fun, this trip would not be, of that she was certain. There was no telling what dangers the Mage would throw in their path. And then, of course, there was Fox.

To Phylicia, he undoubtedly *was* the fun. She could hardly blame the other Ilina for being excited about a trip through a beautiful forest with an even more beautiful and unattached male, one she longed to seduce.

Have at him, Melisande thought as she watched the Greek god push himself to his feet. But the thought of Phylicia and Fox together clawed at her insides. Even as she scowled at the thought, the male in question turned her way, his gaze locking with hers. Desire curled deep inside her, heating her, annoying the hell out of her.

As their gazes met, his expression gave way to one of smug satisfaction, the smile spreading slowly across his finely shaped mouth as if he saw exactly what he did to her, as if he fully believed she was more interested in him than she pretended. When, of course, he knew nothing. Nothing at all.

She wasn't interested. She wanted nothing to do with him. If only her traitorous body would concur. If only she could stop *feeling.*

How she wished it were the other team on Castin's

trail. She'd happily accompany Lyon, Wulfe, and Kougar. She and Lyon had come to something of a truce in the past weeks, each agreeing not to try to kill the other. He hadn't appreciated that she'd led an attack on Feral House though she'd been utterly justified. Kougar had kidnapped Ariana, and Melisande had had every reason to fear for her queen's safety among the shape-shifters. Ultimately, Kougar and Ariana had reclaimed the love they'd once shared, and now the two races worked together closely. Too closely.

"Fuck." Jag pushed himself to his feet beside Fox. "Next time I'm taking the Hummer. Every time I travel by Ilina, I swear I'll never do it again."

"We just saved you hours of travel time," Melisande snapped.

Jag glared at her. "What are *you* doing here?" Like most of the Ferals, Jag didn't like her. Unlike most, he had no bridle for his tongue.

"Jag . . ." Olivia punched her mate in the arm and turned to the two Ilinas. "We're grateful for your help."

"Just don't stab us in the back," Jag muttered, then turned away, dismissing them as he looked around. "There." He pointed down the hill to a dirt road some hundred yards below. "Is that Castin's truck?" He grabbed Olivia's hand and started forward.

Fox winked at her . . . *winked* . . . then smiled at Phylicia as if she were the darling of his heart, before he turned and followed Jag.

Oh, she was going to rue her decision to join his team, that was already blindingly clear. Swallowing another huff, she started after them, Phylicia at her side. The sun was shining, the late-spring day warm but lacking the summer humidity that would arrive soon enough. She breathed in deeply, savoring the smells of the forest. No plants grew in the Crystal Realm, no trees, no flowers. She'd missed them bitterly during the long years they'd been forced to fake their extinction.

Minutes later, the small group fanned out around the late-model blue Chevy pickup with Canadian license plates. Plates they'd already confirmed were registered to Castin. She tried to imagine the male she'd known in those prehistoric times driving a pickup truck and failed, utterly. She'd never lost her heart to him, thank the heavens, but she'd liked him. A lot. And never imagined he was capable of such savage betrayal.

Jag threw Fox an expectant look. "Time to shift, Foxy. Let's see if we can pick up a scent."

"After you, boyo."

The two shifters moved a little deeper into the trees, and Jag began to strip off his clothes. They must be hiding from prying human eyes, though she'd seen nobody out here, because none of the Ferals possessed an ounce of shyness about their bodies. Shifters never had. And no Ilina was ever offended by a bit of male nudity. Far from it. A quick glance at Phylicia told her she was waiting avidly for Fox to begin to strip as well. But when he made no move to do so, Melisande suspected he was one of the Ferals who retained his clothes and weapons through the shift.

Jag disappeared in a spray of colored lights, and moments later, a full-sized jaguar stood in his place—his head nearly black, his rosettes becoming more and more pronounced the farther they moved down his body.

Foxy? the jaguar shifter prompted, telegraphing his thoughts to all of them.

As she watched, Fox closed his eyes, began to sparkle, then disappeared. In his place stood a huge fox, the size of a Great Dane, with glorious red fur, black legs, and a face that was far too engaging.

Might want to downsize it a bit, Foxylocks. Don't want to scare the humans if we run across any. Even as Jag spoke, he shrank himself to the size of a jaguar-shaped housecat.

Feck. Give me a minute. I still haven't gotten the hang of this.

Melisande found herself biting back a smile, which was a novel experience.

Slowly, the fox began to shrink.

That's it, Jag coaxed. *A little more. It's harder than it looks. It took me several years to get the hang of it. You're a natural. There,* he said when the fox looked just about right. *That's enough.*

But Fox apparently wasn't any more adept at turning

off the sizing than turning it on because he just kept shrinking. *Bloody hell, I'm the size of a squirrel.*

Jag's laughter rang in her head. *Hey, Itty-bitty. You get any smaller, and you're going to have to ride on my back.*

The fox sneezed . . . or snorted. But a moment later he was growing again.

There! Jag said. And this time the fox stopped. *Perfect. You look like a run-of-the-mill red fox.*

Together, the two animals trotted out of the thicker trees and back to the waiting women. His mouth open, the fox appeared to be grinning as his gaze met hers, intelligent laughter lighting those eyes. Yes, entirely too engaging.

Jag paced in circles, close to the truck, then looked at the fox. *Got his scent?*

Feck, no. The animal closed his mouth and began to sniff at the ground. *Wait . . . I smell something. Therian.*

You've got him, then. Let's go.

As the four-footed pair loped into the woods, Olivia followed them, Melisande and Phylicia bringing up the rear. Melisande had seen the Ferals shift often enough, particularly in recent weeks, but she'd never watched a new Feral. And she'd found Fox's struggle with his newfound powers surprisingly winning, which she'd never admit to him in a thousand years. He'd turned neither angry nor embarrassed, and he appeared not to care at all that Jag continually called him by some ridiculous nickname or another.

Clearly, the Greek god didn't take himself too seriously. If he weren't a shifter . . . or a male . . . she might actually find that she liked him.

The shifters moved swiftly, but the women had no trouble keeping up even at a walk. They'd traveled more than a mile when she began to hear the shifters' conversation in her head. They must be broadcasting it to all of them.

We'd make better time with longer legs, boyo. There's no sign of humans.

Can you upsize without turning into a horse this time?

Fox laughed, his animal making that snorting/sneezing sound again. *Probably not.* A moment later, instead of growing, he shifted back into human form in a spray of colored lights. "Feck."

Sensual energy slid over Melisande's skin as it always did whenever she first came near the male in human form. As if he felt it, too, his gaze swung back to her, heat leaping into his eyes, a heat that spiraled deep down inside of her.

She scowled at him, which only earned her a knowing smile. Looking away from her, he winked at Phylicia. Did he think he had to spread his attention evenly? He could give it all to Phylicia. All of it, and she'd be happy if he did.

Marguerite appeared at her side suddenly. "Hawke and Falkyn are having trouble."

Jag shifted back to human form without warning. "What kind of trouble?"

The Ilina eyed his naked form with appreciation. "Trouble flying. Every time they lift off, they get dizzy and have to land again or risk crashing to the ground. It's apparently the Mage warding around this mountain."

Jag grunted. "Which means we're in the right place, boys and girls. What about Lyon, Wulfe, and Kougar? Are they having any trouble on foot?"

"Not yet, no. But they wanted you to know that Hawke and Falkyn won't be joining you. And there's no cell service up here. We're your only means of communication."

Jag slugged Fox lightly in the arm. "Let's get going, Goldilocks. Kara needs us." In the blink of an eye, Jag was once more a jaguar.

Fox eyed the other Feral with obvious envy, shifted into his too-large fox, and stayed that way.

I'm glad you decided to join us, pet. Fox's voice caressed her mind as he took off after Jag.

I'm not your pet.

He chuckled in her mind. *Aye. Are you anyone's pet?*

No. Go away.

That chuckle again. *You intrigue me, little Ilina. So much spit and fire in such a pretty little package.*

Quit calling me little. I'm tall for an Ilina.

Ah. This time the laughter was in his voice. *That explains your not even reaching my shoulder.*

It's not my fault you're a hulking brute.

The fox looked back at her, mouth closed, eyes intense. Inside her head, his voice turned soft, surprisingly serious. *I'll concede the hulking. Therian males tend to grow large. But I'm not a brute, pet. Never a brute. Except to my enemies.*

She wasn't sure what to say to that. She'd held shifters in such contempt for so very long, unable to see them except through the lens of cruelty visited on her by Castin and his clan all those centuries ago. They weren't all like that, she knew that. Especially not the Ferals. But that didn't mean she would ever fully trust them.

Come walk beside me, Melisande. The flirtatious quality was back in his tone.

Why would I want to do that? she snapped.

Because then you could touch me, stroke my fur. I've never had a female's hands in my fur before. I'm curious to know how it feels.

Ask Phylicia. She'll put her hands on you any way you like, and we both know it.

He didn't reply right away, and she hoped he'd finally given up talking to her. She studied the landscape, reveling in the beauty of the Allegheny Mountains, the wildflowers dotting the ground beneath the spruce and hardwoods. The leaves were still the light green of spring against a bright blue sky. Below, running parallel to the road, a creek glittered crystal clear between a border of large, dramatic rock formations. The place was stunning.

So how long have you been an Ilina, pet?

She rolled her eyes. The male was relentless. *All my life. I'd appreciate it if you'd disconnect me from your inane, rambling thoughts, Feral.*

If I'm inane and rambling, it's because your beauty is stealing all deeper thought from my head, Melisande.

She snorted. *Do women really fall for that drivel?*

Truth be told, women usually appreciate my attention. You're something of a rarity.

A challenge, you mean?

Aye. But more than that. There's something between us, you can't deny it. Something happened when you blasted me with that pleasure. Or perhaps your blasting me with pleasure instead of pain was simply a factor of whatever was meant to happen all along.

Melisande growled low with frustration. *I don't want you, Feral. I don't know how to make that any clearer. I don't want your voice in my head, I don't want you smiling at me, I don't want anything to do with you. Nothing. And that isn't ever going to change.*

For a moment, he was silent. Then the fox paused and swung his head back, watching her once more with those probing, serious eyes. *Is your antipathy toward me specifically, Melisande, or toward all Ferals?*

Does it matter?

Perhaps not, though it would be a salve to my battered ego if you said it was all shifters and not just me.

There's not enough salve in the world to cover your massive ego, she replied tartly.

Now you seek to wound me. But the laughter was back in his voice.

You're still in my head.

Aye. I'm thinking it may be the only way I'll ever get inside you.

You've got that right. Now go. Away.

You'll push me into Phylicia's arms, he warned.

Good. She wants you. I don't.

Very well. He sighed dramatically. *You wound me, pet. My heart may never heal.* Once again, the fox paused to look back at her, laughing. Then his mouth snapped closed and he eyed her with an intensity that told her he hadn't given up. Not at all.

And she groaned.

He wouldn't succeed. Certainly not in any way he was hoping to. But he scared her all the same. Because he stirred things inside her that had lain dormant for so long, she'd thought them gone forever.

Things that could, if she wasn't careful, destroy her.

"**W**ant to tell me what's going on?" Lepard asked after they'd left the Washington, D.C., suburbs far behind.

Grizz's hands tightened on the steering wheel of an old Toyota sedan he'd appropriated in Leesburg. He'd never been particularly strong at mind control, but the attempt had worked well enough. The Toyota owner now believed he was the owner of a Ford Escape. The Ferals wouldn't be able to track them via the vehicle. Not right away, at any rate.

"I overheard them talking," he told his companion, surprised Lepard had been content to wait this long before demanding an explanation for their sudden flight from Feral House. "All the newly marked Ferals are either the best of our lines or the worst. There were no accidents. Since the originals have no way of knowing for certain which is which, they've decided to imprison us all. Once they have all seventeen of us accounted for, they'll kill us and start over."

Silence. *"Hell."*

"Our replacements should, theoretically, be free of the dark infection. They should all be the best of the line."

"So we're just running away?"

Grizz admired the thread of disgust he heard in Lepard's voice. "You have a better idea?"

The snow leopard shifter ran a hand through short, snow-white hair. "There's got to be a way to figure this out."

"I agree."

Lepard turned to him, his eyes sharpening. "You have a plan. We're *not* just running."

"We're not just running, no. But I'm not sure it's much of a plan."

Lepard sank back against his seat. "At least it's something. Of course, the fact that we've run is going to be damning in the Ferals' eyes."

"We can't be of any help in their prison."

"So where are we going?"

"Amarillo."

"Texas?"

"I need to talk to someone. If anyone knows of a way out of this, it's him."

"You couldn't use a phone?"

Grizz didn't answer. There was no use trying to explain his relationship with the Indian he needed to talk to.

After a few minutes, Lepard said, "You trust me. At least you must not think that I'm the worst of my line. Why?"

"Just a hunch. I saw your eyes when you were under the thrall of the darkness. You were fighting it. You let the Ferals capture you."

"I did. You did the same." Lepard frowned. "But I heard that Rikkert accused you of murder."

"He did." Rikkert. He wondered idly which animal had marked the male and if they'd ever know.

"What's that about?" Lepard persisted.

The old ache pulsed painfully. "I killed his daughter. And his grandson."

Silence. Lepard's eyes narrowed on him. "You say that so matter-of-factly. But your hands are about to snap that steering wheel into fragments. You didn't mean to."

Mean to? He'd sell his soul if he thought it would bring them back. "No. The boy was mine. But they're just as dead."

Fox followed Jag, keeping his animal ears open for sound of trouble, or Mage, and his nose down for the scent of the one they tracked. But his man's mind remained firmly on Melisande. He longed to strip that neat little mist-warrior uniform off her and unbraid that tight plait of pale hair. In his mind's eye, he could see her lying in the grass, graceful limbs in casual abandon, her hair fanned out around her like a silken curtain as he licked her from head to toe.

He longed to touch her, to kiss her, to make wild love to her. But beyond that? With most females, there was no "beyond that." They wanted him for his beauty and his body, and he wanted them for the same. Period. End of story. But with Melisande, he wanted more. She tugged at him in all kinds of ways he didn't understand. He wanted . . . to talk to her. To know her. To understand her. To make her smile.

And he felt this need to protect her because there was something wrong. He sensed a vulnerability in her that he hadn't seen the first time he met her. Something . . . wounded.

It was an odd thought to have about a female so hard and sharp that her every word, every glare, cut. But he'd seen confusion in her eyes and glimmers of fear. And he didn't like it, not at all.

He wanted to understand, especially if he was somehow at fault. And then he wanted to make it right. She fascinated and confused him, infuriated and excited him almost in the same breath. He wanted to kiss her until she smiled at him with damp, swollen lips and watched him with eyes drunk with passion.

And then he'd send her on her way. Because he'd be damned if he wanted more.

On four feet, he followed Jag onto an outcropping of rocks overhanging a wide, if shallow, creek a half dozen feet below. Jag padded across the rocks, then turned to continue up, away from the creek, Olivia walking at his side.

Fox hesitated, looking down at the creek, wondering where the desire came from that had him wanting to leap down into the water. It wasn't a gut thing. He felt no goose bumps, or shivers, for that matter. Just . . . a tug. Odd. Perhaps it had something to do with his fox. Did foxes like the water? He wouldn't have thought so, but maybe his did. With a mental shrug, he followed Jag.

It was strange and amazing being both man and animal like this, and for the hundredth time, he marveled at his changed existence. He marveled at the thought that at one time all Therians had been shifters. How awful it must have been to lose that ability after the Sacrifice all those millennia ago. For him this was still brand-new. The other Ferals had told him that it would take some time for the man and animal to get used to one another and to learn to work together. They'd warned him about a lot of things and informed him that he'd probably develop one or two abilities that he hadn't had before. Lyon was said to be able to steal the emotions of another, particularly a human. Tighe was good at clearing the mind of a human who'd seen things he shouldn't have. And they'd hinted that Jag could do something with his hands, something the females enjoyed. He wasn't about to ask for an explanation of that one. Apparently sometimes these gifts were new, sometimes just a deepening of talents the Feral already possessed.

So far the only thing he'd seen new was that premonition. And it was bothering him. A lot.

How you doing, Foxylocks? Why don't you walk on two feet for a while, take a break?

I'm fine, Jagabelle, but thanks for the concern.

Yeah, well I wasn't really asking, Fox-man. Maintaining the shift can be taxing for a new Feral, and the last thing we need is for you to do a face plant from exhaustion just as we cross a traveling party of Mage.

That would be poor strategy, wouldn't it?

Jag chuckled in his head. *Yes it would. Besides, Cas-*

tin's trail is clear and easy to follow. There's no need for us both to stay in animal form. We'll take turns from here on out.

Since you put it that way . . .

The change flowed over Fox in a heady torrent and a rush of relief. He hadn't realized how much effort he'd been putting into holding the shift until he stopped. But the moment he was a man again, Melisande's sensual energy rushed over his flesh, heating his blood.

He longed to walk straight to her, take her in his arms, and kiss her until she melted. And he might have considered it if he didn't suspect he'd get a knife in the gut for his efforts. He might do it even then if he didn't sense that odd note of vulnerability in her. Despite the tartness of her words and the coolness of her gaze, he felt the need to treat her carefully. Something told him that she was not a woman to be seduced, but instead slowly and carefully gentled. Which was an extraordinary thought given her indisputable strength.

But his instincts with females were usually dead-on.

Olivia patted his shoulder. "Are you okay?"

He smiled at his old friend, throwing his arm around her shoulders and hauling her close for a quick hug. "Jagabelle suggested I take a break and two-foot it for a bit."

She snorted. "You two amuse me." But there was a sadness in her eyes that tugged at him.

"What's the matter, Olivia?"

Her red hair gleamed in the sunlight, but her eyes suddenly turned bright with unshed tears. "Kara. I'm so worried about her."

"We all are." He squeezed her shoulder. "You've become close friends, haven't you?" He'd known Olivia for more than a century and knew her well.

"More than friends. The Feral wives . . ." She shook her head. "We've become sisters. That sounds silly, I know, but it's true. I love her, Fox. *They can't have her.*"

"We'll get her back." And they would. The need burned inside of him as it did all the Ferals.

He glanced over his shoulder at the two Ilinas walking close behind, unable to ignore Melisande even if he wanted to. She glared at him, but the glare didn't quite reach her eyes. Was it possible she was beginning to soften toward him?

Olivia caught the glance back. "Determined to tame that tornado, are you?"

"I'm not sure *tame* is the right word. To be truthful, luv, I'm not sure what I'm doing. I just can't seem to look away for long."

"Smitten," Olivia whispered.

"Never," he whispered back.

With a smile and a shake of her head, she pulled away. Catching up with Jag, she slid her hand along her mate's spotted tail, running her fingers through his fur.

Fox watched, filled once more with the desire to know the feel of Melisande's fingers in his own fur. He paused long enough for the two Ilinas to catch up with him, then fell into step beside them.

"And how are you ladies holding up?" he asked, even as his gaze scanned the surrounding vistas, searching for signs of Mage. Or Castin. Or Kara. His warrior's instincts were so well honed he didn't even have to consciously pay attention. He was always aware of what was going on around him. Always. Regardless of whether or not there was a female in his company he badly wanted to bed.

Phylicia slipped her arm in his, her long, black hair brushing his hip. "You've no idea how wonderful it is to be able to walk the Earth freely again. We were trapped in the Crystal Realm, hiding for so long that I thought we'd never be free."

"You've a lot to make up for."

She cut him a seductive look. "I do indeed." Her mouth tilted attractively. "You know, if we were to take a little break, I could mist you right back to your companions the moment we were through."

"Phylicia . . ." Mel warned.

Did she really think he'd abandon Jag? "A tempting offer, pretty one."

Phylicia beamed at him.

"But my duty is here. Kara comes first."

She smiled, the heat never leaving her eyes. "I'm here whenever you have time, warrior."

"Speaking of Kara," Melisande said coolly. "Go

check on the other team, Phylicia. I want to know if they've found anything."

Phylicia rolled her eyes and, a moment later, disappeared.

Fox eyed Melisande wryly. "Jealous, pet?"

She huffed. "Hardly. She's distracting you. And Kara doesn't deserve that."

They needn't worry. He'd miss nothing. But he leaned toward her, his voice a whisper. "You distract me far more. You distract me just by breathing."

With fascination, he watched her cheeks pinken. No, she wasn't immune to him, not at all, no matter how much she tried to pretend otherwise.

"Then I'll go."

He grabbed her arm. "Don't." At the feel of her soft skin beneath his fingertips, attraction spiked, slamming him with need.

Melisande gasped, her eyes leaping with heat and dismay, and dashed through with wisps of fear.

Fox snatched his hand back. "I'm sorry."

She glared at him, her eyes once more cool, her jaw hard. But, to his relief, she didn't stalk . . . or mist . . . away. Her expression turned to one of long suffering. "I can't leave even if I wanted to. Not with Phylicia gone."

Wisely, he didn't comment, pleased that she deigned to walk beside him. It was the first time they'd walked together, the first time he'd gotten close to her for more than a moment or two. It surprised him how natural it felt. The scent of wild heather wrapped around him, *her* scent, enveloping him in a sensuous fog of want that had his hands clenching at his sides from the desire to touch her again.

Deep inside, his fox snarled as if he disagreed, as if he didn't like her so close. As if he didn't like her at all, contrary animal.

She was so small compared to him, stirring his protective instincts even as he laughed silently, knowing what her reaction would be if he told her so. Pound for pound, she just might be the fiercest person he knew. But, goddess, she was all female, her stride confident and graceful, her features beautifully delicate. He loved the curve of her jaw and the slender beauty of her throat, the skin satin smooth. How he would love to press his mouth against the hollow at its base, to taste the warmth of her flesh and feel her beating heart beneath his lips.

Unfortunately, not only her body language, but that sense he had that he needed to be careful with her precluded any overt action on his part. Even though he was certain that she felt the sensuous energy that leaped between them as strongly as he did.

There's a truck down there, Jag exclaimed suddenly. *Fuck! It's Castin's.*

They all joined him to stare down the steep hill.

"That's impossible," Olivia said incredulously. "We're right back where we started."

Anger clawed at Fox's insides, his equanimity blowing apart in the nonexistent wind. No fecking way. He turned, scanning the forested foothills all around them. Until that moment, nothing had looked familiar. And now everything did. It was plain as day that this was the very spot where they first arrived in West Virginia.

He shook his head. "How could we have circled back without realizing it? My sense of direction is excellent, and we should have been traveling straight." It didn't make any sense.

Jag shifted back to human form in a spray of colored lights and whirled toward them. "I *smelled* him. I know I did. I was on his fucking trail. He must have circled the lake." He turned on Melisande, an accusatory glint in his eyes. "Did you know we were circling back?"

Melisande shook her head, looking around with as much disbelief as the rest of them, the frown on her face for once having nothing to do with anger and everything to do with confusion. "No. This shouldn't have happened."

"Damned Mage warding." Jag's gaze met Fox's. "Did I screw this up?"

"No. But . . ." Fox hesitated.

Jag's gaze narrowed. "But what, pretty boy? If you've got an idea, spit it out."

Fox wasn't even sure why he'd said "but." He didn't have any ideas. He didn't have anything at all, except

. . . "Back at the creek . . . I wanted to leap down into it. And I have no idea why."

Jag studied him. "Your intuition?"

Fox started to shake his head, then hesitated. "I didn't think so. But maybe it was. Or maybe my fox just felt like a dip in the water."

Jag let out a noisy sigh. "Yeah." He looked at his wife. "What do you think, Red?"

Olivia frowned. "Clearly the warding is screwing with us. I say we follow Fox." Olivia crossed her arms, her gaze worried and frustrated. "We have to find a way through this."

"We'll find Kara," Fox assured her, though how, when they couldn't even find their way across the mountain, was anyone's guess.

"You take the lead this time, Foxy." Jag grunted. "Let's hope you have better luck than I did."

Fox nodded, his heart rate jumping. It was up to him, now. He sure as hell hoped he didn't get them *completely* lost.

Or captured by the Mage.

Wulfe stared in disbelief at the now-all-too-familiar rock formation, a pair of rocks sitting at an angle he'd thought interesting the first time he saw it. This was now the third. Dammit!

At the roar rumbling out of Lyon's throat, he knew his chief had seen it, too. The sound, more animal than man, raised the hair on the back of Wulfe's neck. It was a roar filled with a pain and fury no man should suffer, especially one as fine as the Chief of the Ferals.

This mountain was messing with them big-time. They'd picked up Estevan's scent without too much trouble, but it just kept circling back to this rock even when they felt certain they were traveling in a different direction. Twice now!

Lyon went feral, his eyes turning to cat eyes, his fangs and claws sprouting. He turned on Ariana even as Kougar stepped between them.

"Find. The. Way," Lyon growled.

Ariana met that dangerous, furious visage without an ounce of fear. Instead, she shook her dark head with mounting frustration. "I can't, Lyon. I can't sense the way through this mountain's magic any better than you can. You *know* I'd take you to her if I could. You *know* that."

Lyon dipped his head and swung away, his body radiating barely contained rage as he lifted a small boulder and threw it as hard as he could, taking down two pines with a pair of echoing snaps.

Wulfe ached for his friend. They were all desperate to find Kara. They loved her, every damned one of them. And the bastard Mage, probably Inir himself, had her.

"Why can't I sense her?" Lyon released a roar of such anguish, such rage, Wulfe felt gut-punched.

If only they knew. Lyon was the Finder, the one Feral among them all capable of tracking down the Radiant, even if he weren't mated to her. If Kara died, goddess forbid, it would be Lyon who would have to search out her replacement if she didn't come forward on her own.

He physically hurt for his old friend. Lyon wouldn't be right again, *nothing* would be right again, until Kara was once more safely back at Feral House.

Wulfe felt an echoing ache at his own empty arms and was ashamed to admit it wasn't for his dead mate, Beatrice, but for another. For Natalie, a woman who'd never been his and never would be. A woman he didn't even want to be his, not really. She was human. And he . . . He wasn't fit to be any woman's mate.

The Ilina, Brielle, fell into step beside him, surprising him. Few women ever came to him freely, most too put off by the riot of scars that crisscrossed his face.

"Who is she?" Brielle asked quietly, soft understanding in her eyes.

"Who is who?" he growled, nonplussed when she didn't mist away in fright.

Brielle didn't so much as blink. "The woman who lives in your eyes."

It was tempting to tell her that she was mistaken. Or that it was none of her business. Instead, he found himself answering. "She's human. Marrying another."

"Why?"

"Why what?"

"Why is she marrying another when you're in love with her?"

He scowled, wishing he hadn't said anything at all. "I'm not in love with her." It was ridiculous to think he was in love. He just wondered how Natalie fared. He was worried about her. "Besides, I wiped her mind. She doesn't remember me. She . . . can't. For her own safety."

"I'm sorry, Wulfe."

"It doesn't matter." But the words felt like glass in his throat.

"Do you know where she lives?"

"I . . ." He wanted to deny it and couldn't. He'd been to her house once, in wolf form, on the pretext of keeping an eye on her for her brother, Xavier, who was now a guest and prisoner of Feral House since they'd been unable to steal his memories of the horrors they'd both seen. "I know where she lives."

"I can take you there," Brielle said softly. "Anytime you like."

He met the Ilina's vivid gaze. But though he searched for subterfuge, or agenda, all he saw was soft understanding.

"Thank you. But no." Hell. The longing to see Natalie again was an ache inside of him that never went away. But no good could come of it for either of them. Even if she never saw him as anything other than a friendly wolf.

No, after that last visit, he'd promised himself he wouldn't go near her again. And he'd meant it.

Deep inside, his wolf howled, a pained, mournful sound. And his heart ached.

Nearly an hour and a half later, they still hadn't found the creek again. Nothing looked familiar and hadn't for most of the trip. Yet the two shifters insisted they were following Castin's scent.

Melisande ground her teeth in frustration. It wasn't that she didn't believe them, it was just that she didn't trust this mountain. Not at all. None of them did.

Over the last hour and a half, Fox had quit trying to flirt with either her or Phylicia, his mood deteriorating just as hers was, if in a different way. He walked ahead now, at Olivia's side. Melisande's gaze caught on his back, lingering over the snug, perfect fit of his army green tee, which so beautifully defined the shape of him—his broad shoulders, trim waist, and the thick, muscular arms. As much as she told herself to ignore him, her Ilina's eye for fine male flesh had reawakened, and there was no turning a blind eye to so magnificent a specimen.

By the mist, in another time, another world, this shifter would certainly have become her lover and might have become her mate. The energy that continually leaped between them told her that. An Ilina rarely found such a connection with a male, but when she did, it was rarer still for her to be able to walk away from it. The Ilina ended up forming a mating bond with the male, a bond that destroyed her when her mate died, as males often did.

As she watched, that fine back bowed, Fox's biceps flexing, his hands fisting until he looked like he was ready to let out a massive roar. Which would not be a good idea in enemy territory, and the male surely knew it.

"Jag," Olivia called quietly.

The jaguar shifted back to man, turning to Fox. "You okay, Fox-man?"

"The mountain is messing with us, and I've *fecking* had it!" His voice remained low, but so tight with fury that Melisande could hardly believe the words were uttered by the same man who'd charmed her so relentlessly a short while ago. That fury slid over her, wisps of smoke. Deep inside her the need to ease that fury stirred. She tamped it down, shoving back the gift she hadn't used since the softer parts of her died all those years ago. She wanted nothing to do with her softer self.

As she and Phylicia moved far to the side, Melisande caught sight of Fox in profile, his teeth clenched, his eyes taking on an animalistic light. He was shifting. No . . . *going feral* . . . that in-between place where the shifters could fight as equals regardless of the animal spirits who'd claimed them. Fangs sprouted from his mouth and claws from his hands.

Jag watched, a smile slowly spreading across his face. "Feel like another fight, Foxy-boy? I'm more than happy to give you one." Without further warning, Jag leaped at Fox, drawing his own fangs and claws, tearing a chunk out of fox's shoulder.

The two powerful males threw one another to the ground, ripping at faces, arms, chests as if they fully intended to kill one another. Melisande watched them with a mix of disgust—they were *animals*—and fascination. She'd seen shifters fight like this in the old days, but to watch a male as calm as she'd believed Fox to be turn so . . . *feral* . . . was surprisingly exciting.

"It's a wonder he's able to hold it together as much as he has," Olivia said, joining her. "Kieran . . . Fox . . . is more even-tempered than most males, an incredibly controlled fighter, but he's still a new Feral."

The fight didn't last long. Minutes later, they were pulling apart, grinning like a pair of idiots as their claws and fangs retracted.

Jag wiped the blood from his chin. "Feel better?"

"I feel brilliant." Fox turned to her, his face still wreathed in a grin, battle lust lingering in his eyes. "Give me a kiss?"

"Not even in your dreams," she retorted.

To no one's surprise, Phylicia took him up on his offer, running to him lightly, pulling his head down, and kissing him soundly.

Even with his mouth pressed to Phylicia's, Fox's gaze remained locked on Melisande. Then his eyelids dropped closed and his arms went around the other woman, pulling her close.

Jealousy flared bright green behind Melisande's eyes, but she bit down on the need to rip her sister from the troublesome male's arms. They were welcome to one another. Melisande had no use for men, and every one of her sisters knew it.

Fox released Phylicia, slamming Melisande with both his gaze and a grin that crowed victory, as if he could see the jealousy smoking inside of her.

Damn Feral.

Her fingers curled, and she barely resisted the need to press her fist to her stomach, to ease the ache of all the emotions clawing at her insides, fighting to get out. With dismay, she sought the anger, the rage that had been her constant companion for so long, and found it distressingly absent.

What was happening to her? She could never again be the woman she was before her capture. That woman had died in too many ways to count.

But who was she if not the warrior who hated shifters?

I smell water, Jag said nearly two hours later.

Why it had taken so much longer this trip around, Fox had no idea. Well, that wasn't true, was it? He knew exactly why. It was the fecking mountain and its fecking magic. Goddess only knew what kind of danger Kara was in, yet they'd made no progress toward finding her. None whatsoever.

Still, if Jag smelled water, hope stirred. *Maybe that's our creek.*

Give that intuition of yours some leeway, Goldilocks.

Will do, boyo.

Minutes later, they came upon a creek similar to the one they'd seen before . . . or perhaps the same creek, just a different spot along it. Fox stopped beside the stream and reached out, desperate to feel his gut stir, or tug, or wave its hands in the air and sing the Irish National Anthem at the top of its lungs. Anything.

And he got nothing.

Let's follow it a ways, Jag suggested. And not ten minutes later they found that rocky overhang he'd been searching for. *This is the place.* And damn if he didn't feel that same urge he had before to leap down into the creek. *We're crossing.* He shifted back into human form and got body-slammed by Melisande's sensuous heat flowing over his skin, sinking into his pores, into his blood, blasting him with the need to feel her against him, under him, tight around him as he thrust deep inside her wet heat.

Dammit. To. Hell. It was no wonder his frustration kept building out of control.

He looked back to find her watching him with a heat that mirrored his own. A lost look raced across sapphire eyes a moment before her shields slammed down. Everything inside him urged him to go to her, to help her, to comfort her. But those now-frosty eyes and the rigidness of her shoulders told him she wanted nothing more than for him to leave her alone.

There would be time aplenty in the months to come for him to solve the mystery of Melisande. Once Kara was safe.

Is that your gut talking? the jaguar asked, looking up at him.

"I believe so," he hedged, because at the moment all he was hearing was his body's screaming demand to touch the lovely Ilina.

He shivered. And suddenly he *knew.*

Finally. "I'm completely sure. This is the way." Shifting back into his fox, he leaped off the rock and into the water, splashing through the creek on fox paws and climbing out the other side. Giving himself a shake, he shifted back into a man and got hit with the same bloody blast of sultry energy. If only he could find a way to shut it off.

Or satisfy the need it created.

Out of the corner of his eye, he watched Melisande and Phylicia disappear, and then reappear just as suddenly on the other side of the creek. Olivia pulled off her boots and waded across barefoot while Jag leaped across in his animal, then began rooting around for Castin's scent.

With an effort, Fox yanked his mind off the woman who tormented him and shifted back into his animal. His gut might be telling him to go this way, but why? Was this the direction Castin went? Would this path lead them to the Mage stronghold and Kara? Was it the direction of the juicy chipmunk his fox was hungry for?

Got it! Nice work, Goldilocks.

Castin's trail? Fox asked hopefully.

Yep. Plain as day. How in the hell it's going this way and *circling back, is anyone's guess. Maybe Castin did the circuitous route the first time, too, thanks to the warding, then headed across the creek.*

Fox could only hope that was the reason for the strange trail though it didn't explain why it had taken them nearly twice as long to reach the creek the second time as the first. He was afraid the warding really was screwing with them. Which meant they could still conceivably wander this mountain for days and make no progress whatsoever.

They traveled through sundown and into the evening. For a time, they continued by moonlight, but when clouds began to slide in, shutting out all light, Jag called a halt to their progress.

"Olivia can't see, and neither can I unless I'm in my animal. We'll rest. Get some sleep unless the clouds and moon cooperate a little better." They'd seen no draden, which was good news. The small, gaseous Daemon remnants fed off Therian energy and would attack them in their human forms. Fortunately, they didn't bother the animals or Ilinas, and Olivia was draden-kissed, one of only a handful of Therians who could turn the tables on them, draining the draden before they could harm her.

Jag pulled a small lantern out of one of the packs, built a small berm around it with underbrush and dead leaves, then turned it on low, offering enough light for them to see one another but not so much that it would be seen from a distance if there really were Mage around.

Olivia pulled sandwiches out of one of the packs and handed them out. Phylicia and Melisande settled on a rock nearby, but Melisande was the only one who accepted the food.

"You don't eat?" Olivia asked Phylicia.

"I can. And I do sometimes. There are other ways Ilinas prefer to feed." She glanced at Melisande. "Most Ilinas."

"Pleasure," Olivia said matter-of-factly.

"Yes." Phylicia threw Fox a look of speculation and no small invitation.

But it was Melisande who captured his attention and wouldn't let go. He took the sandwich Olivia handed him and bit into it as he tried to keep from staring at the blonde. Legend called them sex sirens and he'd come to learn that for many of them, that was true. They fed on pleasure of all kinds—music, dance, art. Especially the pleasures of the flesh. And they were reputedly skilled and inventive lovers.

If only it were Melisande who wanted to feast on him. They'd be away from here in a heartbeat, and he'd have that trim little tunic and leggings off her so fast it would make her dizzy with delight.

Melisande rose, finished with her sandwich, and turned to Jag. "We'll take watch while you sleep."

Jag nodded. Phylicia joined Melisande and the pair walked away from the campfire. When they were a distance away, Jag glanced at Fox with speculation. "What is it with you and the Ilinas, pretty boy? The nice one looks like she wants to devour you, and the bitch looks like she wants to lop off her friend's head for it."

"Don't call her a bitch." Fox's words were sharper than he intended. No they weren't.

Jag watched him with interest. "Okay."

Olivia nudged her mate with her shoulder as she swallowed a bite of sandwich. "If you tell him you're jealous of all the Ilina attention, I'm going to have to beat your ass, Feral." Her words held a hint of laughter and the utter confidence of a woman well loved.

Jag grinned, cupped the back of her head, and gave her one hell of a kiss. "If there's an ounce of jealousy, and I'm not sure there is, it's a pride thing, nothing more. Not a one of them holds a candle to you, Red. Not a woman on this planet. Or its clouds, for that matter." Though it was clear they were teasing each other, Jag's expression turned intense. "Not a one."

Olivia kissed him back, far more tenderly, then pulled back, laughter in her eyes. "Don't you forget it." Those too-sharp feminine eyes swung to Fox. "So what's going on with you and Melisande?"

Fox shrugged. "Unfortunately, nothing."

Jag snorted. "You just about went feral a moment ago when I disrespected her. Trust me, that's not *nothing*. What does your animal think of her?" he asked with studied indifference.

"He snarls when she's close."

Jag cocked his head, his gaze turning thoughtful. "It's just lust then, Fox-man. I admit, we didn't think it was. Kougar says when an Ilina can't hurt a man, that male is probably destined to be her mate. We've been taking bets on this thing between you and Miss Bitch . . . uh, Miss Melisande. Sounds like I have some inside information now, because the animal spirit is usually the first one to recognize the Feral's mate, usually long before the Feral himself. And if the fox spirit is snarling, that female is not destined to be your mate."

Fox glanced at the lantern. That was good news, of course it was. Great news. He was drawn to her. More than drawn. He was utterly and totally obsessed. But the last thing he wanted was a mate. He wouldn't take her as his mate even if she really was the one.

And she wasn't.

Great news.

Then why did he feel like he'd just been slugged?

Wulfe lumbered through the forest on four paws, his wolf's night vision far better than his man's. Lyon and Kougar, too, had shifted hours back, the two Ilinas accompanying them on foot . . . or floating along beside them as mist. It was impossible to know if they were making any headway this time though it had been hours since they'd last seen that odious rock formation.

Not long after they started off last time, they'd come to a fork in Estevan's scent. One path had headed northeast, the other southwest. Since they'd taken the southwest one the last time . . . they thought . . . they'd headed northeast. And so far, so good. Wulfe could only hope they were on the right track. Finally.

The night was cloudy, but alive with the sounds of crickets and night birds, and the scurrying of the nocturnal animals hunting food and one another.

It was odd to be out at night and not hunting draden. He loved being in his wolf, loved the feel of the breeze through his fur and the soft forest loam beneath the pads of his paws. If only he could lose his mind in the animal's senses as easily as his body. If only he could forget about Natalie for just a little while. Maybe once she married, it would be easier. At least then he'd know she was happy—as happy as she could ever be with her friends dead and her brother permanently missing.

And that was the real problem, he supposed. He knew how sad she was. He'd seen it for himself. And though he'd stolen her memories of that savage battle, and taken the wound on her cheek, adding it to his own gruesome collection, he couldn't take her grief.

She needed to be happy, she *deserved* to be happy. And that was the one thing he couldn't give her.

The sound of voices caught his attention, and he paused, his ears pricking up. But these voices, he realized, weren't coming to him through the air. They were in his head. And they weren't the voices of his brothers.

The Ferals?

I've lost a few. But more Ferals come, my lord. And the originals will cease to be a problem soon.

Good. I've waited a long time for this. Hail the Daemons. Hail the Daem—.

The voices went silent. Wulfe let out a whine.

What's the matter? Kougar asked. In his animal, he slid silently through the forest not far ahead.

I just heard voices, he told his fellow Feral. *Telepathically. Did you hear them?*

No.

Shit. *I think one of them might have been Inir.*

The cougar stopped abruptly and swung toward him, his cat's eyes glowing in the dark. *What did they say?*

That more Ferals are coming. And the originals will cease to be a problem soon.

The cougar stared at him for long minutes, then finally turned away, loping after the lion. *Let me know if you hear anything more.*

As they continued on, Wulfe remained tense, waiting, both wanting to hear more and not. What in the hell did it mean that the Mage was telegraphing his conversation to him like that? Had it been a mistake? Did this mean they were near?

But he heard nothing more, and a couple of hours before dawn, they rounded a corner that felt too familiar. With a sick punch to the gut, Wulfe looked up at that same fucking, idiotic rock formation.

Dammit. To. Hell.

Lyon went berserk, and it was all Wulfe could do not to join him. They'd traveled more than twelve hours . . . *twelve hours* . . . and they were right back where they'd started. They'd made no progress in finding Kara. None!

Kougar's voice rang quietly in his head. *Get some sleep, Wulfe. We'll try again in a few hours, when the sun rises.*

And they'd make another useless circle around this godforsaken mountain before winding up right back here again.

Shall we try to calm Roar?

No. Let him rage. I'd be doing the same if it were Ariana lost to me. I have done the same.

As would he, if it were Natalie. Even though they weren't mated, even though she wasn't his, if she was in trouble, he'd go crazy trying to reach her.

Somehow, they had to find a way to reach Kara.

If only that didn't seem like quite such an impossible task.

Chapter Seven

Fox, Jag, and Olivia ate the rest of their sandwiches in silence, gathered around the small lantern deep in the mountains of West Virginia. The night-insect chorus was in full swing, the air moving and comfortable.

Jag stood up and stripped off his shorts.

Olivia's eyebrow shot up. "Are you trying to tell me something?"

Jag snorted. "Always, my love, but not yet. I want to have a sniff around just to make sure we haven't missed anything."

Fox watched as the man shifted into the jaguar. "Do you want some help, Jagabelle?"

Keep my mate company, Foxy. I won't be gone long.

"Aye." As the jaguar disappeared into the night's shadows, Fox glanced at Olivia sitting across from him, her red hair gleaming in the lanternlight. He rose and joined her on her log. They'd been friends for more than a century and lovers a few times, though neither had felt any emotional attachment beyond the friendship. Therians were notoriously nonmonogamous. They slept around often and freely unless they found the one meant to be their mate, which was rare.

"You're happy," he said, bumping her shoulder gently with his. It wasn't a question. Happiness and contentment radiated from her.

Her grin was slow to bloom, but all the more breathtaking for its depth and completeness. "I am. Never in a million years would I have thought to find such contentment, especially with that Feral. He was an ass, Kieran. He had the worst mouth on him." She laughed. "Well, he still does, but it's just habit, now, not designed to antagonize."

"He's changed." Fox looked at her thoughtfully. "You changed him."

"No, that's not entirely true. He changed, yes, but much of it was his own doing, coming to grips with a past that had haunted him for too long."

"Which he'd not have done if not for you."

"No, probably not." Her hand curled around his forearm. "I hope you find your mate someday. I never knew what I was missing, and it's a good thing. But now that

I've found him, I wonder how I ever survived my cold, solitary existence."

Fox lifted his brows with a slow grin. "Your existence wasn't entirely cold."

She laughed. "No, it wasn't. And yet . . ." Her gaze turned knowing and wise. "When you find the right one . . . the *one* . . . everything that went before pales to nothing. I can't explain it better than that. You'll have to experience it for yourself, and I hope you do someday, Kieran. I truly hope you do."

Fox hooked his arm around her shoulders and pulled her against his side. "You're the only one I ever wanted, Olivia."

She laughed. "Liar."

Fox smiled. "I'm happy the way I am. Some males are suited to mates and some are not. I'm one of the latter."

"You're wrong about that," she said softly, tipping her head against his shoulder. "You'd make the right woman a wonderful mate, Kieran. You'll see."

In the darkness, Fox saw glowing cat eyes. Jaguar eyes. And he was suddenly conscious of just how close he was holding Jag's mate. He started to release her, not wanting to risk the friendship that had developed between them. But the jaguar sat back on his haunches, his stance blatantly nonthreatening.

The warmth of Jag's voice in Fox's head a moment later confirmed it.

*You're okay, Fox-man, you know that? I like know-
ing that Olivia has a friend among the Ferals, someone
who's known her for decades. Every one of the Ferals
will defend her to the death, but you'll be watching
her back even before the trouble starts. And if I'm not
there, you'll be the first one fighting at her side.*

I will, Jag. Absolutely. She's a fine, fine woman. Fox
placed a quick kiss on the top of Olivia's head, then
released her and stood as Jag strode into the camp, a
man once more. Their gazes met, understanding and
friendship passing between them as Olivia rose to meet
her mate. As the couple moved together into the shadows, Fox headed in the other direction and settled on
the ground half a dozen yards from the lantern. Lying
on his back, his hands beneath his head, he stared up
at the clouds scuttling across the faint light that was all
that was visible of the moon.

He'd heard the others say they found it far more comfortable to sleep on the ground or floor in their animals,
but he'd been sleeping like this in human form for centuries and for now, he'd stay with what he knew.

He'd only been lying there a few minutes, hadn't even
closed his eyes, when the premonition hit. One moment
he was staring at the night sky, the next at a stained
ceiling and a single too-bright lightbulb. Like before,
he felt as if it were real. His arms and legs were pulled
outward, spread-eagled, aching as if they'd been in this
position for far too long. Cold stone bit into his hips

and bare shoulder blades. He was sweating, gasping, trying to gain his breath after . . . something. Something horrendous. Pain radiated through his mind, echoes of what he'd just endured, but even the echoes were enough to make him sick.

His vision swam, clearing slowly, revealing once more a world where everything was beige and gray like an old photograph. Sepia tones.

A man walked into his line of sight, the same one he'd seen in his last premonition. Inir? A chill of dread skated over his scalp as he stared into those cold, soulless copper eyes and saw his own death.

"Good news, Feral. It's almost done. Soon, there will be no more pain. You and your animal will be separate entities, the animal spirit mine." The Mage smiled, and it was a terrible thing. "Your animal spirit will be my greatest weapon against the Ferals, while you, of course, turn to dust."

Like hell. He wanted to tell him to go fuck himself, but his vocal cords were too raw to make a sound. From screaming?

Just as quickly as the premonition began, it ended, and Fox found himself staring at the moon overhead as it peeked out briefly between the clouds. His pulse began to hammer. After all Inir had done to destroy the Ferals and free the Daemons, *he* was to deliver that bastard his greatest weapon?

Goddess help him. Goddess help them all.

He sat up, feeling sick to his stomach, and wondered if he should tell Jag now, or wait until morning. Someone needed to know what he was seeing.

He sensed he wasn't alone a heartbeat before Phylicia took form. "Warrior," she whispered softly, and knelt at his side. "I can give you great pleasure if you'll let me. And I'm so hungry. I want you."

For a moment, he ignored her, his mind crowded with the damned premonition that hinted of disaster, yet told him nothing. Maybe what he needed was a distraction.

"Where's Melisande?"

"Keeping watch. And not on us."

"She knows you're here? With me?"

"Yes. She knows."

It was Melisande he needed, dammit. He didn't even need to touch her, just . . . to be near her. But she didn't want that, didn't want *him,* at least not that she was willing to admit. And Phylicia did. He held out his hand to the dark-haired beauty, and she was instantly in his arms, straddling him, her hands sliding over his shoulders, her mouth dipping to find his neck.

Perfume exploded his senses, a rich, musky scent he found pleasant, but little more. If this was the legendary Ilina mating scent that was reputed to drive a male mad with wanting, it was missing the mark. No blood filled his loins.

With a groan of frustration, he gathered the woman against him, pressing his mouth against hers, seeking a passion that wouldn't come. Phylicia rocked against him, making a sound of disappointment when she found no erection to greet her.

She never would. This wasn't going to work. She simply wasn't the woman he wanted.

He lifted her off his lap and set her beside him. "I'm sorry, Phylicia. You're a beautiful woman."

"But you've only eyes for Melisande."

He looked at her, unable to see her eyes in the dark. "Goddess help me if that's true."

"She won't have anything to do with you, warrior, not in that way." She stroked his cheek, her voice sad. "Melisande has no desire in her for anyone. It would be a shame if you, of all males, turned celibate because of it."

Celibate? He'd rather be dead.

Then again, if his visions came true, he might soon find himself exactly that.

They set out again the moment dawn began to lift the night's dark cover. Fox led the way this time, in his animal, while Jag and the others followed on two feet. Fox was antsy this morning, as if he'd woken with an itch beneath his fur. Everything was wrong out here. They'd found nothing—no sign of the Mage or Kara or Castin. Nothing but more fecking mountain.

He couldn't even summon the will to engage Melisande. All he could think about was finding the way out of this godforsaken useless loop of a trail.

They'd only traveled a short distance when the blindness hit him suddenly. One moment, he was following Castin's scent beneath a dawn sky, and the next, he had no sight at all. He hoped to hell it was another premonition and not something worse, something more sinister. With a whimper, he lay down on his stomach, afraid to move forward when he couldn't see.

"Fox-man?" Jag asked.

He smelled Olivia beside him, felt her hand stroke his head, and wished it was Melisande's. "Kieran? What's the matter?"

He couldn't focus enough even to speak telepathically. And then he couldn't think at all as a scene opened up before his sightless eyes.

In the vision, he was walking down a hallway that looked to be one of the upstairs halls at Feral House. He recognized the wallpaper and the paintings on the walls, faintly lit by electric sconces. It was night. Stopping before one of the doors, he reached for the handle and turned it slowly. Quietly. Then let himself inside, closing the door behind him.

The room was huge—far bigger than his own—decorated with heavy wallpaper and dominated by a large bed draped in dark red and gold. He'd seen this room before though only from the doorway. The Radiant's bedroom. Lying in the bed was a woman he didn't know, a woman whose hair appeared, in the moonlight, to be red.

His heart clutched at the sight of this stranger in Kara's bed which could only mean she was Kara's replacement. The new Radiant. *They were going to lose Kara.*

He padded quietly to the bed, but even as silent as he was, the woman's eyelids fluttered up. "Fox? What are you doing here?"

Without answering, he sat on the edge of the bed beside her. But when he lifted a hand as if to stroke her face, she jerked away and sat up.

"What's the matter with you? I'm a mated female and well you know it. Wulfe would not be happy to find you here."

Wulfe. This woman would be Wulfe's mate?

Saying nothing, he pulled his hand away, then suddenly lunged, grabbed her, and shoved his thumb beneath her ear, knocking her out. The woman crumpled, hitting her head on the headboard with a dull thud. Lifting her, he positioned her on the bed just as she'd been when he first arrived until she looked like she was sleeping. Then he rose and opened the window. Wide.

What the hell? It was nighttime. The draden were drawn to the Radiant's energy above all others. If they got in, they'd drain her life in minutes.

But without a backward glance, he left the room, closing the door quietly behind him.

"Kieran?" Worry laced Olivia's voice. The stroke of her hand over the top of his head jerked him back to the present. "Are you okay?"

He shifted into man form, then rolled onto his back, covering his eyes with his arm, shutting out the people standing over him, trying to shut out the vision he'd just seen. He was going to kill her. The new Radiant. Was *that* what the Mage would do to his animal? Turn him evil, too?

"What happened, Fox?" Jag's voice was, for once, warrior hard.

Fox sat up, blinking, and found Melisande watching him from behind the others. Golden brows were drawn in worry, a hint of compassion softening hard sapphire eyes, and he held onto that, his gaze clinging to hers, feeling it like a lifeline pulling him from the chaos of the vision, tethering him to the here and now. Slowly, as he stared at her, the confusion slipped away.

But not the despair.

"I've been getting premonitions," he admitted, shifting his gaze to Jag. The scene played out all over again in his head, holding him hostage. *I'm a mated female and well you know it. Wulfe would not be happy to find you here.* Wait. Wasn't Wulfe the mate of the previous Radiant, the one before Kara? Could he be chosen again? Or . . .

Holy fecking goddess.

Leaping to his feet, he swung toward Jag. "How did the previous Radiant die? Wulfe's mate." What if he hadn't been seeing the future but the past?

Jag eyed him keenly, as if he wasn't entirely sure Fox

hadn't lost his mind. "The Cub killed her. The damned Mage had gotten to him months ago and cut out his soul without anyone's knowing, including him. He acted the same as always, but he was partly under the thrall of the Mage. He killed Beatrice, our Radiant, six months ago. He opened the window of her bedroom one night. The draden, of course, came right for her."

"What color hair did Beatrice have?"

"Why?"

His patience snapped. "Just answer the fecking question, Jag. It's important."

The other Feral held up his hands in a sign of surrender. "Red. Not as bright as Olivia's, but she was a redhead. Again, why?"

His gaze slid back to Melisande, an inner need to connect with her pulling at him. If she were his, he'd have her in his arms right now, tight against his side, her heartbeat steadying his own.

Slowly, his gaze returned to Jag's. "I think I just saw the Cub kill her. Through his eyes."

"Shit, Fox. Has this happened before? These . . . sight things?"

"Twice in the past twenty-four hours. I thought I was starting to get premonitions, but now . . . I'm not so sure."

Jag turned all warrior. "Tell me about the other two."

"I was captured. By the Mage. And they were trying to separate me . . . him . . . from his animal."

"The Cub?"

"I don't know. I don't think so. The vision looked completely different. Like I was seeing the world in sepia tones."

Jag frowned. "Color-blind, maybe? Sly, the fox shifter who preceded the Cub, was color-blind. Sounds to me like you're getting flashbacks from your animal. I've never heard of that happening before. We never knew how Sly died. He was one messed-up fuck."

"How long was he missing?"

"About a year. He'd been a Feral for almost two millennia, second-oldest of the bunch, but a real loner. A year after he disappeared, the Cub showed up, twenty years old and newly marked. The new fox shifter. That's how we knew Sly was dead." He looked at Fox carefully. "Do you think the Mage succeeded? In separating animal from Feral?"

"In other words, do I think my animal was compromised, too?" Bloody, fucking hell. He'd been so sure he was the lucky one for not being marked by one of the seventeen. Instead, he might be as damaged as the rest of them. "I don't know. So far, all I know is they had him and were torturing him."

"Kieran should be fine," Olivia said, but there were traces of worry in her eyes. "Haven't you all decided that a dark infection transferred to the new Feral through the animal marking would only affect the next one marked? That the one marked after him should be fine? The Cub was the infected one. Not Kieran."

Her loyalty warmed him. But Jag didn't look entirely convinced, and Fox couldn't blame him. Why would an unaffected Feral be getting sudden flashbacks from his animal?

There was no doubt in his mind that something more was going on. He just hoped to hell the Ferals didn't decide to toss him in prison, too.

Jag clasped him on the shoulder. "Let's get going. We can think about what it all means as we walk."

Fox nodded, glancing at Melisande, who watched him with eyes once more cool and enigmatic. The compassion he'd briefly glimpsed in her was gone. Shaken and unsettled from that vision, he turned to follow Jag, remaining in human form, while Jag took the lead in animal.

They hadn't traveled long when Jag let out a frustrated sound. *I've lost the fucking trail.*

Fox immediately shifted and joined him in the search, but there was no sign of it nearby. None.

"What now?" Olivia asked, her voice ripe with the frustration they were all feeling.

As one, the two males shifted back into human form. Fox felt the trip of sexual energy and glanced unerringly to where Melisande stood behind him, noting with satisfaction the way her chest rose, the way her eyelids drooped even as those sapphire eyes speared him, hot and frustrated.

Goddess, he wanted her. He wanted to haul her into

his arms, to claim her mouth as his fingers loosened her braid and buried themselves in her beautiful hair.

Instead, he turned back to Jag. "I suggest we track in wider and wider circles. The trail has to be here somewhere. The male didn't simply up and disappear."

"I agree. I'll take the north and west, you cover the south and east."

As Jag headed left, Olivia at his side, Fox turned right, Phylicia and Melisande following him. He and the Ilinas hadn't gone far, maybe ten yards, when Fox shivered, his gut offering him up a truth.

The trail is this way, according to my intuition, he said to all of them at once.

Hot damn, Jag replied.

But half a dozen steps later, a strange sensation lifted the fur on Fox's body, starting at his nose and traveling toward the tip of his tail. It almost felt as if he were moving through . . .

His gut roared, his intuition exploding. *Danger!*

Behind him, Melisande and Phylicia began to scream. He whirled and leaped, knocking Melisande to the ground beneath his huge fox form.

But Phylicia continued to scream, and when he turned his head, he saw why. The dark-haired Ilina was engulfed in flame.

Chapter Eight

Agony blasted through Fox. Screams filled his ears as he lay on top of Melisande in his animal form, covering her, protecting her. One moment they'd been walking through the mountain forest and the next all of them were screaming with pain, Phylicia on fire. He'd recognized the thrill of magic too late. Too late.

"Get off me!" Melisande pushed at him, pounding at his sides. "Get off me, I have to reach Phylicia."

No, you can't go near her. We hit warding. Mist, Melisande. Get the hell out of here.

"Can't mist." The words came out on a gasp of pain.

What the fuck? Jag yelled in his mind.

Jag, help me get Melisande away from the fire. If I get up, I'm afraid it'll take her, too.

Don't shift! Your animal form may be all that's keeping you from flaming.

The jaguar stumbled forward, lurching as if he'd suffered a near-fatal blow. Grabbing Melisande's arm in his mouth, he tugged and began to pull backward. Fox grabbed her other arm in his mouth and joined Jag, hauling her back away from the warding, away from her burning Ilina sister.

"Save her, Fox!"

Melisande's plea tore at him. It was her he needed to protect. But she appeared to be safe enough. For now. He swung to Phylicia, his stomach plummeting, clenching with horror as he stared at the woman. Her dark hair was now locks of flame, her clothes on fire. The scent of burning flesh raked at his nose, her screams tore at his eardrums as he leaped at her as he had Melisande, into the flames, taking her down. Fire scorched his fur, a second blast of burning energy plowed through his body.

But the fire didn't go out.

Beneath him, the woman screamed and screamed as the fire leaped out from beneath him, licking at his snout, singeing his fur. But not catching.

Jag nudged him with his nose. *Let's move her.*

Fox leaped up, and together they grabbed her burning arms in their mouths, dragging her from the warding as they had Melisande. Her screams quieted suddenly, the woman falling unconscious. The taste of burning flesh filled his mouth, searing his nose and eyes.

As they dragged her to Melisande, the blonde Ilina turned toward her friend, agony etching her face as she took Phylicia's limp hand.

Through his animal's keen vision, Fox stared at Phylicia's devastated form—her hair and clothing all but burned away, her skin patches of blackened leather. *Goddess.*

The fire was all but gone, now centered in only one place—the hole in her chest where her heart should be. As Fox watched, the unconscious Ilina's flesh turned suddenly, ghostly gray.

Melisande cried out, then fell back, closing her eyes. "She's dead."

Fox stared, stunned, meeting first Jag's, then Olivia's pained gazes. Olivia was on her knees, clearly in physical agony. As Fox shifted back to a man, he understood why. The pain he'd felt in animal form was ten times worse in human, a stinging, slicing energy as if the warding were trying to fry him alive even without flame. Oddly, he felt fine tendrils of pleasure darting through that energy, almost as if one of Melisande's pain bombs had locked in permanently.

He blinked. That might be what had happened.

Kneeling beside her, he touched her shoulder. "Mel,

we're all in pain, Jag and Olivia most of all. But I think the energy is coming from you."

She opened her eyes, revealing a storm of emotions so strong he was amazed she wasn't screaming, crying. Grief, pain, terror. He heard every one of them in her voice, when she spoke.

"It is. The warding triggered my pain blast." Her eyes turned bleak. "I can't turn it off, I can't mist, I can't call Ariana. I can barely move."

"We've got to get away from here," Jag growled, in human form again, kneeling beside Olivia. "The warding's killing us." They were worse off than he was, perhaps because Melisande's energy wasn't designed to hurt him.

"It's not the warding, it's Melisande. The warding triggered her energy, and she can't shut it off."

"We can't . . ."

"Go," Fox told him. "Get Olivia out of here. Let the other team know we've found the warding and warn them to keep the Ilinas away."

"You're staying?" There was disbelief in Jag's tone, resignation in his eyes.

"Melisande can't move and can't mist. I'm staying."

"The Mage . . ."

"Will have felt it, I know. They'll be swarming soon. We'll follow once you're out of range. Or once her energy turns off."

Jag looked at him like he wanted to argue . . . it wasn't in a Feral's nature to leave a brother behind, Fox had learned that much in the short time he'd been one of them.

"We'll hide," Fox told him. "Now, go! Get word to Kougar before Ariana meets the same fate as Phylicia."

With a nod, Jag looped his arm around Olivia, and together they stumbled back the way they'd come.

Fox turned back to Melisande who was trembling, her face white as snow. "I'm going to carry you, Mel."

"No."

But he saw no alternative and scooped her into his arms.

She began to struggle. "Let me go."

"I'm not going to hurt you. We've got to get out of here before the Mage find us."

At first, she was stiff in his arms, but as the tremors wracked her slender frame, she began to soften, curling her arm around his neck, tipping her forehead against his jaw. A feeling of rightness poured through him, followed by a raging rush of protectiveness.

The Mage weren't going to touch her. He'd kill them first. Every bloody one.

Kara stood in the center of the circle of Feral Warriors in bare feet, jeans shorts, and a T-shirt, shivering even though the day was warm, the sun hot on her arms and shoulders. This was all so wrong. These weren't *her* Ferals. Yes, she'd brought them into their animals on the goddess rock near Feral House in Great Falls several days ago. But they weren't in Great Falls any longer. Instead, they stood on a rocky ledge overlooking a mountain hillside deep in a forest . . . somewhere. She had no idea where. Behind her loomed a castle built into the mountainside. The stronghold of the Mage Elemental, Inir.

The four Ferals—Polaris, Croc, Witt, and Lynks— circled her now, their chests bare, their eyes cold as a winter sky. Their golden armbands, each with the head of the shifter's animal, gleamed in the sunshine as Polaris chanted the ritual to bring a new Feral into his animal, a ritual he'd learned during his own *Renascence*. There had been such joy during that ceremony as the animals they'd thought long lost returned to mark Feral Warriors once more. They hadn't yet realized the new ones marked by the lost spirits had been infected with dark magic.

This ceremony was even more of a travesty, for it wasn't being led by her beloved Ferals at all but by the evil ones, with the express purpose of adding another warrior to their vile army. And they expected her to participate. The new Feral wouldn't come into his animal without her radiance.

The thought of helping them made her skin crawl. The stronger the evil Feral army became, the better the chance they would destroy the men she loved. But the males were three times her size, every one of them. And a hundred times as strong.

And so she shook.

If only the good men inside them would fight the darkness as a couple of the other new Ferals had. Grizz had allowed himself to be captured. As had Lepard. But she saw no struggle against the darkness in the eyes of any of these four. She feared that Inir's control over them was complete.

Her gaze slid beyond the circle of evil Ferals to Inir, and her gut cramped. He stood in a ceremonial robe of blood red, his arms crossed, his face a cold mask of authority. His face was round and plain, forgettable but for the eyes, which gleamed pure copper. His hair, cropped close to his head, appeared to be almost the same shade as his eyes.

Beside Inir stood another man, the newly marked Feral they intended to bring into his animal. A tall, lanky male with fear in his eyes.

Polaris took his knife to himself, carving a bloody line across his chest, then slapped his hand to it, fisting the blood as he handed the knife to Lynks.

It was Lynks's fault she was here, the traitor. He'd been cleared of the darkness, yet somehow Inir had kept his hooks in the man. He'd knocked her out as they'd descended the stairs to the basement of Feral House, and she'd awakened, bound and gagged, in the back of a minivan barreling down the interstate.

How he'd gotten her away without Lyon's knowing, she couldn't guess. The thought of what her beloved must be going through tore her heart to shreds.

Unless . . . No he wasn't dead. She still felt their mating bond strong and bright inside her, and she wouldn't if he were dead. Would she?

Tears burned her eyes, and she struggled against them, blinking them away. A warm breeze caressed her cheek as gently as Lyon's thumb might have, and she felt him within her, filling her with his love, giving her strength. No, he wasn't dead. Crazed, perhaps. Frantic with his inability to find her and almost certainly blaming himself for her capture. She knew her lion.

The white tiger shifter, Witt, cut his chest, the last of the four to do so, and handed the knife back to Polaris.

Polaris turned to her. "Call the radiance," he commanded. Locked away deep inside him was a good man. Ewan, he'd been called before he was marked by the infected polar bear spirit. He'd been a friend of Olivia's, one of her soldiers, for decades. But he was captive of the darkness. A good man no longer. And she would not do as he demanded.

"I can't." She lifted her chin. "I can only go radiant near Feral House, where the earth's energies are the strongest." It was a lie, and they all knew it. She'd already gone radiant once here, attacking one of her captors.

Unable to hold his gaze, she looked up at the sky, wishing with all her heart she'd see a hawk or falcon, that they might be shifters who would lead Lyon and the others to her. Why couldn't they find her? It had been two days since she'd been taken. Two days. But looking to the skies, all she saw were crows.

"Do it, Radiant." Inir's voice was soft and chilling.

Kara set her jaw. "No." Her gaze found the newly marked Feral, her gaze catching his. "I won't help you turn this man evil."

The new Feral's face paled, glistening with sweat, as he looked from her to the bloody warriors, to Inir, and back again. "Yeah, I . . . don't think this is such a good idea."

Inir ignored him, his copper gaze focused solely on her. "Hurt her."

Kara gasped, then clamped her jaw shut as terror bolted through her. But she made no sound as Croc stepped forward, a gleam of pleasure in his eyes as he balled his fist and plowed it into her cheekbone. Pain exploded as she flew, landing on the rough stone.

"Go radiant, and he won't do it again," Inir said evenly.

Oh, God. "No." Thankfully, she was immortal and could already feel her injuries knitting. As the pain began to recede in her face and hands, Croc brought his boot down hard on her leg, snapping her femur in two. Agony turned her vision white, and she screamed, unable to hold back the cry. Turning watery, furious eyes on the evil Mage who commanded them all she snarled between clenched teeth, "Kill me if you want to. I'm not helping you build your evil army."

As her leg, too, healed, she tensed for the next blow, but it didn't come. When the pain was gone, she warily pushed herself to her feet, wondering what torture he'd devise for her next.

A moment later, she knew, as one of the sentinels led a little girl with flyaway hair and missing front teeth to Inir. The child, no more than six years old, looked at the bloody warriors with wide, terrified eyes.

Inir took her hand and she allowed it . . . until he pulled a knife and cut a gash across her palm. The child screamed and screamed, trying to tug her injured hand away from him, but he held it fast, and open, facing it toward Kara.

"She's mortal," he said without emotion.

Kara's head began to pound. "Leave her alone, you bastard." With righteous fury, she lunged forward, but Croc grabbed her arm and held her back.

Inir smiled, and she realized she'd given him exactly what he wanted. A way to get to her. She felt the blood drain from her face. For most of her adult life, until Lyon found her and the Ferals ascended her to Radiant, she'd been a preschool teacher. Children, human children, had been her life. And the thought of standing coldly by while one was hurt . . .

Inir yanked the girl's dress up and over her head, stripping her of everything but a pair of cotton panties with blue butterflies on them. Inir hooked one arm around the tiny girl, pinning her arms to her sides as she cried and struggled to get away. His tanned and hairy arm looked obscene across the child's pale, skinny belly.

Kara shook, torn as she didn't think she'd ever been before. Giving in to Inir, bringing one more evil Feral into his animal, could cost the lives of the men she loved. Yet how could she allow this child to suffer?

Inir began cutting a shallow furrow across that pale belly. Blood welled and ran, turning blue butterflies purple, as the child screamed, slicing Kara's heart into a million pieces. "Stop!"

Inir lifted his knife, glanced at her, then began a second cut parallel to the first. "Go radiant."

Closing tear-filled eyes, Kara pulled the power from the earth. In an instant, she felt the warmth slide through her flesh as she went radiant. The four Ferals closed in on her, clamping rough, punishing hands around her wrists and arms, drawing from her power.

Blinking hard against the moisture, Kara opened her eyes, found Inir, and shot daggers into his chest. If only she could kill him for real.

The villain dumped the bleeding, screaming child onto the stone and motioned to one of his sentinels. "Get her out of here."

Polaris released Kara and turned toward the new Feral. "Hold him," he told the sentinels.

The male blanched. "What are you going to do?"

Polaris lifted his knife and cut a shallow furrow across the man's chest, then grabbed one of his hands and forced him to slap his palm against his own bleeding chest. "Make a fist."

"Why?"

"Just do it."

When the man had, Polaris opened his own bloodied fist and placed his palm on top of the new Feral's. The other three stepped forward and did the same, one atop the other.

Polaris resumed the chant, and the others slowly followed. "Spirits rise and join. Empower the beast beneath this sun. Goddess, reveal your warrior!"

Thunder rumbled, the ground shaking as if furious at this sham. The new Feral threw back his head with a look of surprise and dawning excitement. Then he disappeared in a flash of colored lights, shifting into his animal for the first time. A moment later, an unnaturally large wolverine stood in the middle of the rock, snarling. And a moment after that, he was a man again, fully clothed, a look on his face entirely different from the one he'd worn before. Gone was the fear. In its place, evil slid across eyes gone cold.

Kara swayed, feeling suddenly clammy and light-headed.

Croc grabbed her arm, tight enough to leave bruises. "Back to your room, Radiant."

At least if she stumbled, there would be someone to catch her. Tears burned her eyes. If only that someone were her beloved Lyon.

Lyon, where are you?

But no one answered.

Melisande clung to Fox, her arm wrapped around his thickly corded neck, his soft hair brushing her cheek as she shattered. Emotions locked beneath the ice flayed her alive. The grief. The crushing guilt. Pain.

Only the panic had eased, lessened momentarily by the strength of Fox's arms. Her thudding heart merely raced now, the terror no longer trying to claw its way out of her throat. But the white fear was far from gone because she couldn't mist. She couldn't defend herself.

Trapped. Again. The last time . . .

Memories rose up, and with them a terror that stole her breath. She felt weak, sick at her stomach. She had to mist, had to escape. She would not be captured again!

"You're safe, Mel," Fox said quietly against her temple.

"If the Mage find us . . ."

He pulled back, forcing her to look at him. Too close, his sky blue gaze gripped her, forcing her to hear him, to believe him. "I won't let anything happen to you, I promise." Pain radiated through those eyes, his jaw tensing.

"I'm still hurting you. My energy."

His mouth twisted ruefully, and she found herself admiring the strong curve of his jaw and its light dusting of golden beard stubble. "Your energy isn't all pleasure this time, that's for sure." That stubbled chin brushed her temple. "But it's not your fault."

It was the fault of the Mage and their warding. But his low voice soothed, and she found herself holding on to him harder, his warm, masculine scent wrapping her in a sensual cocoon that almost . . . almost made her feel safe.

But safety of any kind was an illusion.

The emotions tore at her, and she struggled to contain them, to control them. She couldn't live with them, not this way. Not this way. Too much.

"Bloody hell," Fox muttered.

Melisande opened her eyes, peering in the direction he was looking and stilled, stunned as she stared at the beautiful lake far below, sparkling beneath the sunny sky.

"What's the matter?"

"This is the way we came."

She frowned. "There was no lake the way we came."

"Precisely."

"Are we lost?"

"Not lost, no. I have an excellent sense of direction, and I know exactly where we should be. It has to be more of the mountain's magic." He turned his face, once more brushing her temple with his stubbled chin. "I'm going to put you down. I want to take a look around and try to pick up our trail. I need to shift."

He lowered her to the ground atop a soft bed of leaves and moss beneath a tall oak. But the moment he released her, she began to shake again, the panic crawling up her throat. What if the magic swept him away?

"Mel?" he asked worriedly.

"I'm fine," she snapped.

He eyed her for a moment more, then nodded. "I won't be out of your sight."

In a flash of sparkling lights, he shifted, then began sniffing, moving slowly away.

Melisande clutched her knees to her chest, shivering from a cold that burrowed deep inside of her as if the shards of shattered ice were rising to the surface. Phylicia's face, her death mask, blazed across her mind, searing her with loss and a fury too deep to voice. Ever since that first alliance between Ferals and Ilinas a thousand years ago, the Mage had been determined to destroy the mist warriors. They'd taken one, now. And what of Ariana and Brielle? Would Jag reach them in time to warn them, to keep them from suffering the same fate?

Fear for them pressed down on her until she could

hardly breathe, until she felt as if a Feral stood on her chest, crushing her.

She struggled for control, struggled to feel nothing, as her gaze followed the huge red fox. Finally, he shifted back to human form. As he started back, Melisande pushed herself to her feet, then sank back down when her legs refused to hold her.

A moment later, Fox was at her side, gripping her arm carefully. His brows drew down, the back of his hand pressing against her cheek. "You're like ice." Without a moment's hesitation, he sat beside her and pulled her onto his lap, wrapping his thick warm arms around her. Palming her head, he pressed her cheek to his shoulder.

Her warrior's pride demanded she push him away. Instead, she shuddered with relief and curled into his warmth. *For just a few minutes,* she told her pride. *I need this.*

"You're still shaking like a leaf. You're in shock, Mel," he said quietly. "You can cry you know." His nose nudged her forehead. "I won't tell."

She almost smiled. "I don't remember how to cry." As the moments passed, and she soaked in the warmth and strength of Fox's arms, her tremors slowly calmed. But as her own tension melted, she began to feel his. Not a warrior's alert tenseness, but pain.

"I'm still hurting you, aren't I?"

"Your energy is, aye."

"You should have gone with Jag and Olivia."

The hand palming her head began to move, stroking her with a care that felt alien . . . and disturbingly sweet. "I would never leave you here, alone and defenseless."

She pulled back until she could see his face. His brows were pulled together, small furrows of pain between his eyes.

"Would you have left Phylicia if I'd been the one who'd died?" she asked.

He was silent for a moment, his hand sliding down her braid, curling it around his hand. "No. I would never abandon any female like that." The truth of his words shone in his eyes. "Or any male, for that matter."

"Why do you have to be so damned honorable?"

A smile tugged at his lips. "Do you wish me dishonorable?"

"I could dislike you easier if you were. You're a hard man to hate, Feral."

"Thank you. I think." He tugged gently on her braid. "You're no longer shaking."

"No. But I'm still blasting the energy. It's weakening me." She frowned. "I don't know how to shut it off."

"Hopefully, it will stop on its own. I'll carry you until you're stronger."

"I think I can walk, now. Did you find our trail?"

His jaw tensed. "No. The trail is gone, both forward and aft. It's as if we misted into this spot."

"That's impossible."

"Aye, but it's a fact. We're not where we were."

Cold dread trickled down her spine. "Then where are we?"

He shook his head. "I've no bloody idea." Lifting her off his lap, he rose, then pulled her to her feet beside him, keeping his arm around her.

Her legs wobbled but managed to hold her this time, her body's healing abilities fighting the weakness. Pulling away from him, she met his gaze. "I can walk."

He held out his hand to her, his blue eyes glittering with a fierce protectiveness. "I want you to hold on to me and not let go. The mountain is fecking with us, and I wouldn't put it past it to try to separate us."

She'd had the same thought and took his hand without hesitation. His warm fingers closed firmly around hers, and she breathed more easily. What was he doing to her? He was a man, a shifter, and she had no business trusting him. None at all.

Except she did.

But there would be time to think about that later, when they weren't in quite so much danger. When she could mist again and no longer needed him. Her plan to keep him at a distance had failed spectacularly.

"If we don't know where we are, then we don't know where the warding is," she murmured.

His jaw clenched. "No. Hopefully it's nowhere near here." Hand in hand, he led her up the hill, the opposite direction they'd been going. She managed to keep one foot in front of the other though the effort cost her. She was so damned weak.

Melisande had no idea how far they'd traveled when, once more, all hell broke loose. Something hit them, hard, and they were flying backward, their hands coming unlinked.

Pain screamed through her body, a hundred times worse than before. Fire licked up all around her.

They'd hit the warding.

Again.

Chapter
Nine

"**M**elisande!"

Fox shifted into his animal right where he landed, leaping at Melisande, covering her as he had the first time he'd run her into the warding. *Bloody hell.*

She was engulfed in flame.

Terror ripped through his mind, a terror that he wouldn't be able to save her, even as blazing agony tore through his body nearly short-circuiting his brain. Beneath him, Melisande screamed.

Don't you dare die on me, angel. Don't you dare.

The unnatural fire seared his nerve endings, right through his fur, until his animal whimpered, until he wanted to howl.

Mel, we're too close to the warding. I've got to move you.

She didn't answer, and he realized she'd gone still beneath him. *Just as Phylicia had moments before she died.* His heart seized. Panic clawed at his mind. Should he continue to cover her and hope the fire went out, or try to move her? And if he did try to move her, which direction? He wasn't even sure where the warding was, and if he pulled her through it again, it was all over.

It might be already.

Goddess, goddess, goddess. If only his gut would give him a clue. He turned his frantic mind inward, searching for some sign, and got nothing. But his instinct was to stay put and continue to blanket her with his monster fox form as he had the last time.

His heart pounded, fear ripping a hole in him as he pressed his fox face against Melisande's flesh, praying, *praying,* he'd covered her in time. He couldn't see the flames and had no idea if they continued. All he knew was that the pain continued to sear him alive, on and on and on. At least she'd fallen unconscious and wasn't suffering.

Finally, *finally,* the searing heat began to ease away. Beneath him, Melisande's chest continued to rise and fall, her heart beating steadily against his own. He made a whimpering sound in his fox's throat, his muscles going lax in relief.

Thank the goddess.

He had to get her out of here. If only his intuition would tell him in which direction lay safety. Lifting himself up slowly, he looked down at her through his fox's eyes, relieved to the depths of his soul to find no hole in her chest. The damage to her had already healed. Even her clothes appeared barely singed.

Backing off her, he turned away, nosing in every direction, seeking the warding. There. The buzz zapped his nose no more than three feet from the soles of Melisande's boots. He followed it a couple of yards in both directions, needing to make sure, then shifted back into human form and lifted Melisande into his arms. Tucking her tight against his chest, he strode hard and fast in the opposite direction. He couldn't get her away from that deadly energy fast enough.

But as he strode across the forest floor, suddenly everything changed. Stone walls appeared out of nowhere, thirty feet high, at least fifteen feet long, as if he'd walked through an invisible portal into another world.

What the hell?

He tried to back up and return to the forest, but instead he slammed into stone. The walls hemmed them in on all sides. *Impossible.* High above, blue skies peered down.

He'd walked them into a bloody prison.

This was *not* possible. His heart began to thunder in his chest.

In his arms, Melisande stirred, her eyes fluttering open, then snapping wide as she struggled to pull herself up.

"Where are we?" she demanded, groggily.

"I've no bloody idea." Pulse pounding, he set her on the cobblestones at his feet. "Wait here."

She snorted. "It doesn't look like there's anyplace to go."

He strode forward, slamming his palms against rough, cool stone liberally covered in soft moss. "It appears to be real," he muttered.

Melisande pushed herself slowly to her feet. "You thought it wasn't? How did we get caught in here, anyway?"

She swayed, and he rushed back and grabbed her arm, steadying her. With surprise, he realized he felt no pain.

"You've stopped blasting energy."

"Yes." Confusion clouded her eyes. "We hit the warding again."

"Aye."

Sapphire eyes lifted to his. "You knocked me down. I don't remember anything after that."

"There's not much to remember." She seemed steadier, if still in shock. He released his grip on her, running his hand lightly up and down her tunic-clad arm instead. "I picked you up, carried you away from the warding, and here we are. I saw this place appear out of the corners of my eyes between one step and the next."

Fear bolted through her eyes. "Magic, then. When we hit the warding, we must have ended up inside it."

The thought chilled him to the bone. If the magic could displace them, it could certainly toss them into this prison. Just where the Mage wanted them, where they could slaughter them like pigs.

No bloody way.

He tugged on a springy lock of golden hair that had pulled loose from her braid. "We'll get out of this, Mel." But he wasn't so sure, and the look she gave him told him she knew it. And agreed.

"It's too bad you can't shift into a bird," she muttered, then turned toward the nearest wall, kicking and pushing, running her hands along the stone as if looking for a fingerhold that might allow her to start climbing.

There was no doubt in his mind she was still in shock, yet she'd pulled herself together, and he admired her for it.

Joining her, he, too, sought a loose stone or a way out, but nothing moved, and the wall was too tightly built to allow for climbing. Inside him, anger sparked, frustration growing until he found himself growling low in his throat, until he feared his claws and fangs were about to erupt.

Bloody fecking hell.

He had to get control. Or instead of protecting Melisande, he was going to wind up hurting her.

As they beat helplessly at the stone walls, as escape appeared less and less likely by the moment, Melisande fought back the panic that once more stalked her. Deep within her mind, the screams began to rise, and she pushed them away, struggling to build a mental wall or a box, anything to keep them away from her, to keep them buried. So many emotions. How had she ever lived beneath the onslaught of so much *feeling*?

Slowly, she managed to force the emotions into an imaginary box where she locked them up tight, then prayed she could keep them there, keep them silent, or she didn't know how she'd function at all. As it was, she had more than enough to deal with. With the return of her emotions came the memories, a flood of them. Miserable memories, filled with pain and grief. Raw, even after centuries.

Being unable to feel had allowed her to be strong, so incredibly strong. She'd been able to do what had to be done to protect her queen and her race. Feelings— compassion, sympathy, pity—invariably got in the way of that. She did not want to be the woman she'd once been, softhearted, *weak*. She liked being the warrior, liked being untouched emotionally by what went on around her.

The emotions were back now, in all their miserable color. Most of them, at least. But she would go cold again, once she found Castin. As long as she didn't allow Fox to soften her more.

She watched him beat at the stone, then run at it, full speed, ramming it with his shoulder. Bone crunched and he grimaced, then returned to his starting point and ran at it again. Over and over, he hit the wall until his shirt was bloody, until the sounds coming from his throat were more animal than man.

He whirled on her suddenly, the fangs dropping from his gums, his eyes turning to yellow animal eyes.

"Fox?"

She swallowed as she stared at his fearsome visage, at the wild male trapped within the stone walls with her, a shifter gone feral, half-out of his mind with the need to tear something apart.

And she was the only thing within reach.

As she watched the fury and struggle war in his eyes, her old gift raised its head once more. The need to ease the torment of others. The last time she'd felt it, when Fox went feral in the woods, she'd ignored it. Calling forth her gift was not something she wanted to do if she sought to turn back the tide and return to the cold warrior she'd been for so long.

But it didn't appear that she had a choice. This time he didn't have Jag to fight, and an out-of-control shifter was the last thing they needed. Especially if he started turning those claws on her.

As she started toward him, he shook his head.

"Stay back," he growled around those fangs.

"I'm not seeking to fight you, Feral," she said calmly, evenly, staring into those savage eyes. Though they looked more like cat than fox eyes, she was prepared for that. She knew from experience that all shifters, except the vipers, looked the same in this half form, allowing them to fight as equals whether bird or tiger, gazelle or wolf.

"I'll hurt you, Mel!"

"No, you won't." She approached him slowly, carefully, nerves snapping despite her outer calm. "I trust you, Kieran."

His eyes flashed with surprise at her use of his old name, distracting him long enough for her to slip in close and lift her hand to his face, her palm against the soft golden stubble that covered his jaw.

He was shaking in his fight for control, but she called on her gift, wondering if it would even come to her after all this time, especially when she had such mixed emotions about using it. At first, her gift failed her. Though she'd begun to feel it stirring deep inside of her, trying to awaken, it was buried deeper than she'd realized. But she closed her eyes and reached down. As she touched that gift and began to pull on it, her hands against Fox's cheeks slowly began to warm and she felt a softening inside her, a need to help him that she didn't want.

The moment the tension began to seep from Fox's arms and shoulders, she snatched her hands away. Stepping back, she watched as his fangs began to recede, as his eyes changed back from animal to sky blue. She'd done it.

Fox released a shuddering breath, reaching for her and taking her hand. "What did you do?"

"It doesn't matter."

"You stole the fury." He lifted her hand and began to pull it toward his mouth as if he meant to press a kiss to her palm.

She snatched her hand away, glaring at him. "We need to get out of here."

Fox watched her for several moments more, as if trying to decipher her lightning mood swings, then nodded, once, decisively. But frustration once more leaped into his eyes.

They'd tried. There was no way out.

"You still can't mist?" he asked, running a hand through his hair.

"If I could, I wouldn't still be here," she snapped.

He glanced at her, his expression turning wry. "If you could mist, would *I* still be here?"

She cut her eyes at him, her temper sliding away. "Tempting as I might find it to be rid of you, Feral, no. I won't leave you behind."

He smiled at her, a quick grin that lit up his face, stealing her breath, and sending the butterflies to flight in her chest. *By the mist,* his smile flipped her end over end, leaving her with no memory of which way was up.

Wrenching her gaze from his far-too-handsome face, she stared at the stones with consternation, trying to catch her breath. "Sometimes shifters can breach warding in their animals when they can't get through in human form," she murmured.

"And if I get out, what happens to you?" He reached for her, tugging lightly on her braid. "I'm not leaving you behind, either, angel. There's got to be . . ." A funny look crossed his face.

"What is it, Fox?"

"My gut." He turned and strode to the far corner, bending low and reaching his hand straight through solid stone.

Melisande gasped. "So it isn't real."

"Most of it is. Or, at least, it's solid." But when she joined him, he held out a hand, holding her back. "Let me test it first. There could be more warding." On his hands and knees, he pushed his arm through up to his shoulder, then pulled back. Meeting her gaze, triumph leaped in his eyes, satisfaction pulled at the corners of his mouth.

And it was all she could do not to stare at those perfectly sculpted lips.

Reaching out like a blind man, he slowly determined the edges of the passage he couldn't see, then dipped his head beneath and looked through.

"Bollocks," he muttered and pulled back again. "It's a way out of the prison, but it's no escape. We're definitely in some kind of game. Test it first before we go through."

Without hesitation, Melisande knelt beside him, brushing his hard chest with her shoulder as she pushed her hand slowly into the invisible void. Nothing blocked her way or caused her any alarm, so she scrambled through the opening. Pushing to her feet, she found herself within a long passage lined by two stone walls, as high as the prison's, which appeared to run parallel to one another for as far as the eye could see in either direction.

With a grunt, Fox crawled through after her, then rose to stand beside her. "This place is one big mind fuck." He pulled one of his blades out of his boot.

Melisande curved her hand around her sword, and together they started off, shoulder to shoulder, her back and muscles tense with the knowledge that Mage could jump out at them at any moment, without warning.

But not twenty yards in, another path suddenly appeared on the left.

They exchanged wary glances. Fox shrugged, and they followed that path instead—a path that turned at right angles every ten to twenty paces, the stone walls remaining perfectly uniform.

"It's a labyrinth," she murmured, a trace of fear scuttling up her spine. "We could be lost in here forever."

And hadn't Paenther warned of just that? People disappearing. And perhaps not victims of Mage violence at all, but simply lost in the maze.

"We won't be." Fox's warm hand slid beneath her braid, curving around the back of her neck, his thumb stroking her, featherlight.

She stiffened at the touch, surprised . . . *appalled* . . . that she liked it. But of course she did. She was losing the cold veneer that had protected her for so long.

Desperate to cling to her shields, she jerked away, and he let her go.

Around the next corner, the labyrinth veered in two different directions, left and straight ahead.

Fox held out his hand to her, and she looked at him askance. Had she not just made it clear she didn't want him touching her?

His gaze chided. "My gut's telling me I'll lose you if I'm not holding on to you, pet."

Oh. She wasn't convinced he was telling her the truth, but neither was she willing to risk it. With a huff of resignation, she slid her hand once more into his.

Sky blue eyes crinkled at the corners, laughing at her prickliness even as his large hand engulfed hers, squeezing gently, his fingers curving around her with fierce protectiveness. And she had no desire to pull away.

A moment later, she was giving thanks to the ancient queens when they passed, suddenly and startlingly, into another world.

"**N**ever thought I'd see you again," the old Indian said, as Grizz led Lepard into the small antiques shop in Amarillo. Of course, the Indian didn't look old—he was immortal—but he played the American-Indian card to the hilt with his buckskin pants and vest thick with intricate and colorful beadwork. His black hair hung in a long braid down his back revealing a strong-boned face and skin a shade darker than Grizz's own.

"I need help," Grizz admitted.

Black eyes flashed. "Never thought I'd hear those words from *your* mouth." He turned away as if dismissing him.

Grizz's temper, always a volatile thing made all the more hair-trigger since he'd been marked a Feral, exploded. Fangs dropped from his gums, claws erupted from his fingertips. Gripping the edge of the nearest table loaded with junk, he flipped it, sending dozens of ceramic tchotchkes flying in a crash of breakage.

The Indian whirled, his face a mask of outrage that quickly morphed into one of shock. "You've been marked."

"You don't want to cross me right now." The words came out a growl.

A flicker of fear lit those black eyes. "Never did."

Grizz stepped through the breakage, ceramic crunching beneath his boot. His fangs and claws receded as he leaned his hands on the top of the glass case separating him from the Indian. "Do you know of any way to tell a good man from an evil one—a man born with evil in his soul?"

The Indian held his ground, his mouth tight as his gaze flicked to the wrecked store, then back to Grizz. "Which animal marked you?"

"The grizzly."

The Indian snorted. "Figures."

"Well? Can you help?"

The Indian shrugged. "I know of someone who might be able to. But she won't do it."

"Tell me more."

"She's ancient."

"That's not helpful, old man. Is she Therian?"

"Mage. Part Mage, at least. It's said that Sabine can see all the way into a man's soul."

And what exactly did that mean? "Tell me where to find her."

"Last I heard, she was living up north. The Rockies." The Indian held up his hand, forestalling Grizz's anger. "I know someone who might know where she is. He's an artist. Lives in Montana. I hear he saw Sabine a while back—sixty or seventy years ago, now."

"His name?"

"Yarren Brinlin." He pointed to the painting of wild horses that hung above the table Grizz had overturned. "That's his work there. I bought it from a gallery in

Bigfork. Ordered it over the Internet. You can probably track him down without much trouble. Don't tell him who gave you his name."

With a brief nod, Grizz turned and left.

When they were back in the car, Lepard peered at him, a hundred questions in his eyes. "Can you trust what he says?"

"I wouldn't have asked if I couldn't."

"There's bad blood between you. How far back do you go?"

"All the way. He's my father."

"Shit." Lepard sighed. "So we're driving to Montana, now?"

For the first time in a long time, Grizz smiled. Lepard was okay. "No. There's a jet charter outfit near here. I know one of the owners."

"Thank the goddess. So we find this Sabine and take her back to Feral House?"

"Got a better idea?"

"No. But if the original Ferals can't tell if we're good or bad, why are they going to trust the woman we bring back? They'll probably toss her in the prisons right along with us."

"That's assuming she'll help us."

"That's assuming we can find her." Lepard ran a hand through his hair. "This mission has *failure* written all over it."

"You're welcome to leave at any time."

Lepard turned away, staring out the window. "Let's go find this witch."

Yeah, they'd find her. And she'd tell Grizz his soul was black as tar. But he already knew that. It wasn't himself he was determined to save.

It was Rikkert.

Fox's pulse pounded in his ears as he stared at the impossible sight. As cleanly and suddenly as they'd walked into the labyrinth, they'd left it again. But not for the woods. He didn't know where in the hell they were.

Shops lined the street in both directions, pedestrians scurrying through the light rain over the wet cobblestones, covered in worn peasants' cloaks and hats from centuries past. A man driving an oxen cart yelled at them as he neared. Fox yanked Melisande back out of the way, the cart splashing them both with dirty rainwater.

Melisande turned to him with eyes as wide as saucers. "Have we actually time-traveled?"

"I've no bloody idea." But it smelled like it—the fish and rotting meat, the excrement, the unwashed human bodies interspersed with the tang of sea air and the sweet scent of the flower seller's bundles of blooms. Dublin in the early eighteenth century had smelled just like this.

"We're not in the past," Melisande said, as if suddenly certain.

"How can you be sure?" He noted the place where they'd first arrived, the middle of the street in front of a shop with the sign *Cobbler* swinging from twin chains.

"Because if we'd simply time-traveled, I would be able to mist again or communicate with my sisters in this time. And I can do neither."

He turned his attention back to her, something he constantly fought, and resisted the urge to let go of her hand and stroke that long, gleaming braid. Goddess, he longed to touch more than just her hand, but he wasn't willing to risk letting go of her just yet.

"You were injured," he reminded her.

"I was. I'm not any more. The warding has me locked down just as it has ever since we first hit it."

"If we're not in the past, then none of this is real." His gaze darted again, his senses taking in everything—the people walking the streets eyeing them with curiosity, the clank of rigging on the harbor nearby, the utter lack of birds, even seagulls.

"My thought exactly."

The hint of impudence in her tone had him turning back in time to see a twinkle of mischief in her eyes as she lifted one blond brow. He stared at her, struck by the incongruence of Melisande with a twinkle in her eye. Goddess, he wanted to kiss her.

"But obviously some of it's real," she continued.

"Like the water. The splash from that puddle soaked through my clothes." Taking a step away from him, she tugged on his hand, apparently no more eager to let go of him than he was her. Which pleased him more than it probably should.

He was about to ask her where she was going when she released him to quite intentionally bump into one of the street sellers.

The woman turned with a frown, then, sizing them up, began to smile with a mouth missing half its teeth. "Fresh fish?"

"No, thank you," he replied, then ushered Melisande past her.

Melisande whirled on him, that twinkle of mischief giving way to a gleam of laughter, and it was all he could do not to grin, or haul her into his arms. Goddess she was a beauty when she wasn't glaring at him with kill-you-in-your-sleep eyes. Well, she was a beauty either way, but he rather preferred the laughter.

"She felt real enough." The laughter in those sapphire eyes died abruptly on a gasp of horror. "I know what this is." She stopped beside a broken wheel leaning against the brick and turned to face him, her color turning ashen. "It's what used to be called a *temporal cage.*"

"Which is . . . ?" He didn't like the sound of that, not at all.

"A temporal cage is essentially a Daemon mind

game. In ancient times, when the Daemons still roamed the earth freely, they would create worlds with horrific creatures—things not seen in real life—then send their human captives into them to suffer, to die, while they watched . . . and fed."

"This place doesn't seem so bad." He swallowed. Yet. "There has to be a way out."

"I'm sure there is, but few ever escape the cages." Pulling her hand from his, she crossed her arms. "We have to find the key."

"What kind of key?"

"I don't know. It could be anything—animal, mineral, or vegetable. Perhaps something that doesn't look right, like a flower blooming out of season, or a rock with an odd glow." She met his gaze, her own ripe with dread. "We have to find the key and destroy it before this world destroys us . . . as it was almost certainly designed to do."

*Chapter
Ten*

Fox didn't like the way the inhabitants of this strange seaport were beginning to eye them. Not as potential customers but as a potential threat. He liked even less Melisande's suspicion that they were in a Daemon temporal cage. Unfortunately, he believed her. Too many things over the past months pointed to the likelihood that Inir had acquired Daemon magic. It made perfect sense that he'd use the strongest of it to guard his stronghold.

"Let's find that key and get out of here." He glanced at Melisande and she nodded, but when he held out his hand to her, she ignored it and set out ahead of him as if she were determined to get them out of here. Or determined to keep him at a distance. Probably both.

Truth be told, he was as anxious to get out of here as she was. Kara needed them. They sure as hell couldn't rescue her trapped in a place like this. He wondered if Lyon and the others would find themselves trapped in here, too. He wouldn't mind the help in finding the way out. But, *goddess*. What if all of them wound up wandering this godforsaken place for the rest of their lives? Lives cut short by lack of radiance unless they were actually close enough to the stronghold . . . and Kara . . . even here.

Side by side, they wandered the seaside village, drawing more and more attention. An attention that was beginning to claw at his nerves. How many more eyes would he draw if he suddenly went feral? If only he could be certain they weren't in any kind of real world of the past. Giving himself away as inhuman could bring down disaster upon the entire immortal world.

"I don't like the way they're looking at us," Melisande said quietly.

"Me either. Just keep walking." Unable to resist, he ran his hand down that silken braid.

She threw him an enigmatic look but said nothing, and he curled the braid around his hand, loving the feel of it wrapped around his fist. Releasing the long, golden length, he watched it fall down to the curve of her back, swaying to mimic her hips.

With effort, he tore his gaze away, concentrating on their surroundings, on finding the key.

The air was cool and damp against his cheeks, a far cry from the late May temps they'd left behind in the mountains.

But when he shivered, it was not with cold. His gut was delivering up another truth.

"This way," he said, eyeing an intersection up ahead, knowing they needed to turn right.

Melisande glanced at him but said nothing, her gaze on the people who were beginning to throng the street, her hand on the hilt of her sword.

True humans couldn't hurt them easily and would never overcome either of them one-on-one. But an angry mob could kill even an immortal. The last thing he wanted was to be forced to cut down humans, but he'd not allow either of them to be taken. He couldn't, whether or not this place was real. And if that meant shifting into his animal, so be it.

All at once, the humans . . . dozens of them, now . . . pulled knives and swords out of their cloaks and sheaths, turning on them as if a puppet master had given the order to attack. And he probably had.

Melisande drew her sword.

Fox grabbed her free hand. "Run!"

He took off, pulling her with him. Now wasn't the time to stand and fight, not unless they had no other choice. No, this was the time to get the hell out of Dodge and hope his gut would lead him to the key. Or to safety. As the cold drizzle fell on their heads and slicked the cobblestones beneath their boots, they dodged assailants, street carts, even a goat.

That intersection. They had to reach the intersection.

"Sooner or later, we're going to have to stand and fight, Feral," Melisande said beside him.

"Not if we're lucky."

"Let go of my hand. I can run faster." She tugged her hand free and he let her go, knowing she was right.

At the intersection, he turned right, not even looking first. This was the way they needed to go. He *knew* it. The cobbled street tilted precariously downward toward the waterfront. A vast expanse of water lay beyond. What would happen, he wondered, if they were to steal a boat and sail away? Would they eventually come to the edge of this magical world and be forced to turn back? Or was the bay even part of the world to begin with?

Side by side, they started down the hilly street, a street blessedly devoid of people or assailants of any kind. Escaping that mob had been too easy.

Too easy.

No sooner had he acknowledged his disquiet than vines began to seep up from beneath the cobblestones, dozens of them, reaching for his ankles, his legs.

Fox pulled his knives and began hacking at them. Beside him, Melisande did the same, but the vines were too quick, too strong, and even as he hacked, they curled around his legs and feet, until he couldn't move, then began to climb up his body.

"Fox!" The thread of panic in Melisande's voice tore at him, but there was nothing he could do to help her when he couldn't help himself. The magic was too fecking strong!

As he fought and hacked, the vines curled around his torso, his arms, his hands, his neck, yanking him back, pulling him down until he was flat on his back, sealed to the cobbles like Gulliver in Lilliput. With a furious roar, he went feral, but neither his claws nor fangs could find purchase to cut at the vines.

"Fox."

He managed, barely, to turn his head, to look at Melisande who was tied to the street as he was, not four feet away. In her eyes, he saw a raw terror that made him crazed . . . and that helped pull him down because, goddess, *she* needed *him* this time. She was struggling against the hold of the vines, her eyes bright with tears that were beginning to leak down into her hair.

"Mel," he said around the fangs still protruding from his mouth. He wanted to offer her comforting words and had none to give. They were caught, ripe for the slaughter.

"I can't be captured. I can't, Fox. *I can't.*"

He didn't want to tell her that capture was the least of their worries. Except, when he managed to glimpse back over his head, the mob was gone. They'd driven them into the trap and served their purpose. Why? So the Mage could come collect them?

"I *can't*, Fox."

She was panicking. His fangs receded. "Melisande . . . *angel*. Look at me. Can you turn your head and look at me?" When she managed, he caught her gaze and held on tight. "I'm here. I'm here, sweetheart. We're going to get out of this. The mob's gone. They're not going to hurt us. We're going to escape."

"No. We're not. *Fox* . . ."

What would make such a fierce warrior panic? But he knew. Being a captive like this was something she'd done before.

Goddess.

He had to get her out of here.

And he didn't have a clue how to escape.

Panic welled, ripping at Melisande's breath as she struggled against the vines that held her fast, just like the chains that had trapped her so long ago. Memories reared up . . . terror . . . betrayal . . . *pain*. She fought them back, fought . . . and lost.

"Mel, I have a plan," Fox said quietly beside her. "Trust me."

Trust him. A shifter. The thought was nearly laughable, and yet . . . she did. And a moment later, Fox disappeared in a spray of sparkling lights, shifting to a mammoth fox, then downsizing faster than she'd ever seen him. The vines tried to tighten around him, she could see them contracting, but Fox was faster. And suddenly he was bounding free, a tiny fox, racing away from the grabbing foliage.

Away. Leaving her behind.

Trust me, angel, he said, as if he'd heard her thoughts. *These damned vines!* Moments later, *There! I'm free of them. I think. Don't go anywhere, Mel. I'll be back.*

Don't go anywhere? Hoarse laughter burst from her throat, then died a quick death as terror overcame her again. Sooner or later, someone would come. Perhaps Mage sentinels, perhaps just more people of this odd, magical world. They'd take her into captivity. And then what? Hurt her? Kill her?

Sweat soaked her back, a cold sweat that had her trembling even as she struggled against the iron hold of the vines.

Fox, if you leave me, I'll kill you, Feral. Someday, I'll escape, and yours will be the first life I take.

I'm not deserting you, sweetheart. I'm grabbing weapons against the vines. I'll be back in a minute.

And suddenly her fear shifted. *Fox, you can't come back here! The vines will catch you all over again.*

Melisande, tell me what you know of Daemon temporal cages. Are they always accessed from a labyrinth?

She thought about it. *No, I don't think so. I've never heard of the Daemons using a labyrinth, though there are old stories of ancient Mage creating magical gauntlets with them.*

It makes sense that a Mage would use Daemon magic to create that which he knew. In other words, a labyrinth. Tell me about the gauntlets.

It occurred to her that he was intentionally turning her mind from her predicament, forcing her to think of something else. Easing her panic. And it was working.

She thought about the old stories, from the times before the Sacrifice five thousand years ago, a time when the Mage still had full access to their great store of magical power. And as she thought, her breathing began to even out, her trembling to quiet.

The gauntlets were a series of trials. Usually horrific trials. If the captive . . . almost always a shapeshifter . . . survived or escaped one, he was thrown into the next. Eventually, most died. The few who made it through the entire gauntlet alive were experimented on, then killed.

Fox made a noise in her head that sounded like a grunt. *No reward for the strongest and most clever.*

No, she agreed. *Not when they're your enemy.*

She felt something slide against the side of her neck as if rising from the cobbles, then gasped as it turned razor-sharp, cutting her flesh. It rose, briefly, into her line of vision, a bright orange vine where the others had been green, sliding across her throat and down the other side, sharp, cutting, deeper and deeper.

Fox! I'm out of time. One of the vines means to take off my head.

Wulfe whined at the sound of the buzzing. It tickled his wolf's ears, vibrating through his head and body like an electrical charge sprinting along his skin.

Do you feel that? he asked his companions.

Feel what? Kougar asked in reply.

It sounds like we're getting close to a power station.

I don't hear it, Kougar said. He and Lyon hadn't heard the voices, either.

With a mental frown, Wulfe continued on, following Estevan's trail through the mountain forest, praying to the goddess they were on the right path this time. About an hour ago, they'd come upon a lake they hadn't seen before on their perpetual loop around the mountain, and for the first time, they were slightly hopeful they'd finally penetrated the mountain's mischief.

But that hope did little to lift their spirits. Several hours ago, Ariana had felt one of her maidens die, one of the two who'd gone with Jag and Fox. Assuming the group had come under attack, Ariana had tried to mist Kougar to them, but she'd been unable to find any of them. Ever since, they'd been riding a knife's edge of tension, worried their friends were no longer alive. The only thing that kept hope from dying was the fact that Ariana was certain Melisande still lived even though she could neither find her nor communicate with her. If she was lost, but alive, so, too, they reasoned, were Jag, Fox, and Olivia.

All they could do was keep going.

It was midday, the sun high in a sky dotted with wispy clouds, the day warm, though not hot, even though Wulfe had spent the entire morning in his fur. The wolf was the best tracker of them all. If anyone could follow Estevan's scent, it should be him.

Even with the mountain fucking with them.

I sense one of mine.

Shit. The voices were back.

That's not possible. The Ferals killed them all.

Not one of those. This is different. Blood calls to blood.

The voices faded away, the same pair he'd heard before, leaving Wulfe more perplexed than ever. And far more disturbed. Who had the Ferals killed? And they'd killed them all? What did that mean? They certainly hadn't killed all the evil Ferals. Perhaps all those with true evil inside? But they'd only killed two of them. If he'd meant those two, wouldn't he have said *both*?

A dog barked in the distance, a familiar bark echoing down from the rise above. A bark the Ferals mimicked when they wanted to call one another when speaking telepathically wasn't necessary, or possible.

Relief swept through Wulfe as he followed the direction of the sound to find Jag and Olivia starting down the slope.

Where's Fox? Lyon demanded.

Alive, Jag replied. *I'll tell you more when we reach you.*

Thank the goddess.

All three Ferals shifted into human form as Jag and Olivia joined them. Ariana moved close to her mate, and Kougar pulled her against his side.

"What happened?" Lyon sounded almost like his old self though Wulfe knew that was an illusion. The Chief of the Ferals was practically shaking with the need to continue forward, to snatch Kara out of the enemy's hands.

"We hit some serious-ass warding," Jag told them. "The two Ilinas burst into flame on contact. Fox body-slammed the blond bitch . . . I mean Melisande . . . and somehow took the fire for himself. Phylicia's dead. I'm sorry, Ariana."

Ariana nodded. "Thank you, Jag, but I felt her death the moment it happened. Are Melisande and Fox all right?"

"Fox is hurting, but he's okay. Melisande is injured, I think. She's emitting energy like a nuclear reactor, and she can't mist, but her vocal cords were working just fine." He pulled Olivia against him. "We've been trying to frickin'-ass find you for hours, to warn you to get your Ilinas off this mountain before they fry, too."

Kougar squeezed Ariana's shoulder, then released her. "Go."

"Take Olivia," Jag said.

Both females, warriors through and through, scowled at their mates. Olivia crossed her arms. "No way."

Jag hauled her around to look at him. "Liv, the magic on this mountain is fucking powerful, you've seen that. We can usually get through warding in our animals. What if you can't? What if you go up in flames, too?"

Kougar nodded. "We're not risking your lives." He turned to Ariana. "Find Hawke and Falcon and let them know what's going on. Have them continue to patrol the periphery, but stay off the mountain. They'll be able to find cell service to get word to Feral House if they think backup will do us any good."

Jag kissed his frustrated mate, and she kissed him back after only a moment's hesitation. "Be careful," she whispered.

Kougar kissed Ariana. She pressed her hand to his cheek, then handed him the backpack with Wulfe's and Lyon's clothes. A moment later, the two Ilinas and Olivia disappeared in mist.

The four Ferals shifted back into their animals and continued on. Wulfe felt the weight of worry lifted a little bit, knowing Fox and Jag were fine. But Kara was still in the hands of the enemy, and they had no idea where Fox and Melisande had gone. Deeper into the mountain's sorcery?

Less than a mile later, they crested a rise. Wulfe gave a mental gasp as he stared at the sight below. In the valley, hung a curtain of shimmering color, blues and purples and reds, rippling and flaring as if the door behind it had been left open on a windy day.

To his surprise, his three companions continued forward without comment. A chill ran down his spine.

Don't you see that? he asked all three at once.

See what? Jag replied.

Dammit. As he loped forward to catch up with them, energy charged his skin, making his fur rise, and he realized the buzz had been getting steadily stronger.

The cougar gave him a quizzical look. *What exactly do you see?*

And suddenly he knew. *The warding.* The curtain stretched as far as the eye could follow in either direction, curving back on the ends as if enclosing the mountain. *It's moving, rippling.*

Why in the hell was he the only one who could see it? Why was he the only one hearing the voices? He didn't like it, not at all. Then again, it was probably a good thing someone could.

More than a little fascinated by the sight of the warding, he started forward, leading the way down the hillside. The buzzing grew more intense the closer he got, until he was less than a body length away.

Where is it, Lyon demanded, the African lion coming up beside him.

Right in front of us.

Lyon leaped through it with a single bound. Kougar and Jag followed, Wulfe bringing up the rear. But beyond the first warding curtain, he saw another not a dozen feet away.

There's another one, he told his friends. And, like before, they leaped through it, one after the other, Lyon leading the way.

What the fuck? Jag exclaimed.

Wulfe understood a moment later when he joined them. They weren't in West Virginia any more. Instead, they stood on a cobblestone path between two high stone walls. A short distance ahead, an opening in the wall offered a choice.

Kougar and Lyon shifted into men, pulling knives from the backpack Kougar alone was able to carry through the shifts.

"Where the hell are we?" Lyon growled. But none of them had an answer. And a moment later, Wulfe realized, all three of his companions were giving him guarded looks.

What? he demanded, still in wolf form.

"Why you?" Kougar asked quietly.

Hell if I know. A chill slid down his spine. But he was pretty sure it had something to do with the voices he was hearing in his head. What had the one said? *I sense one of mine. Blood calls to blood.*

For the first time in centuries, he remembered the old tale of the origin of the wolf clan. A horrific tale he'd never given any credence to.

Until now.

Fox ran down the empty road, along the deserted waterfront, and back up the steep cobblestone street, where even now, Melisande lay trapped by the vines. Vines almost certainly designed to kill her.

Bloody fecking hell.

The street was now clear of vines except the swath around Melisande. But he knew with certainty that the moment he stepped into their path, they'd rise up and try to snare him just as they had before. This time they would fail. In one hand he held a torch, in the other, a jug of oil, both of which he'd just snatched from a nearby saddlery. This place might not be real, but much of it was realistic down to the finest detail.

I'm coming, pet. Hang on for me.

Taking a deep breath, he launched himself forward, running as fast as he could, covering as much ground as possible before the vines started snaking upward. They caught him not six feet from where Melisande lay, the blood coating her neck and running into the cobbles beneath her.

His heart pounded and he knew he was going to have to be quick and careful or he'd wind up setting himself on fire, which would help her not at all. He sprinkled the oil on the roots of the vines just below him on the hill, then stabbed them with the burning torch.

As he'd hoped, the vine disappeared, snaking back into the street. In a wide swath behind him, he sprinkled more oil, setting it on fire. Instantly, the vines there disappeared as well. The oil burned, the fire not large enough to hamper his movements.

But the vines were climbing his legs, now, coming at him from the front and below. He dispatched those in front of him as he had the ones behind, letting the oil run beneath his feet . . . carrying the fire. And suddenly he was free. He leaped forward, battling back the vines as he had the others until finally he reached Melisande.

"I'm here, luv."

Her eyes fluttered open, their sapphire depths dark with agony. His heart contracted as he spied the orange vine around her neck. It was already halfway through. *Goddess,* it would soon sever her head completely. With a speed borne of desperation, he transferred the jug to his torch hand, pulled his blade, and attacked the orange vine viciously, hacking it away. But as it lost its grip on her, half a dozen more of the serrated vines rose up to take its place.

Goddess, goddess, goddess.

Fox yanked and pulled, stabbed and burned, care-ful not to catch Melisande on fire in his haste. Finally, *finally*, he had her loose. Even as badly injured as she was, she scrambled up, her immortal blood quickly healing the damage done by the orange vines.

"Stay close, Mel. We're heading downhill. Watch behind."

As she leaped beside him, he dribbled oil over the

vines that had held her, that still reached for her, setting them on fire. Together, they eased their way down the hill following the same path he'd traveled up, burning and hacking their way through.

Until, finally, they were free.

At the bottom of the empty street, yards past the last of the vines, Fox finally set down the jug and torch and hauled Melisande to him, studying her face, her neck. "Are you all right?"

She trembled beneath his hands, the shadows of terror still in her eyes. A softness filled those sapphire depths, suddenly, taking his breath away.

Small hands pressed against his chest. "You saved me."

"Of course." He cupped her soft cheek in his hand.

The moment grew thick. The need to touch her, to taste her, nearly overwhelmed him. He lifted his other hand, framing her delicate face, watching for her surrender, waiting for her to pull away. Heat and confusion warred in her eyes, but when he lifted his thumb and stroked it lightly across her plump, pink bottom lip, her breath caught. And then she was reaching for his face as if to pull him down, and he was dipping his head.

Lips brushed, passion exploded, sweetness drenched his senses as Melisande melted in his arms, her own arms slipping around his neck, holding him tight. All thought fled, all caution, as her fingers dove into his hair and her mouth opened to his, seeking a deeper kiss, one he gladly gave her. Pure, unadulterated desire tore through his body as her tongue stroked his. She was heaven in his arms, small and precious, her taste like fresh, cool water to a man dying of thirst.

As her tongue thrust into his mouth, her hips rocked against him, stroking his cock, nearly making his eyes roll back up into his head. Goddess help him, she was on fire, and he quaked with the need to give her exactly what she wanted.

Her scent tore through his senses, the soft smell of wild heather, but a thousand times more erotic until his mind was so clouded with passion he couldn't remember where he was or who he was. The need to touch her *everywhere* was almost more than he could control.

His hands roamed her back, falling to her small, perfect ass as he hauled her against the erection that was demanding release.

"I have to be inside of you," he groaned against her lips.

In his arms, Melisande froze, turning to stone.

Fox pulled back slowly, easing his hold on her, letting her go when she pulled away.

"Mel . . . ?"

"This isn't the time, Feral," she snapped. "We need to find that key and get the hell out of here. Kara's in need of rescuing, or had you forgotten?"

He felt as if she'd slapped him, and at the same time

knew he'd needed the reminder because he'd absolutely been lost within the pull of passion.

"You're right."

She looked at him with surprise, then nodded.

Extending his hand to her, he smiled, because they were free . . . for now . . . and because, despite the abrupt ending of their passionate interlude, sooner or later, the woman was going to be his. When the time was right. He knew that now.

When she cut those sapphire eyes at him, then, with a small huff placed her hand in his, he felt the world right itself.

Hand in hand, they strolled along the wharf, where people once more worked—unloading crates from a boat, cleaning fish. All ignored them as if they weren't even there.

Fox's senses remained on high alert, as they had since the Ilinas first dropped them in West Virginia. If the populace of this strange place had turned on them once, they could do so again. But even as his senses traveled outward, seeking danger, part of his torn attention remained firmly on the woman at his side.

Something was bothering him mightily. Something he needed to understand. "You've been captured before, haven't you, pet?" he asked quietly, uncertain how she would take the question.

She glanced at him with surprise, one golden brow lifting.

"I sensed your panic when the vines had you. And you're not a woman to panic."

With a sigh, she looked away, out at the water. "It was a long time ago."

"And yet some things we never forget."

"No. That's true. I was captured by Therians." She said the words so matter-of-factly, but he heard the pain behind them. And he finally understood her hatred of shifters. He waited for her to continue, but when she remained silent, he asked, "Are any of them still alive? Because if they are, I'm going to kill them."

She glanced at him, an odd look in her eyes. Surprise, perhaps. And steel. And something that almost looked like chagrin. "I wreaked my vengeance, Feral. Without mercy. Every one who hurt me, I killed. The only one I never found was the one who betrayed me in the first place."

He glimpsed the warrior capable of hauling innocents into the Crystal Realm to die because she saw it as the only way to save her race. A hard woman. But not all there was to her, not even close. And that hard veneer had come at a terrible cost, he was sure of it, now.

"Is it possible he still lives?"

She looked away. "I know he still lives. And he's going to die." Slowly, she turned to meet his gaze, her eyes glittering sapphire diamonds. "It's Castin."

Ah, *"Feck."* His stomach flipped.

"I recognized his picture when Hawke flashed it on the screen in the war room yesterday."

"You can't take him on alone."

"He's mine," she snapped.

"He's also a Feral Warrior, if one who has not yet been brought into his animal. And you're an Ilina who cannot mist."

She scowled at him. "Don't remind me."

Fox's mind was spinning from Melisande's words. *Everyone who hurt me, I killed.*

Goddess. Had they raped her? Was that the reason she'd turned to stone as he'd kissed her, the moment he'd said he wanted to be inside of her? The thought slammed him with a fury that had his free hand fisting. Had Castin raped her? If so, the male was going to die, either by Melisande's hand or his own. But he would die.

How had she been captured when she could turn to mist in a heartbeat and escape?

They were difficult questions, and he wasn't at all certain she was ready to share the answers with him.

But before he could pose a single one, everything around them changed. As cleanly and suddenly as they'd walked into the medieval seaport, they walked out of it again.

And into chaos.

Chapter Eleven

They'd walked into a bloody hurricane.

Battering wind slammed into Fox, flaying him with sharp, stinging sand, knocking him back a step. He grabbed Melisande's hand, pulling her against him, shielding her as a palm frond sailed at them, striking him in the hip before tumbling away. Behind them, the roiling ocean sent pounding surf to scour the shore. Water rushed over his boots, then receded just as quickly.

They'd stepped into yet another world, this one far from the medieval seaport. A tropical island, from what he could see. And, apparently, right in the middle of one hell of a storm.

Squinting his eyes against the blowing sand, Fox searched for assailants along the beach or hiding among the trees, certain they were around somewhere. But he could see nothing but the angry ocean, dark, swirling clouds blocking out midday sunshine, and a tropical island under full-scale attack by Mother Nature.

The sand blowing in his face annoyed him. The impossible nature of this mission infuriated him. That quickly, he felt the anger building inside of him—that new Feral edginess that had him feeling like he wanted to crawl out of his skin. If only Jag were here to give him a good fight.

He pressed his mouth close to Melisande's ear and yelled above the gale, "We've got to find shelter. Somewhere defensible."

Glancing up, she met his gaze with a tense mouth, hard agreement in warrior eyes. He tightened his grip on her hand with an instinctive need to protect. She couldn't weigh much more than a hundred pounds, and he feared that the wind would lift her up and send her flying. Together, they ran from the beach toward the tree line above.

A shiver took hold of him, one he'd come to recognize as the kind that preceded some of his intuitions, now. And sure enough, as before, he suddenly *knew* where to go.

"This way!" He tugged on Melisande's hand. Within

the forest, debris flew, branches snapped, trees bending as if pushed low by a giant hand.

His gut led him toward a particularly thick clump of trees in which they could find some shelter. He pulled back a wide palm frond for Melisande to precede him through. She stepped forward, then froze and began to backpedal.

"What's the matter?"

"Look. Carefully!"

He leaned forward to see what the problem was. A pit. *Bloody hell.* By the looks of the trampled palm fronds around it, and the fronds lining the bottom some twenty feet down, the pit had been hidden. Before the storm? No. By the track marks up one side and the badly disturbed ground on top, whoever, or whatever, had fallen in had been hauled out again. And recently.

Why in the fecking hell had his gut brought him this way?

"Look!" Melisande yelled above the howling wind, pointing.

He followed her gaze to where someone lay sprawled and motionless a short distance away, partially hidden by a downed palm tree. Castin? Carefully avoiding the trap, they made their way to him. But as they approached, Fox saw that the body was missing its head. And it wasn't alone. There were three in all, the heads scattered nearby like so many bowling balls.

A suspicion tugged at him and he nudged one of the heads with the toe of his boot, turning it until he could see its sightless eyes. The brown irises were ringed in shiny copper. Mage eyes. Approaching the second, he lifted one closed eyelid. Mage eyes again.

Melisande checked the third. "Mage."

"Three dead Mage. No wonder there's a hurricane." Mother Nature got angry when her Mage were killed. Millennia ago, the Mage had been the closest to true nature spirits that existed on Earth. Now they were, more and more, a bunch of soulless bastards trying to free the Daemons to destroy the Earth they'd once protected.

"Who killed them?" Melisande asked.

"Damned good question." And he had an idea. "Hold on to a tree. I don't want you blowing away." When she'd done as he commanded, he pulled on his own inner power and shifted into his fox, startled by the feel of hurricane-force winds through his fur. Opening his senses, he began to sniff around the bodies. Sure enough, he caught the scent they'd been following before they entered the labyrinth.

Castin, he told Melisande. He followed the scent straight back to the pit. *He's the one they caught, I'd wager. The question is, did he get away or were there more Mage than these three?*

As he shifted back to human form, a strong gust

knocked Melisande sideways, and she barely hung on to the tree. He grabbed her against him. "We've got to find shelter."

"Yes."

The storm's fury was leaching into him, stealing his equilibrium. He was struggling to stay in his skin, to keep from going feral.

Hand in hand, they pushed into the forest of tropical trees, climbing over downed palms. Fox continually scanned for any sign of Castin or Mage, but he saw no one, nothing but flying trees and palm fronds.

About fifty yards in, he found what he'd been looking for—several boulders clustered together, surrounded by brush and trees forming a natural shelter from the worst of the storm. They ducked into the space, tucking themselves against the rocks as the wind continued to howl.

Melisande glanced up at him, old hatred in her eyes. "Castin's here."

"He *was* here. He may not be any longer. It appears your suspicion of a Mage gauntlet is accurate."

Melisande nodded. "A gauntlet usually follows a single path."

He longed to put his arm around her, to hold her close, but he didn't trust himself not to draw claws. Even now, they were throbbing beneath the surface of his fingertips.

"The question is, where does it end?" he asked.

Melisande pursed that kissable mouth, drawing his attention, making him long to taste it again.

"It's delivering us to the Mage," she said. "To Inir. At least it's delivering you there. Me, it's trying to kill." Her words were without emotion, but he felt the shiver go through her. And he knew an answering rage that only fueled the loss of control he was already struggling against. Because it was true, and they both knew it.

She leaned against him with a trust that curled around his heart and was utterly misplaced. *"Don't."* He pulled away. "I'm losing it again, pet. If I go feral, I'm going out into the storm. Stay here. Stay safe."

How was it that this fierce, vulnerable, prickly woman, had come to be so important to him? All that mattered was protecting her.

Even . . . *especially* . . . if that meant keeping her safe from him.

As the howling wind threw palm fronds in every direction, uprooting trees and slamming them to the ground, Melisande watched the agitation rise in the shifter at her side and saw the moment Fox's eyes changed from sky blue to yellow animal eyes.

Accessing her gift was a risky game, one that would sooner or later almost certainly derail everything she wanted in her life. But a shifter gone feral was a dangerous companion. And she didn't want him out in the storm alone. Not when she had the power to help him.

Taking a deep breath, she turned to him, reaching for his face just as he started to move as if to rise.

"Fox, let me help."

Feral eyes turned to her. "Too dangerous."

It was, actually, but not in the way he thought. Never one to take no for an answer, she grabbed his face in both hands, forcing him to hold still for fear of hurting her with his fangs or claws. She knew he wouldn't intentionally harm her. And for a reason she didn't entirely understand, she couldn't let him suffer.

Closing her eyes, reaching down deep inside of her, she opened that door and found the energy of her gift, pulling it forth as quickly and strongly as she could. It came more easily this time, more forcefully, and she felt her hands heat at once. Beneath her palms, Fox's tension slowly drained away.

When she opened her eyes again, Fox was staring at her with wonder and gratitude, his own eyes once more blue. And slowly filling with heat as his gaze roamed her face, as it dipped to her mouth.

Her breath caught, and she tore her gaze away.

Without warning, he pulled her onto his lap, tight against him, tucking her head against his shoulder as he wrapped his arms around her. Pressing her face against the warm flesh of his neck had her mouth hungering for a taste. She curled her arms around his neck and felt his hands slide over her, one along her thigh to cup her buttocks, the other sliding over her breast.

Little by little, the pleasure of Fox's touch, of his nearness, of his hand in hers, had been seeping into her, trickling deep down inside of her. Feeding her. And awakening her deep Ilina nature, so much of which had been frozen after the attacks.

Even with the storm screaming around them hunger flared. Her mating scent released. Between her legs, she began to burn. No, she didn't want this!

But even as the cry sounded in her head, her mouth found his, her control broke, and she was kissing him. And then his arms were around her, pulling her close, his mouth fusing with hers in a passion as wild as the storm. As one, their mouths opened, their tongues finding one another, drinking from one another, a heady taste of sweetness and lust. His hands gripped her tight, one at her back, the other cupping her head.

His mouth tore from hers to rain kisses along her cheek, her jaw, the curve of her shoulder. She arched, tilting her head, giving him access as his mouth suckled at the flesh along the side of her neck, erasing the phantom pain of the vine, a wound now fully healed.

"Fox," she gasped, as his touch sent passionate flames licking her insides, melting her from the inside out, filling her with a need, a hunger, that she'd thought never to feel again.

The pleasure grew inside her, changing, distilling

into the finest of nectars, feeding her body and soul and setting up a craving for more. In a distant part of her mind, she railed at the foolishness of feeding this hunger. Did she not want to return to the way she'd been, to the warrior unable to feel?

But she was lost to Fox's touch, to the feel of his silken locks beneath her fingertips, to his masculine scent and the taste of his kiss and the brush of his whiskers against her sensitive neck.

She was on fire for him and he was equally crazed with need for her.

The hand at her back, slid lower, down to her hip, strong fingers flexing into her butt cheek, pulling her against him as he rubbed his thick erection against her hip.

His mouth reclaimed hers, and she drank of him all over again as his tongue invaded her mouth, as her tongue slid against his. She was on fire for him.

Barely registering her actions, she twisted on his lap, straddling him, rubbing herself against his hardness. Fox groaned, pressing her closer. And then his hand was at her waist, his fingers sliding down inside the front of her leggings, down between her legs, one finger diving deep inside of her.

Her cry of pleasure strangled in her throat as her body froze, memories rearing up, terrible and terrifying. *Chained, spread . . .*

Melisande froze, pushing off of Fox's lap, her heart

pounding. Shaken, she sat back against the rock, struggling to breathe, curling into herself beside him as another tree cracked and fell nearby.

"Melisande?"

She didn't answer, didn't know what to say because even as the memories crashed over her, her body, fully awakened, wept with need. The passion continued to swirl in her blood, stretching and growing, flowing into her limbs, deep into her core. She wanted, *needed,* to be back in Fox's arms, to feel his mouth on hers again, to feel his body inside hers.

And the thought of it both excited her and terrified her.

Stars in heaven, she didn't want this.

The wind whipped around them, branches and entire trees tumbling end over end, flying past. The storm raging outside was nothing compared to the one raging within her. The hunger burned until she feared she would turn to ash. She needed release, and she needed it now, but the thought of being covered, of being entered . . .

A deep quaking began in her limbs, her stomach souring even as the heat raged between her thighs. She wanted Fox, desperately. If only she didn't. If only she could turn it off. She wasn't at all sure how much longer she could stand this, or what she would do when she couldn't.

She pulled her knees against her chest and dipped her

forehead onto them, curling tight, struggling to ease the terrible need. But nothing worked.

Feeling a gentle tug on her hair, she opened her eyes to find that Fox had wrapped a lock that had escaped her braid around his finger. Her heart squeezed, recognizing the need to comfort in his expression, even as he refrained from touching her more directly.

Tilting her head sideways to look at him, she found him watching her with blue eyes deep with longing and gentle understanding. Even as desire leaped like an electrical arc between them, he caressed the back of her head.

"I would never hurt you, pet. Never."

Somehow, he saw the battle inside of her. Could he also tell she was coming apart at the seams? That she wanted him as badly as she wanted to run the other way?

He leaned forward, pressing his lips ever-so-briefly against her temple. When he pulled back, his gaze was soft as down. "You looked in need of it."

Pressure welled in her chest. He was stealing her heart.

He lifted his hand and lightly stroked her head, and she melted against his side. Slowly, he curved his arm around her shoulders and pulled her against him, giving her a dozen opportunities to pull away. But she didn't. She needed his strength, his comfort.

For so long, she'd felt nothing, nothing but rage and

hatred. Now everything had changed. The rage toward the shifters was gone. Certainly the rage toward this shifter. How could she hate a man who'd risked everything to save her, and not just once? He was a good man, a kind man whom, against all reason, she was coming to adore.

Her mate. That's what he might well have become if she were different. If she could be the woman she'd been before. But she couldn't, she knew that. And she didn't want to be. She wanted to reclaim the coldness, to once more become the unfeeling warrior. But to do that, she had to get away from Fox, and that wasn't going to happen. Not now. Not within the Mage labyrinth.

So for this time out of time she would enjoy the closeness of another, the feeling of no longer being alone. And try to keep from destroying herself in the process.

As loose brush swirled into their small windbreak on the howling gale, she closed her eyes, hiding her face against Fox's shoulder. Thank the ancient queens that he'd been caught with her, for she'd never survive this alone. If only he weren't tearing down her defenses, brick by brick, awakening a desire and a need inside her that she feared would tear her apart.

Fox held Melisande against him, his hand on her shoulder, his body on fire, his heart breaking because he got it now. For a moment, when she first pulled away from him, she'd let her shields down, and he'd felt like he was staring into his sister Sheenagh's eyes again in those horrible months after she'd been attacked. The fear. The anger.

Goddess. He'd already figured out Melisande had been captured. Now he'd seen blaring evidence that she'd been raped. No wonder she froze every time they got too close. His heart squeezed with pain at her suffering even as the rage stirred inside him.

If Castin was to blame, the male would die a thousand deaths before Fox handed him over to Melisande for the killing blow.

Finally, he understood how she could be so hot for him, so *wet*, yet push him away. But she hadn't pushed him away at all, not really. He'd scared her. No, the situation had scared her. But, goddess, she wanted him. One moment she'd smelled of wild heather and the next her scent had exploded, turning lush and carnal—wild heather crushed beneath writhing bodies deep in the act of sex. And still it filled his nose, his lungs, making his cock throb with wanting. It was her mating scent, he was sure, and it was driving him insane. Goddess in heaven, he hoped it went away soon because her arousal was sending his into orbit.

Finally, the winds began to die down. High above, the sun peeked out.

"Mother Nature appears to be over her pique." Fox placed a soft kiss on Melisande's head, then released her and pushed himself up, rising from the small wind-break to make certain they were still alone. The small, tropical forest was a shambles, but he saw no sign of life.

"Let's take a look around." He held out his hand to her.

As she placed her hand in his, Melisande met his gaze. Heat remained in her eyes, and a wealth of frustration. But as he smiled at her, the sapphire warmed with a hint of an answering smile. He resisted the need to haul her into his arms and against his heart for about four seconds, then did just that, pulling her close for a simple hug.

To his relief, she wrapped her arms around his waist and returned his hug briefly before pulling away, but not before he felt the way she still trembled. And not before he was enveloped, all over again, with that lush, carnal scent.

Her arousal hadn't died at all. He watched as she fought for control, her jaw hardening, her back straightening as she turned to survey the area. A tough little warrior, despite everything. Tough on the outside, aye, but beneath that hard façade, he was beginning to see a different side of Melisande, one filled with a sweetness the other Ferals would never believe.

Deep inside, his fox snarled, a possessive sound this time. *Mine.* And he knew it was true. This woman was coming to mean far too much.

Moving out from the trees, they once more came upon the dead Mage.

"I'm going to see if I can pick up a trail," Fox told her, hoping the shift to his animal might douse the sensual fire in his body, at least for a little while. He shifted, sighing with relief as the sexual need died away, then he turned his attention to the task at hand. He began sniffing around the bodies, then followed the trail back to the pit, padding all around the two sites.

Finally, he returned to her, brushing against her hip with his side, delighted when her fingers dove into his fur, stroking him.

Ah, that feels good, pet.

"I'm thinking you're the pet."

He grinned at her. *Keep your hands on me like this, and I'll be whatever you want me to be.*

He tensed slightly, worried his words would drive her away after what happened in the windbreak, but the look she gave him was one of wry amusement and her hand continued to stroke him.

"I like the feel of your fur. It's incredibly soft."

Her hand moved to the top of his head and he pressed into her touch, loving it.

"Did you find the trail?" she asked.

Aye. Castin's scent doesn't extend beyond this small area. It's as if he appeared at the site of the pit and left this world immediately following the battle with the Mage.

"Perhaps that's what happened." She moved to the front of him, running her fingers along the side of his neck as he melted from the sweet feel. "Or perhaps the labyrinth is messing with us just as the mountain did. If the labyrinth is part of the mountain's magic, it probably is."

Aye.

"So, what now? Someone is bound to come after us again. Maybe Mage."

I agree. I suggest we stay close to the beach, where we'll have plenty of warning of anyone's approaching. In a spray of sparkling lights he shifted back to human form. The sensual energy he always felt upon turning human in Melisande's presence hit with a blast of desire that nearly drove him to his knees. *Goddess.* He found her with his eyes, saw the answering flare of heat, and he had to fist his hands at his sides to keep from hauling her into his arms. The need to touch her, to taste her, to mate with her was burning him alive.

With an audible groan, raking both hands through his hair, he turned away and started toward the beach. Melisande fell into step beside him. He eyed the ocean, wondering if it was cold enough to douse the fire in his loins. As they walked, he curled his hands into fists, fighting the natural inclination to hold out his hand to her. Touching her in any way was a bad idea right now.

"Do you see anything living?" he asked, trying to shift his thoughts to something other than the fire burning in his blood. The sun, now fully out, beat hot on his scalp and shoulders adding to the sense that he was burning alive. "I've seen no wildlife, not even a seagull."

"There was a goat in the seaport, but he was tied to one of the carts." Melisande's voice sounded as strained as his own, her words laced with a huskiness that did nothing to ease his discomfort. "So is this an ocean without fish? And if we had a boat, how far could we sail before this world ended? Would we hit the edge of the warding and burn? Or slide right through into yet another world?"

He didn't answer. He'd barely heard her questions through the need pounding through his body. From the water's edge, he turned back, observing the landscape, to all appearances, a deserted island.

But he knew it was more than that. It was a trap. Another stop along the gauntlet.

While his warrior's brain constantly logged senses and impressions, searching for threats of any kind, his man's brain was wholly on the woman at his side. A woman so ripe with need for him that they were both shaking from it. Yet she was a woman who wouldn't . . . couldn't follow through.

"Melisande, was your capture by the Therians part of the reason the Ilinas faked your extinction a thousand years ago?" He was treading on delicate ground, but he wanted to understand.

"No. They had nothing to do with one another. My capture by the Therians happened lifetimes before the Mage attacked us. We never intentionally faked our extinction, by the way. Not at first. A thousand years ago, Ariana and Kougar fell in love. The Mage feared the Ilinas and Ferals would join forces and sought to keep that from happening. Up until then, the Ilinas had stayed out of the war between the shifters and the Mage. We tended to prefer the more virile shifters in our beds, but we'd never fought beside them, not since the Daemon Wars. And never against the Mage.

"The Mage . . ." She stopped abruptly. "They attacked us," she said harshly. "Their poison killed ninety-six Ilinas, more than two-thirds of our number, leaving the rest of us clinging to life for several centuries. When we emerged again, we realized the immortal world thought us extinct, and finally understood why the Mage had not finished us off as they could so easily have done. They'd tapped into Ariana's queen's power and had fed the poison to the rest of the race through her. And they still possessed that ability. It became critical that the Mage poison master not learn that Ariana still lived before I could hunt him down and kill him."

"And did you?"

"No." The word was filled with acid. "The poison had some kind of magic in it that kept me from ever finding him no matter how close I got. Ariana and

Kougar finally tracked him down not long ago. And they killed him."

Fox frowned. "I don't understand. If Kougar and Ariana were mated a thousand years ago . . . did Kougar know what had happened?"

"No. He thought their mating bond had severed. He believed Ariana dead all that time."

He'd never heard of a mating bond severing without the death of one of the pair. "Then how . . . ?"

She scowled and turned away. "I don't want to talk about it anymore."

Fox swallowed his questions with difficulty, for he had a cartload of them. But he'd clearly hit on another traumatic event. *Goddess.* Two-thirds of her race wiped out in a single attack. He couldn't fathom the scope of such a tragedy. Yet she'd lived through that after being captured and, almost certainly, raped by Therians. So much misfortune. Then again, she'd lived over a thousand years. Lifetimes more than a thousand, by her own account. And what that meant, exactly, he had no idea except that the woman had history, and baggage, in abundance. Reason aplenty for the hard shell she'd acquired, a shell that appeared to be disintegrating around her.

With everything he learned, with every glimpse he got into who she was and the events that had formed her, the more intrigued he became. He wanted to know more. He wanted to know everything.

She turned back to him, her temper of a moment ago gone, a wry smile tilting her mouth to one side. "Sorry. Tender subject."

"I'm hopelessly nosey when it comes to you." He grinned at her, and to his utter delight, a full smile bloomed on her face, transforming her features from merely beautiful to exquisite. His pulse raced, his knees weakened as he basked in the glow of that smile.

"You should do that more often, pet."

"Do what?" But an impish light lit her eyes, making them sparkle, and he thought he just might have heart failure.

"Smile."

"I'd forgotten how. Until you." She frowned, but it was a quick, unheated thing, as she shook her head. "You're making a wreck of my life, you know that, don't you? I liked not feeling. And you're making me feel again. Too much."

He stopped her, his hand on her arm, and turned her toward him, caressing her cheek with his palm. "You make me feel things I'm not comfortable with either, Mel. If I'm upending your life, so, too, are you upending mine. What the future brings, I can't fathom, but I hope you're part of it."

Her eyes turned serious. "That's not the plan."

"I hope you change your mind." He cupped her face. Heat flared in her eyes. The hunger that had yet to die ran, hot and thick, through his blood. His heart began to pound.

No, not his heart. Not just his heart. His warrior's senses went on high alert.

The vibrations he was feeling . . . *footfalls*.

They were no longer alone.

Kara lay on the bare cot in the small prison cell, her arm across her forehead as she stared at the stone walls, feeling heartsick, scared, and ill. Was this how a human felt when coming down with a virus, all clammy and gross? She'd heard them talk about it often enough, for she'd grown up with humans. Not until recently had she realized she was immortal.

The thick wooden door rattled, and she sat up, wondering who was coming for her this time . . . and why. She knew it would be one of the evil Ferals. When she'd first arrived here, bound and gagged in the back of a vehicle, a Mage sentinel had pulled her out of the car. She'd gone radiant on him, pulling the energies, electrocuting him. Only a Feral Warrior could withstand such a blast, and only one with his armband firmly in place to channel it.

Only Ferals had touched her since.

Lynks opened the door, a tray in his hand. Her dinner. The man was big, as were all Ferals, but unlike the others, there was a softness to him, as if he was a man unused to hard work. And in his eyes, where she should see guilt for his betrayal, she saw only shiftiness.

"You were cleared of the darkness, Lynks. Why did you steal me from Lyon?"

He wouldn't meet her gaze.

"How did you know Inir wanted you to kidnap me?"

"I'm not sure," he mumbled. "Just did."

"Does he control you?" she pressed. "Are you sorry for kidnapping me or were you glad to be able to pull it off?"

Impatient eyes cut to her and away again. "You wouldn't understand." He set the tray on the floor and rose.

"I'm trying to," she said softly. Because it was absolutely critical that the good Ferals understand the men they had among them. If all the new Ferals were going to betray them as Lynks had . . . Dear God, the males she loved could all be dead.

"I have . . . needs," Lynks said. "People don't get it. Inir does."

"What kind of needs?"

He shrugged. "I like kids. I like them . . . you know. I like to fuck them."

Kara closed her eyes against the image, the blood draining from her face. "You're a pedophile."

"Whatever. Inir lets me do what I want with the kids he has here."

Kara thought of the poor little girl Inir had cut up

and had to swallow down the bile trying to rise to her throat. "Has Inir been communicating with you all along?"

Lynks glanced at her, his eyes belligerent, then looked away. "I know what he wants me to do though I don't know how. The first time it happened was with you. I knew I needed to follow you down the basement stairs. Then halfway down, I suddenly knew he wanted me to knock you out, say that ritual with your flip-flop, carry you out the cellar door and through the woods. There was a car waiting right where I knew it would be."

She frowned. "What ritual with my flip-flop?"

"I don't know. Something about your essence. I think it was so that Lyon would still sense you there and wouldn't know you'd been taken." He reached for the door as if to leave, and Kara stopped him.

"Lynks, when Inir told you what he wanted you to do, could you have said no? If you'd wanted to?"

He looked at her thoughtfully. "He promised me all the kids I want to fuck." He shook his head sadly. "I'm not cut out to be a hero, Kara. I am what I am."

When he'd left, Kara stared at that closed door, sick to her stomach, her mind whirling. Because of that ritual with her shoe, Lyon hadn't been able to sense her leaving. And now? If he couldn't sense her, he couldn't find her. She might never be free.

No, she didn't believe that. Lyon would find her. He wouldn't stop looking for her until he did.

Of more concern was the fact that Inir clearly still had his claws in the new Ferals, even those that the good ones believed were free of the darkness.

And she had no way to warn them that they had traitors in their midst.

"We've got company." Fox whirled, spying three males running toward them dressed in nothing but loincloths, their faces and bodies liberally painted in hues of blue and yellow, their hair matted and long, their swords gleaming in the sun.

Fox pulled his knife. Beside him, Melisande drew her short sword and threw him a savage grin. "I'm ready to spill some blood."

He met her grin. Goddess help him, he could fall in love with this woman. "You're good with that sword?"

"Damn good."

He nodded. "All right, then. I don't think they're real. But we kill them, either way."

"I'm right beside you."

The painted trio were closing the distance fast, their swords raised. As one, Fox and Melisande surged forward. Melisande's sword was small, but a deadly little thing. He himself had only a pair of knives. Long knives. Good knives. And his animal. He'd shift if the battle went poorly, but he was still far more comfortable fighting in his human form. He'd been doing it for three hundred years.

The savages came at them, two of the three diving for Melisande, which made little sense, given her size. Unless their goal was to kill her quickly, then turn their attention to him. Bloody hell. That was exactly what they intended.

"Mel, it's you they want," he said, parrying the first blow from the one who'd targeted him, probably intent on keeping him too busy to defend her. Screw this.

In a single furious pull of magic, he shifted into his fox and leaped at his opponent, tearing off his head with one bite. He turned to find Melisande holding her own, dodging and ducking, striking thighs and wrists and abdomens until the two men were ribboned in blood and wounds that weren't healing. Were they human?

He snarled, but the sound did nothing to turn them from their attack. They were focused on Melisande and only her. And they weren't getting her.

As he leaped, the male he'd targeted swung toward him, catching his front leg with his blade in a wash of pain a moment before Fox caught the painted bastard's head between his jaws and bit down, hard.

Two down.

He was so tempted to leap in and kill the final savage, saving Melisande from any chance of injury. But she was no damsel in distress and would likely be furious if he tried. Instead, he shifted back to human, gripped his knives, and prepared to back her up.

His forearm burned and he glanced at the cut he'd taken to his fox's front leg, a cut that had yet to entirely heal. And what in the hell did that mean?

Melisande and her opponent engaged, their swords clanging before she spun away to attack again, a fierce, determined light in her eyes. The male was a skilled fighter, but his strength appeared to be no greater than human. Could these three really *be* human?

He tensed as Melisande's attacker lifted his sword as if he intended to cleave her in two. It was all he could do not to rush in. But he forced himself to stay where he was and not interfere. When the male brought that blade down only to strike air . . . and to find Melisande's blade protruding from his chest, Fox began to breathe again. *That a girl.*

The male fell, dead, from that simple strike to the heart.

But as Melisande pulled her blade out, blood spraying, she stumbled back, her face going pale.

"Mel?"

"I'm fine."

But she wasn't. Something had happened as she'd fought, and he needed to understand. "Mel?"

She whirled on him, her mouth hard, her eyes snapping with temper. "I said, I'm fine. I killed him, didn't I?"

Aye she had, but she was not fine and he wished to hell he knew what was going on in that lovely head of hers.

Melisande gasped, he gaped, as the three dead savages suddenly disappeared, leaving not so much as a trace of blood on the sand.

"They're gone," she murmured, staring at the sand where her opponent had fallen. "They weren't real."

No. He glanced at the wound on his forearm that still hadn't healed. But their swords sure as hell were.

Chapter Twelve

"**K**eep your eyes open," Fox said, as they started walking along the beach again. "Three attackers likely means more, especially since they failed."

Melisande fell into step beside him, fine tremors passing through her limbs. For one harsh moment, as she'd pulled her blade from the dead savage, memories had reared up, ugly memories of horror, of death. And for the space of a few heartbeats, she'd heard the screams again, the screams she'd tried to box up and bury deep in her mind. They'd torn at her psyche, flaying her, before dying away and disappearing again.

But the attack had left her shaken.

Why had she reacted like that? Was it because her old

self—the kind, loving person she'd been before Castin's betrayal—had never killed anyone, not even during the wars? Was that old part of her suddenly having qualms about killing? Violence had once been antithetical to her nature. Long ago, she'd been a bringer of peace. But she was no longer that woman, and hadn't been for a long, long time. She was a warrior, through and through, now. Except . . . she wasn't entirely that unfeeling warrior anymore, either.

By the mist, she didn't know who she was anymore. She knew who she wanted to be, but with each passing hour, she lost her grip on the woman she'd been for so long, a woman who'd felt no passion, no remorse, who'd never even been able to smile. And it scared her that she might never be able to reclaim her.

What would happen when she faced Castin? Would she be able to fight him to the death as she intended? Yes, Castin she'd be able to kill without a qualm. She'd hated him for so long for what he'd done. The bigger problem was her ability to kill him. Full-fledged, shifting Feral Warrior or not, Castin had always been a powerful male. And she could no longer mist.

Determination set her jaw. It didn't matter. One way or another, she'd take the bastard down and make him pay for what he'd done to her and her sisters.

Fox slid his palm across the back of her neck, the slide of flesh on flesh triggering that deep, aching need for him all over again. With the battle, the hunger had slid away, pushed aside by more pressing concerns. But he'd renewed it with a single touch.

How was she supposed to function when all she could think about was having sex, and the very thought of it sent chills crawling over her flesh?

By unspoken consent, they walked in silence for a while, then began to speak of innocuous things—more speculation of what the ocean would look like if it were truly empty of life. All the while, they kept their senses tuned, but saw no more sign of attackers.

They'd traveled the beach for more than an hour when Fox suddenly stumbled to a stop beside her, then sank slowly to his knees, a look of pain creasing his strong, handsome features.

"Feral, what's the matter?" Her heart plummeted, and she grabbed his shoulder. "Were you hit?" She saw no arrow, no bloom of blood that might indicate he'd been head- or heart-shot. Again she looked around, searching for Mage, or Castin, or some other assailant, but she saw nothing. "Fox?"

But he didn't answer. With one hand she gripped his thick shoulder, with her other, the hilt of her sword, as she prepared to defend him while he was down. No one was going to hurt him. *No one.* Her head pounded as her gaze swung from one part of the island to the other, ready for an enemy that had yet to show.

If only she knew what was happening! Fox swayed, reaching for her blindly, his fingers grasping her hips as he steadied himself. He groaned, dipping his head.

Instinctively, Melisande reached for him, feeling the need to ease his torment. Her fingers slid into his soft locks, caressing his skull as she called on her old gift. Warmth suffused her hands as she sought to ease his torment.

He pulled her closer, wrapping his arms around her, pressing his forehead against her chest. Slowly, the terrible tension in his shoulders and neck began to ease, and his breathing started to come more easily. "You have a magic touch," he murmured at last, without moving.

She stroked his golden head, loving the feel of his silken hair between her fingers, adoring the scent of him. "What happened?"

For long moments, he didn't reply, just knelt before her, holding on to her as she became more and more aware of the hands at her back, of the face pressed between her breasts.

"I had another flashback. A tunnel beneath a wall. Maybe Inir's stronghold. I don't know."

Though she heard his words, it was the location of his face that had her full attention. Desire, already ripe and lush within her, erupted in a torrent of damp need. Between her legs, she throbbed and ached, hot . . . *needy.* She began to tremble, her mating scent erupting all over again.

His head came up, golden lashes rising over eyes as hot as molten lava. Slowly, his breathing grew more shallow until it tore in and out of his nose. His hands began to shake as badly as her own, gripping her hips. Keeping her close? Or holding her at bay?

Her breath hitched, the need to taste him again almost a physical pain. She trailed her fingers down his sculpted cheek, then traced the fullness of his lower lip with her thumb.

"Mel . . ."

"I can't help it," she gasped. "I can't stop it. I haven't had a male since the attacks, haven't wanted one. In all this time, I've felt no desire, Fox. Not until you. And now I'm crazed with it."

He stared at her with those hot eyes. "It's not going away." His grasp on her hips tightened, his own trembling need telegraphing to her plainly.

"No. It's getting worse. Why do you have to be so damned beautiful?"

His mouth tilted into a semblance of a smile, but sympathy shimmered within the fire in his eyes.

"Can you . . . pleasure yourself? Will that help?"

"It will only make it worse." In the old days, the only thing that had brought her true pleasure was the touch and possession of a male. Touching herself, bringing herself to release, only drove the hunger higher.

She gripped his face tighter, touching her forehead to his, unable to look him in the eye as she voiced her admission. "I need *you*. But I don't want to. I don't want to do this." It was an admission the warrior she'd been for so long would never have made. Then again, the warrior had felt no desire. Safe behind those icy walls, she'd been nearly impervious to harm. With that icy shell lying in broken shards around her, she'd lost her defenses.

When she pulled back, the tenderness in his eyes made her heart clench.

"What if I lie beneath you, angel?"

She took a shuddering breath, moisture dampening her thighs at the thought of him stretched out like that.

"Here?"

"There's no one here but us."

"For now. What if the Mage come? Or more of those blue-painted barbarians?"

"I can shift quickly. My state of undress won't affect me at all."

Stars in heaven, she was really going to do this. She met his gaze, her body quaking with fear and need. "Don't touch me. Please. I need you to not touch me."

"I'll keep my hands behind my head." He lifted a brow. "But I have one request in return."

"What's that?"

"You give your sword into my keeping. I'd hate to have to regrow any of my more tender anatomy."

She laughed, a quick amused burst of air through her nose. But a moment later, she was shaking, wondering how in the name of the ancient queens she was going to get through this.

Fox stroked Melisande's satin cheek. "Tell me what you want me to do, angel. You call the shots. All of them." Having sex in the Mage's labyrinth was a risk. He knew it. Although, while his shifting skills weren't optimum as yet, his Great Dane size was just about perfect for tearing off an attacker's head. And he could move from sex to leaping in his fox in two seconds flat. He was sure of it. Especially if Melisande's life was at risk.

Besides, this wasn't likely to take long. Not with Melisande about to climb out of her skin and him about to burst from his own.

Leaning forward, she eyed him like a warrior going to battle. And that was just what she was, he thought darkly. How he wished he could take away the misery of her past. But he would do what he could. And if that meant letting her use him for sex . . . ? Everyone had to make sacrifices at some point.

"Lie down in the sand," she directed. "Don't take off your clothes. Just push your pants down to your thighs."

He swallowed, totally turned on by this despite himself. When had he ever allowed a female to take the reins completely? He'd always considered himself a good lover, a considerate one who gave as much as he took. And he was all too happy to let his partner have her way with his body to her heart's content as long as she wasn't into pain. Much. But to let a female order his every move?

Never.

But the thought of Melisande doing so nearly had him spilling into the sand.

He did as she commanded, lying down before her, unbuckling his belt and unzipping his pants. Pushing them down over his hips, he freed the part of his anatomy she needed, then met her gaze, watching her eyes flare with hunger, then tighten with dread.

This was worse than taking a virgin, and he'd generally steered well clear of them. It was worse still, because he couldn't help. At least with a virgin, he could stroke her, gentle her, ease into her. With Melisande he could do nothing but wait for her to come to him on her own. Or not.

"It's okay, pet. My penis is not going to hurt you. It's just going to stand here waiting for you to do what you want with it, though I'd appreciate it if I could hold your knife now, luv."

Wry humor lighting her eyes, she unsheathed her knife and handed it to him, hilt first.

Holding the blade firmly above his head with one hand, he cradled his head on his other arm. Finally, decisively, she sat beside him and began pulling off her boots. A moment later, feet bare, she struggled out of her leggings, revealing pale, slender, shapely legs that he longed to run his palms over. And his tongue. He was starting to shake from the effort to remain still when the most desirable female he'd come upon in as long as he could remember sat within reach, bare beneath her tunic, releasing a mating scent that had been driving him wild for hours.

He'd die if she didn't touch him soon. And he didn't dare say those words out loud.

Slowly, she straddled him, but she just knelt there. Shaking. Tears began to run slowly down her cheeks.

"Mel," he said softly. "Angel, look at me."

She did, her mouth so tight, so furious, her eyes so wounded.

"It's okay. You don't have to do this now. I'll be willing and waiting for you anytime you're ready." And he feared that statement was all too true. If this kept up, he'd wind up with a permanent hard-on.

"I have to do it, now."

He ached for her. And struggled against every natural instinct to grip her hips and drive himself deep into her wet, waiting heat. How in Hades was he going to remain perfectly still when she took him? How was he ever going to keep from thrusting up to meet her when, and if, she ever found the courage to ride him? Yet he must. He'd promised. And he would do nothing to make this any harder for her than it already was.

Closing her eyes, she finally began to lower herself . . . *thank you goddess,* and the feel of her wet heat stroking his head nearly sent him over the edge. With a swallowed sob, she gripped him, too tight, aiming him for her heat.

"Melisande. Look at me. Please."

Slowly, she opened those tear-drenched eyes, blinking to stare at him.

"It's me," he said softly. "Stay here with me." The last thing she needed was to sink back into that nightmare of what she'd endured before.

With a quick little nod, she kept her gaze locked on his as she pushed him inside her. Then he was sliding deep, drenched in her wetness, as she lowered herself all the way down.

"Okay?" he asked, strangling on the groan of pleasure he didn't want her to hear.

Again that quick little nod. "It feels . . . you feel . . . good."

"Thank the goddess. Do you want me to tell you a joke? Keep your mind off it?"

Her laugh lifted his heart even as it forced him deeper and, *oh goddess,* she felt so good. Her tight little sheath clutched him, milking him, as she lifted her hips and lowered them again, undulating in an erotic move that had him clenching his jaw hard, straining his muscles against the need to surge up into her. Even holding himself rigid as stone, he was barreling fast toward release. No! No, he couldn't come yet, not before she'd found her own release, or this whole thing was going to be for nothing.

She was gasping now, moaning, her eyes drifting closed, then snapping open, clinging to him as if he were the only thing keeping the monsters at bay. Finally, she cried out, her inner walls clamping tight around him, over and over. Able to hold on no longer, he poured his seed into her, his fists tight as vises as he staved off the desperate need to hold her as he came.

But the moment it was over, she was off him like a shot. Pale as new snow, she began to pull on her clothes with visibly shaking hands.

Fox took a long, shuddering breath, then rose to his feet and pulled up his pants. They'd made more progress than he'd expected and less than he would have liked. She'd accepted him, and he didn't think she'd been further damaged by the event. But neither was she healed. Far from it. And the truth was, she might never be. His body felt replete, for the most part, but his arms felt achingly empty and his chest hurt. If only he knew what to do to help her. Unfortunately, it was men who'd hurt her. And while he hated being painted with the same brush as those bastards, he got it. He was three times her size and far more than three times her strength. With her unable to mist away, if he wanted to hurt her, she'd never stop him.

No, he understood the problem. What he didn't know was the solution. If there was one. He'd never found it with Sheenagh. Not in time.

Fully dressed once more, Melisande started walking, and he fell into step beside her, handing her the blade. Without comment, she sheathed it.

The need to protect her, to slay her dragons, was

growing in him by the hour. She'd been through so much, yet emerged fire-honed. Too hard, perhaps, but strong as steel.

Until he came along and started screwing everything up.

Sometimes the psyche built defenses for a reason. Sometimes they were the only things that kept people whole. If Sheenagh had been able to erect some in time, maybe she'd have seen her fortieth birthday. Or her sixtieth. Or even her twentieth.

If he could undo whatever it was between Melisande and him, and give her back her ice and fire . . . make her quit hurting . . . he'd do it.

But what was done was done. He just had to find a way to traverse this minefield without hurting her more.

As they walked in silence, she reached for his hand. Without looking at him, she pulled it to her mouth and placed a tender kiss upon his knuckles.

His heart clenched and he tipped his head back, filled with an incredible sweetness. His arm ached to go around her and pull her close, but he would not risk spoiling the moment for anything. Instead, he squeezed her hand, caressing the silken back with his thumb.

How had this small slip of a woman come to mean so much?

Melisande was still shaking inside, her body buzzing from being thoroughly fed for the first time in millennia, her mind in turmoil.

Touching Fox, feeling him as she took him inside her, had sharpened memories she'd fought for millennia to forget. They'd stolen her breath, making her tremble with remembered pain, remembered fear. *The fury.* But then she'd looked at him, seen the gentle, aching look in his eyes, and thought only of him.

For a moment, she'd wanted Fox's mouth on her skin, the stroke of his hands on her flesh. But then the other memories had crowded in again, memories of being violated, hurt, *tortured.* Fox had held on to her, not letting her get lost in them.

He was becoming her anchor, and far too important to her.

"I used to be so innocent, so naive," she murmured as they walked hand in hand across the rain-hardened beach. "I loved to dance, to laugh. To make love. Males adored me and I them." She glanced at Fox and found him watching her intently, listening to every word. "I thought they couldn't hurt me. If a male touched me in any way that I disliked, I simply misted away from him and never went back. No one could catch an Ilina. That's what we all thought."

"How did they catch you?" Fox asked quietly. "Castin?"

"Yes." Her jaw tightened, hating him as much today as she had that day so long ago. We'd been lovers for months and good friends. He'd always been kind to me."

Sky blue eyes filled with pain and fury. "I'm sorry, luv. That's the worst kind of betrayal."

"He gave me a bracelet made of red moonstones, the only thing known to keep an Ilina from turning to mist. They were covered in tar. I didn't realize what they were until it was too late."

"I'm sorry." His grip on her hand tightened. A small hug, and it warmed her. "Why would he do such a thing?"

"His chief wanted more from me than I would ever willingly give." The full story was more than she was up for right now with all the memories so fresh, the old wounds raw and bleeding again. Glancing at him, meeting his gaze, she said, "I'll tell you the rest later. I just can't right now."

He squeezed her hand again. "That's fine, angel. I understand."

She looked at him again, studied him. "You do understand. You've known a woman who suffered the abuse of men, haven't you? Someone you cared for."

"My sister. Half sister. I tried to help her, but . . ." He shook his head, old shadows in his eyes.

"They killed her?"

"No. Not directly. She survived the physical assault even though she was mortal. At eighteen she was gang-raped by seven men. Humans."

"Fox . . . I'm sorry."

A fierce light lit his eyes. "I killed them all." His eyes glazed over as if remembering. "It was the mental trauma she couldn't heal and, as hard as I tried, I couldn't help her with." Old anguish wove within the hard fibers of his voice. "I tried, angel. I tried so hard to reach her, to help her understand that it wasn't her fault. That I'd protect her and wouldn't let it happen again." He shook his head. "Less than a year later, she took her own life. I found her hanging in the barn."

"Oh, Fox. I'm so sorry." She understood now his incredible care with her once he realized she'd been hurt. And how easily he'd figured it out.

He smiled at her, but it was a sad smile. "You're so much stronger than she was."

"I was a lot older when it happened. And immortal."

"I think if Sheenagh had been able to call up the kind of fury you've carried with you, she might have survived, too."

"Yes, but that kind of fury, and what it demands of you, kills the soul."

"It didn't kill yours."

Inside, she trembled. "I'm not sure about that."

He released her hand and pulled her close, his arm around her shoulders. "I'm sure."

Sliding her arm around his waist, she tipped her head against his shoulder. All she'd wanted since Fox first came into her life and she started awakening was to reclaim the fury, the coldness, to go back to the way she'd been. And she might be able to accomplish it. By killing Castin.

But for the first time, she began to realize that she would be giving up as much as she gained. The thought of losing this connection she'd begun to form with Fox cut like a well-honed blade.

A short while later, as they continued down the beach, Fox felt another low vibration. He and Melisande tensed as one, spinning to find more of the blue-faced warriors running toward them.

"There have to be more than two dozen of them," Melisande gasped.

"That's our cue to get the hell out of here." A shiver tore through him, his gut offering up an escape route. He hoped. *Into the trees. Now.*

He grabbed Melisande's hand. "Come on!"

Together, they ran for the tree line. Exactly how this would help them, he had no idea. If they ran through the forest and out the other side, what then?

A glance over his shoulder told him that the savages were coming across the sand quickly and fanning out. He and Melisande would have no choice but to go through the tropical forest unless they wanted to fight. And considering the savages' primary goal appeared to be to strike down Melisande, there was no way in hell they were taking on two dozen of them at once. No way in bloody hell.

As he and Melisande leaped into the trees, they separated, dodging underbrush and fallen limbs and trunks.

"Stop!" Melisande yelled a short distance in front of him, grabbing a tree as if to hold on for dear life.

Fox managed to stop a moment before plowing into her. "What's the matter?" He grabbed her hand, pulling her back against him.

"Another pit."

Sure enough, palm fronds lay across the tropical forest floor, obscuring all but one corner of what indeed appeared to be another pit. But as he looked around, he found palm fronds everywhere, most appearing as carefully laid as the one in front of him.

"It's a minefield," he muttered. And his gut had led him right to it. He couldn't even *think* what that meant, because wasn't it his gut that had led him down that street in the seaport, right into the path of the vines?

Melisande started forward, and he grabbed her arm. "What are you doing?"

"It's either this or fight."

"Okay. You're right. We go forward."

This was the reason they were here—to fall into one of these traps just as Castin likely had. To be captured by the Mage, Melisande almost certainly slaughtered.

He wasn't going to let it happen.

Chapter Thirteen

Melisande's heart pounded as she stared at the pits hidden beneath the palm fronds all around them. The storm should have sent the fronds flying, unveiling all of the holes. But the magic appeared to have restored them to their original place, if it had ever moved them at all.

"Run, Mel," Fox said urgently. "They're here. *Run.*"

Stars in heaven. There had to be paths, but the way the palm fronds overlapped, it was impossible to see where. She began to lift the huge leaves, tossing them into the nearest pit, revealing the holes, one by one. The trouble was, bending, lifting, shoving the fronds down took time. And with two dozen warriors racing to cut out their hearts, there *was* no time.

She prayed to the ancient queens and leaped forward, grabbing one of the long fronds and slamming down the hard stem over and over, walking as fast as she could. Where she hit solid ground, she followed. Where the frond pushed through, she exposed another hole.

At the clash of metal behind her, she whirled to find Fox fully engaged in battle. The only good news was that the savages would be as hindered by the pits as they were. And maybe the pits were the key, the way to even the numbers a little. After a few more yards straight back, she made a hard right. Just as she suspected, with Fox no longer running interference, the painted ones began racing straight for her. Two hit the first pit and fell in with twin cries of fury.

Melisande grinned and kept going. Another three leaped for her and landed in the next pit. Death cries echoed through the tropical woods as Fox made kills behind her. Two more savages leaped to fall in. They certainly weren't the smartest lot. Then again, they weren't real.

She'd sent seven of them into the holes so far. A quick look over her shoulder told her that Fox had killed close to that many, too, leaving . . . ten. Still far too many. But another one cried out. Nine. And another. Eight. Fox was hacking through them quickly, following after the horde that stalked her, taking them out from behind. Seven, six, five.

Suddenly, three of them turned, like puppets pulled by a single string and leaped at Fox all at once. In a coordinated, horrifying move, they tackled him, pushing him into the nearest hole and following him down.

"Fox!" She sprang forward, but one of the two remaining warriors stepped into her path and the other came at her from the other side until she was trapped between them on a strip of ground no more than two feet wide. If she fell in either direction, she, too, would be trapped in one of those pits. And she had little doubt that she'd never leave it alive.

Her only choice was to fight.

Melisande hesitated for only a moment, then lunged. Fear and desperation fueling her actions, she fought for her life and for the life of the man she was coming to care about far too much. She ducked, stabbed, whirled, until sweat ran into her eyes, and her tunic was torn and bloody. But, finally, she managed to hamstring one of her assailants, toppling him into one of the pits. Then she whirled and slashed the other's throat.

With a shuddering breath, she wiped her bloody blades on her ruined tunic and slammed them into their scabbards, then lunged for the pit where Fox had disappeared. But between her first step and her second, the tropical forest disappeared.

And suddenly she stood in the middle of an empty,

snowy plain, at the base of a rocky, frozen hillside. *No.* She turned, trying to return to the island, and failed. There was no going back. And Fox was trapped.

The labyrinth had separated them at last.

It was late afternoon when Grizz and Lepard knocked on the front door of the tan-and-brown two-story frame house in Whitefish, Montana. It sat along a quiet neighborhood street, its front porch overflowing with plants and flowers, in the midst of which sat a padded bench adorned with a fat, sleeping tabby.

In the distance rose the mountains, the Rockies, their snow-covered crowns at odds with the warmth of the late-spring day.

A man opened the door, light brown hair falling straight and shaggy to his shoulders, his beard full and thick. Paint splattered his white T-shirt and jeans and a glass of what appeared to be whiskey sat comfortably in his free hand.

"Yarren Brinlin?" Grizz asked.

Small eyes narrowed. "Who wants to know?"

Grizz pushed his way into the house, startling a squeak of objection from the smaller man.

"Hey! What do you think you're doing?"

Grizz stopped in the middle of the front room and looked around at what was essentially an art studio— two easels with half-painted canvases, a stack of blank canvases propped against one wall. Paints of every conceivable type and color littered every surface. The house smelled of oil paints and paint thinner, with an underlying layer of cigarette smoke and microwaved pizza.

"Get the hell out of my house!"

Grizz's temper ignited, his fangs and claws erupting in a hard growl.

Brinlin gaped, his eyes going wide as dinner plates, his whiskey glass slipping through his fingers to shatter on the paint-splattered hardwood floor. "You're a Feral Warrior."

Grizz felt Lepard's hand on his shoulder. "Dial it back, Grizz."

Wide eyes went impossibly wider. "The *grizzly*? Man alive." His gaze swung to Lepard. "You, too?"

"Snow leopard."

Brinlin took a shaky step backward. "What . . . what do you want?"

"Sabine."

The male's anger-flushed cheeks drained of all color. "No. No way. She'll kill you if you try to go near her. Or she'll kill me."

"She doesn't like Ferals?"

"She doesn't like anybody. She's a loner."

"We need to talk to her," Grizz told him.

Brinlin backed up another step. "I can't help you."

Grizz matched his step, stalking him. "Give me her address."

"I don't know it." The smaller man glanced behind him, unable to back up any farther for the stack of blank canvases behind his heel. "She probably doesn't even have one. She lives in the fuckin' middle of nowhere."

Grizz took another step, until less than a foot separated them, his muscles tense, his patience gone. At seven-foot-two, he towered over the other man and used every bit of that height advantage to intimidate. "Then you'll take us to her."

"No! I mean . . . look." Brinlin visibly swallowed, sweat beginning to glisten on his temples, his gaze darting everywhere but Grizz's face. "There's a lockbox in the woods where I deliver supplies to her once a month and pick up her list for next month. That's it. I never see her."

"When do you deliver the drop-offs?"

"The first of each month."

Which was still four days away. He couldn't wait four days. He was already running out of patience. "Tell us how to reach the drop box."

"I . . ." He swallowed. "She'll kill me."

Grizz's fangs and claws erupted. "It's either her or me," he growled.

The man paled so quickly, Grizz thought he was going to pass out. "Are you going to hurt her?"

"We just need her help."

Despite his obvious shaking, Brinlin scoffed. "Good

luck with that. The only time I ever met her, she pulled a shotgun on me."

"Yet you continue to take her supplies?"

"Providing for Sabine has been my clan's responsibility for as long as anyone can remember. Centuries. Probably longer. She's a loner, like I said. Where she goes, someone in my line follows . . . at a distance. My father was out here first, nearly a hundred years. But he got eaten by a grizzly, and I moved out here to take his place."

"I was told she's Mage. Why is a Therian clan providing for a Mage?"

"She's not Mage. Well, maybe she's part Mage. I don't know. And I don't know how the promise to bring her supplies started. It's just something we've always done."

Grizz felt his claws and fangs retract. He had no control over their comings and goings and wondered if he ever would. "You're going to give me directions to that drop box," he said calmly. "Or I'm going to rip out your liver."

The man blanched. "You can't tell her how you found her. You can't implicate me."

"Directions."

Brinlin took an unsteady breath. "Right." He peered at Grizz doubtfully. "How well do you know this area?"

"Not at all. Print me out a map."

Another shuddering breath. "Okay."

As Brinlin scurried to his laptop, Lepard asked, "What does she look like? Sabine."

"Dark hair, reddish. Pale skin. Pretty, I think, but it was hard to tell since she was watching me through the sights of a gun."

Ten minutes later, map in hand, Grizz and Lepard climbed back into their rental vehicle and left.

"The woman sounds like a real charmer," Lepard commented.

"Maybe. Or maybe she's just being defensive."

"What do you mean?"

"The Indian said she can see into a man's soul. Sounds like some kind of empath to me."

Lepard's mouth opened. A thoughtful moment later, he muttered, "Maybe she senses things about people, and can't turn it off . . ."

"Which would account for her need to protect her solitude, with a gun if necessary."

"Can you imagine the loneliness of that kind of life?"

"I'm thinking more of the kind of welcome we're likely to get. And the chances she'll accompany us willingly to Feral House."

Lepard snorted. "Like negative forty? And I thought this mission had *failure* written all over it. Try *goat fuck*. In great big neon caps. There's no way in hell this is going to work. On either end."

"Probably not. But we don't have a lot to lose at this point."

"Considering that the original Ferals are going to wind up killing us either way?" Lepard gave a humorless laugh. "We are one hundred percent fucked."

Snow was falling lightly, the air frigid, as Melisande looked around, searching for a more defensible position. Because the damned labyrinth would almost certainly send someone to try to kill her again.

Or some *thing*.

She didn't have long to wonder what. Minutes later, the sound of pounding hooves had her turning and staring in rising horror at the beast charging at her from across the snowy plain. The size of a bull, it had a doglike snout with wicked teeth and a thick greenish gray hide. But it was the horns on its head that were scaring her shitless—not two, as a bull would have, but a crown of six, long and narrow, like six short swords ready to cut her into steaks.

She pulled her knives, mentally calculating the beast's speed and the difficulty of ducking the horns to leap on to its back.

The beast let out a bloodcurdling roar and lowered its head, telling her in no uncertain terms that it meant to kill her, that the labyrinth and its Mage masters would not allow her to leave this place alive. And for one dark moment, she feared that was exactly what would happen. That she'd never see Fox again, never see Ariana or her sisters. Fear curled inside her.

She had to kill this thing and kill it fast.

The beast charged, but he was more nimble than she'd anticipated. Pain tore through her side and she looked down to find her tunic torn, blood flowing freely. Dammit! She stumbled away from the beast as he circled around to come at her again. Despite the pulse thundering in her ears, she remained perfectly still as the monster charged her. Ready . . . waiting . . .

At the last minute, she spun out of his reach, striking him, hamstringing him. *So much blood.*

As he went down, he swung his head. She leaped back, but not quite fast enough, her attention stolen for one moment too many. One of those spearlike horns tore through her thigh, flinging her up and over him, into the snow.

The wind knocked out of her, she struggled to her feet, sinking, as her injured leg buckled, watching with disbelief as the beast charged her again, already healed.

Melisande pulled her sword, willing her thigh to knit more quickly. But the beast was nearly upon her. She was out of time.

Fox clung to a thick root protruding from the side of the pit about three feet from the lip. Amazingly, he'd been able to snag it as the four of them tumbled in, keeping the warriors from pulling him down to the watery bottom some twenty feet below. If he fell, there would be no escape. As it was, escape was problematic.

He eyed the lip of the hole just out of reach. So close and yet so far.

And he had to get out, dammit. He had to get to Melisande.

He burrowed his fingers into the dirt wall, down by his knee, seeking another root that might act as a foothold. If he could step higher, he could, pray to the goddess, make his way out. When he'd first fallen, and first caught himself, he'd feared the painted savages would attack him from below, but between falling in and hitting the water, they'd disappeared.

He'd listened to the sounds of battle, desperate to reach Melisande and cover her back. But moments ago, the forest above had gone silent. She hadn't answered when he'd called. And now he was wracked with fear because there was no good answer. Either she'd been taken by those savages, or she'd slipped, alone, into the next world.

Or she was dead.

His heart clenched, his control slipping as a vicious roar built deep inside him. He clamped down on it, struggling to keep his wits about him. He'd do Melisande no good if he fell into this pit.

Finally, he found what he was looking for, a loop of good-sized root still firmly woven into the ground. Stepping on it gingerly, he held on tight to the first root and pushed himself up. *Careful,* he thought. *Go slow.* He could not afford to fall. In both worlds, now, the attackers had fought not to kill him, not even to catch him, per se. No, they'd wanted him caught in the traps. First the vines. Then this pit. And in both cases, the moment he was trapped, his opponents had walked away. Or disappeared.

All evidence pointed to the Mage wanting him taken alive. And he could only assume it was because of whatever it was that Inir had done to the fox animal spirit after he'd killed Sly.

But the Mage didn't want Melisande. The labyrinth wanted her dead.

Goddess, he had to reach her.

He shivered, then wondered what useless bit of untruth his gut was about to offer him this time.

Drop.

Bloody hell. His gut was bent on getting him captured. Why? Had it really turned against him, or was it trying to give him exactly what he wanted . . . a way to find Kara? While he'd never in a million years expected to be the one among them to accomplish that feat, he couldn't deny the satisfaction he'd derive from doing so. The validation. And his gut would know it. But, while getting captured by the Mage might be a way to reach her, there had to be a better way than becoming a Mage captive himself.

If he were to be captured, Melisande would stand no chance.

No. He wasn't giving up and letting himself be caught. Not in a million years.

Painstakingly slowly, Fox dug one foothold then handhold after another until, finally, he was able to pull himself up and out of the pit.

Sweat ran down his back and chest as he searched for signs of Melisande. She wasn't dead. At least he didn't think so. Phylicia had quickly turned to dust after she died. The pain that went through him at the thought that Melisande could already be gone, all trace of her existence wiped from the Earth, was excruciating. She was still alive. He had to believe that.

Maybe she'd fallen into one of the pits and been knocked unconscious. Perhaps that's why she hadn't answered his call.

"Mel!" Still no answer. He began making his way carefully between the pits, peering into each, searching for sign of her. The last thing he wanted to do was to slide into the next world with her still trapped in this one.

But with his next step, snow covered his booted foot, and he knew it was done. He'd left the island. At the same time, he heard the roar of a beast and whirled to see Melisande flying through the air over the strangest creature he'd ever seen—a beastie with six sharp swords for horns. A monster who was about to kill Melisande.

Chapter Fourteen

In a running leap, Fox shifted into his animal, four feet able to traverse the snowy field better than his human two as he raced to save Melisande. Even as he ran, the six-horned beastie turned and began to charge her as she struggled, bloodied, to her feet. She pulled her blade, but though her leg appeared to be healing, it wasn't happening fast enough. Goddess, she wasn't going to be able to move out of the way in time.

He raced over the snow, thanking the goddess that he'd followed her from that world to this. As he neared the beastie, he shifted to human form and pulled his blade, then leaped onto the beast's back and stabbed it through the neck.

But the creature didn't slow. It was almost upon her. Leaning low, he cut hard through the monster's thigh muscle. The beastie went down, tossing Fox over its head into the snow, but as Fox leaped up again, Melisande took his place on the struggling animal's back, stabbing it in the neck over and over.

"It keeps healing," she called to him, annoyance in her voice. "Want to give me a hand with his head?" She asked the question as calmly as if she were asking for help with an unwieldy suitcase.

He grinned, his relief at finding her whole and alive bursting from his throat on a deep chuckle.

"Aye, pet. I'll give you a hand." He strolled to the pair of them and with a pair of hard hacks, cut off the beast's head. A moment after Melisande leaped clear of the carcass, the creature disappeared.

He sheathed his blade and turned to Melisande, barely opening his arms in time as she threw herself at him.

"I thought they'd caught you," she cried, throwing her arms around his neck, wrapping her legs around his waist, clinging to him tight.

He hauled her against him, burying his nose in her hair, shaking from relief and joy and an emotion he was afraid to name. "I thought I'd lost you," he breathed. "I wasn't even sure you'd survived." How had she come to mean so much?

Finally, she pulled back to where she could see him. "I feared the labyrinth had separated us."

"Apparently there's only one path through the gauntlet. Escape the trap, and it propels you into the next world, offering you another chance to fail."

"I need to kiss you," she said softly, fervently.

"Oh, pet . . ." They came together in a blaze of need and thanksgiving, her lips cold, their kiss hot enough to scorch the flesh from his bones. He devoured her, drinking in her taste, her sweetness. The need to keep her with him, safe and protected, trembled through his muscles. As badly as he needed to be inside her again, he longed even more to tuck her within his heart, where no one could ever threaten her or hurt her again.

Snow began to fall as their mouths melded, their tongues twining in a fierce yet gentle dance. She smelled of wild heather and crisp mountain air, and tasted of honey. So sweet, so incredibly precious.

Snowflakes landed on his cheeks, his hands, melting in the heat of their passion. But as he slanted his head to deepen the kiss, their noses brushed and he felt hers, ice-cold. He pulled back. "We need to find shelter, angel." The wind was beginning to whip and the sky to darken.

She gave her head a little shake as if trying to reclaim her equilibrium. "Yes. Shelter." But her mating scent wrapped around him, sinking into his blood, and it was all he could do not to take her mouth again.

"The rocks," he said. "Maybe we can find a windbreak, if nothing else."

She nodded, and he set her on the ground, then took her small, cold hand firmly in his. Together, they climbed into the crags, searching for a cave, or any kind of shelter as the snow fell harder and visibility became so poor Fox could no longer see the snowy plain below the rocks. An army could be approaching, and they'd have little warning.

He didn't like this, not at all. The beast had been sent to kill Melisande, nothing more. But at some point, in some way, the labyrinth would try to corral him into a trap.

"I see something," Melisande said, pulling away from him.

Fox followed her gaze to a low split in the rock, much too small for him to fit through, and watched as she bent low and stuck her arm into it with ease.

He might not fit, but his fox would. "I'll shift and scope it out. I can see in the dark."

Pulling on the power of his animal, he shifted too big, of course, but quickly downsized until he was the size of a small fox. With ease, he trotted through the hole and into a cave about the size of the war room at Feral House, the ceiling high enough for him to stand up in with ease, once he'd shifted back. But as he looked around, he saw something in the corner that made his hackles rise—a large pile of firewood. And a box of wooden matches.

"Fox?" Melisande called softly.

"Come in, pet." He shifted back into a man, and the cave went dark for a moment as his human vision slowly adjusted to the minimal light allowed in through the cave's small mouth. Light temporarily doused by Melisande's arrival.

She'd had to do little more than bend over to squeeze inside. Rising, she looked around, blinking to adjust her sight. "This is perfect. Unless they're my size, or can shift into something smaller, no one else will be able to get in. Certainly, no more than one at a time, and then with difficulty."

"Let's hope we don't have to get out in a hurry." Her mating scent perfumed the air in the small space, igniting the fire in his blood all over again.

"It's better than standing out in the snow. Especially for those of us without fur or coats."

He nodded toward the firewood. "It's a little too perfect. All it's missing is gingerbread walls and candy light fixtures."

Melisande shrugged. "We're not going to escape whatever this place has in store for us, you know that. It won't let us go until we've evaded its traps."

"Walking into one isn't exactly evading."

"No," she said huskily. "But we're safe from the storm. And alone." Sapphire eyes leaped with heat.

She was right. Fox knew she was right. And even if she wasn't, at this moment, he didn't care. He took a step toward her as she moved toward him, and they met in the middle, coming together like two halves of a hole. He pulled her hard against him, devouring her mouth, remembering too late to be careful with her. But as she met him, kiss for kiss, hunger for hunger, he felt a triumphant rush of relief. Her mating scent invaded his senses, sending his already-raging passion spiraling out of control.

"I have to touch you." Despite the need tearing him apart, he forced himself to move slowly, aware she might balk at any moment. He slid one hand to the hem of her tunic, then under, against her cold abdomen, then higher to palm her breast.

The feel of her sweet flesh against his skin pulled a moan of pure pleasure from deep in his throat. "You feel like heaven," he said against her lips. He longed to whip the tunic off of her, to bare her to his sight. But he wouldn't undress her when she was still so cold. And he couldn't see her nearly as well as he wanted in the almost nonexistent light.

It took every ounce of willpower he possessed to pull away from her. It pleased him when she resisted, groaning in protest.

"Let me start the fire, luv. Let me get you warm."

"The fire will lead them right to us." She snorted. "Who am I kidding? They know where we are."

"They do. And they'll come for us. When that happens, we'll fight. Until then, we're going to stay safe. And warm." He cupped her soft cheek, his hand unsteady as the need to touch her everywhere powered through him. "I want to undress you. Will you allow me that?"

She hesitated, tugging at her bottom lip with her teeth. Slowly, she nodded. "If I can do the same to you."

A grin broke across his mouth. "Aye, you can."

The wood was dry, and he built the fire quickly and easily. As the flames began to flicker over the walls, the wood popping and crackling as it took to the flame, Fox turned back to the beautiful woman at his side.

Their gazes met, need leaping between them in a raw, carnal burst. Goddess, he wanted her. And by the passion gleaming in her eyes, he knew she felt the same. He slid both hands to the hem of her tunic and she lifted her arms high, allowing him to pull it up and over her head.

His breath left him on a sigh. It was the first time he'd seen her. "So beautiful." His thumb brushed over one taut nipple. "You wear no bra."

She smiled, a twinkle in her eye that threatened to slay him. "There were no Victoria's Secrets around in my youth. I got used to going without."

He grinned, flicking his thumb across her nipple again as she gasped with pleasure. "So perfect," he murmured, then knelt before her, gripped her hips lightly, and dipped his head, taking one breast into his mouth. She tasted as good as she smelled, like fresh air and wild, sultry nights. As he flicked his tongue back and forth across her nipple, her fingers dug into his hair, holding him close, filling him with a rightness he couldn't explain and didn't question.

He was beginning to tremble with the need to taste her in other places. Everywhere. When he moved to kiss the valley between her breasts, she gasped with pleasure. Fox glanced up at her. "Tell me what you want me to do, angel." If she told him to stop, to leave her alone, he'd do it. He'd expire of wanting, but he'd do it.

"Love me," she said instead, and his knees weakened with relief.

"Aye." He reached down and pulled off one of her boots, then met her heated gaze. "You can tell me to stop at any moment. You know that."

"Yes."

He pulled off her other boot, then reached for the waistband of her leggings and slowly began to lower them, revealing her to his hungry gaze one inch at a time. His heart pounded with fear that she'd tell him to stop, that she'd back away and refuse to let him touch her more.

But she said nothing. Her fingers trailed over his shoulders as he pulled her leggings down to her thighs, then lower, and finally off. Sitting back on his heels, he looked at her thoroughly, in thrall to her beauty, his pulse beginning to hammer in his veins.

"You are so lovely, Melisande."

She watched him in return, a soft smile on her mouth. But there were shadows in her eyes.

"Are you all right?"

She hesitated only a moment before nodding. "Yes. The hunger rages, the desire to touch you is almost more than I can bear."

"But the memories haunt."

"Yes. I suppose they always will." She reached for him. "Touch me, Fox. Make me forget."

And there was nothing in the world he wanted more. "Will you free your hair for me?"

With a smile that was almost shy, and incredibly sweet, she nodded and pulled her braid over her shoulder, unknotting the tie that held it. As she freed her braid, he slid one hand slowly between her legs, pleased when she adjusted her stance to afford him access. She was so wet, so hot for him that he nearly lost the last of his control and pulled her under him. Instead, he stroked her. His finger slid through her wetness, into her body, and she gasped, arching back even as her fingers worked her lovely blond locks from their braid.

Pulling her against him, one arm around her waist, his other hand between her legs, he once more took her breast in his mouth as his finger worked her, in and out, his thumb circling her sweet nub until she was rocking against him, gasping.

He had to taste her. Pulling his hand from between her legs, he gripped her hips with both hands, then kissed her stomach. Slowly, he dipped lower, kissing one thigh, then the other, until finally he found the nectar he sought, licking between her legs, tasting her sweet essence.

"Fox," she gasped, and clung to him, her cry of pleasure the sweetest of sounds. And he had no intention of stopping until he pushed her over the edge.

His fingers pressed into her soft flesh, caressing even as he held her close, her scent invading his senses until she was all that existed—this woman, this moment, and the need to make her scream with pleasure.

As her hips began to rock, he continued his gentle assault, stroking her with his tongue, suckling her, licking her until she was gasping, rocking, digging her small fingers into his shoulders with sweet desperation. And, finally, she was there, arching on a gasping, keening cry, shattering in her pleasure.

Her knees gave way, and he pulled her against him, her glorious hair cloaking them both. She reached for him, her hands on his shoulders, then in his hair, her sapphire eyes blazing as she stared at him with heat and joy.

"I want you, Fox. I need you inside of me." Her temporary weakness evaporated, and she shifted, grabbing for his belt, unbuckling it as she grinned at him, seduction in those marvelous eyes. "There's something you should know about me. Before . . . my captivity . . . I was a woman without inhibitions."

"Thank you, goddess," he muttered, as her sweet fingers unbuttoned the button on his pants and slid down his zipper.

She glanced up, her eyes serious. "Don't cover me with your body, and I think we'll be okay." Then her attention returned to her task, and her cool little hand dipped beneath the waistband of his shorts to slide over his thick, throbbing erection. "If I'm not, we'll both find out." Hot eyes met his. "Let me pleasure you."

His breath hitched as he stroked her cheek. "Is that what you want?"

Her hand slid down over his erection, a shock of pleasure that had him arching back, his eyes dropping closed. When he opened them again, it was to find her watching him with a cheeky smile. "Trust me, Feral. I wouldn't have offered if I didn't want."

Truly, he'd died and gone to heaven.

The next thing he knew, his pants and shorts were down around his thighs and her warm, sweet mouth was on him, kissing the entire throbbing, sensitive length of him. Never had he known anything so erotic. Her fingers closed around him, her thumb brushing the tiny drop of moisture that had escaped the tip. Then she guided him to her lips and closed her mouth around him.

Gripping her small head, diving his fingers into her glorious hair, he struggled not to rock his hips as she licked him, sucking him. And lost. Of their own volition, his hips rose, pushing his erection more deeply

into her mouth and she took him, her free hand finding
his stones, playing with them, wrenching a moan from
his throat. The pleasure built and built until it was all
he could do not to come.

"Enough, angel."

Melisande released him, wiping her mouth, looking
up at him with a sultry, shining joy. "I would bring you
to release."

"I don't want to go there without you."

Melisande slid her hands up under Fox's T-shirt, reveling in the feel of warm skin over hard muscle beneath her palms. "Undress for me," she breathed, her
voice husky, delighting in the rush of pleasure she'd
been denied for so long, a pleasure all the more intense
because of the man she shared it with. A man who
made her smile, who lit her up inside, burning away
the shadows and the darkness, holding the worst of the
memories firmly at bay.

He smiled at her now, a slow, carnal smile that
thrilled and delighted her. Never had she been with a
male who was more gentle, or more considerate. Or
more beautiful.

As he whipped his T-shirt over his head and tossed it
aside, she watched the play of firelight over muscle and
the way his golden locks caught the light of the flame.
He was like an angel in his own right, a warrior angel
if there was ever such a thing.

But her gaze caught on his shoulder where he'd been wounded. And had yet to fully heal. And there was another cut on his forearm. She frowned. "It worries me that you aren't healing."

"Me, too," he admitted as he sat at her feet and began to pull off his boots. "I'm sure it's just the mountain's magic."

She reached for her knife and made a slice across the pad of her middle finger. Pain seared, blood bloomed, but within seconds, the wound closed and she licked the blood away.

"What are you doing?"

"Testing your theory that it's the mountain's magic." She held up her fully healed finger. "It's not affecting me that way."

Fox held out his hand to her. "Do the same to me."

She met his gaze, hesitating for only a moment before she took his hand and cut a far-more-shallow slice, then watched with dismay as the blood welled up, and up, until it ran down his hand, dripping onto the ground.

Her gaze flew to his, and she frowned. "It makes no sense why the mountain would try to kill you this way when it has so clearly been trying to trap you alive." She grabbed the hem of her discarded tunic and wrapped it around his bleeding finger. Moments later, she eased back the pressure to study the wound. "It's starting to heal," she murmured, then pressed the wound some more.

He touched her hand, brushing his thumb across the back of it. "I'm fine, pet. No, not fine. I'm in pain of a different kind."

But it worried her that he wasn't healing properly. Something was obviously wrong with him. And that bothered her far more than she wanted it to.

Fox stood and shucked the rest of his clothes, and she watched, loving him, drinking in the sight of his beauty. He was glorious, his legs thick with muscle, his hips and waist narrow, his chest broad and beautifully sculpted. And his erection . . . as fine as any ever made.

Hunger burned in her belly. Affection and joy built in her chest, a pressure she wasn't sure how to ease.

He pulled her into his arms, and she went happily, loving the feel of flesh to flesh, loving the slide of his hands down her bare back and the press of that protruding thickness against her belly. She drank in the sweetness of being held, of feeling utterly safe even when danger lurked just outside.

The brush of his whiskers and the soft press of his warm kiss to her temple melted her. Nose against his neck, she breathed his scent deep into her lungs, shivering with the raw pleasure it brought her, and pressed her own lips to that warm skin.

His hold on her tightened, his hands once more telegraphing the need that had raged before and that raged again. Lifting her head, she met his kiss in a fiery burst of pure desire, their mouths fusing, their tongues sliding and tangling. He tasted like a clean, fresh spring on a hot summer day, and she didn't think she would ever get enough of him. Reaching up, she gripped his skull, the long, soft strands of his hair slipping sensuously through her fingers. His hands roamed her back, sliding down to cup her buttocks, to pull her tight against his thick erection.

"I have to be inside you," he murmured against her mouth. "I can't wait any longer." He pulled her down with him, lying back with a small smile that wrapped around her heart and squeezed. "Ride me, angel," he said softly.

And there was nothing she wanted more. Straddling him, she lowered herself slowly until the tip of his erection pressed between her legs, seeking entrance.

"Can I hold on to you this time?" he asked carefully. "Will you let me join you?"

"Yes. Please."

He grinned, then gripped her hips and pushed inside her, slowly, carefully, filling her, claiming her.

Melisande arched back, drenched in pleasure. She rolled her hips, sliding him out, then in again in a sinuous move that had always driven her lovers to madness. At the sound of Fox's groan, she smiled, peering down at him, meeting his passion-filled gaze. As she stepped up the pace, his grip slid to her buttocks, his fingers digging into her, driving her own passion higher.

"You're good at this," he gasped.

"Am I?" She laughed, all worries gone for this moment. Her senses swam, overwhelmed by the feel of flesh on flesh, of Fox's wonderful, masculine scent, of his heat, and the sheer perfection of his powerful body. As her need built, emotion welled up inside of her— pleasure, joy. *Love*. How it had happened, she didn't know, but she'd fallen in love with this man.

The passionate storm picked her up. Fox's grip on her tightened. "Look at me, angel." His blue eyes pulled her in, snaring her, holding her with the softest, sweetest touch as he pushed into her, harder and harder, driving her up, and up, and up.

She met him, thrust for thrust, telling him without words that he didn't need to be careful. Not now. Not in this. Together, they mated, sex in its most primitive form, hard, desperate, loving. One. It was glorious, a melding of both flesh and spirit. Grinning at one another, gasping, they screamed their release, her cry to his shout as the storm broke over them.

As her heart began to settle, Fox slid his hands up her side, reaching for her. "Kiss me, Mel."

And she did, lying atop him, stroking his damp face, pressing her lips to his. His hands stroked her back, caressed her head, as her hair fell over them both.

Finally, she tucked her head against his shoulder and knew peace.

"This place could have filled with Mage, and I wouldn't have known it," he murmured against her hair.

"For once, the goddess was on our side." He kissed her forehead with such tenderness that it brought tears to her eyes.

Lifting up, she pressed her hand to his cheek. "That was . . . the very best it's ever been for me."

Pleasure warmed his eyes along with wry amusement. "And you remember those lovers from long ago?"

She smiled. "I do. An Ilina never forgets."

"I thought it was the elephant that never forgets."

"Funny story . . ." She traced his bottom lip with her finger and he pulled her digit into his mouth. "In ancient Persia, the word for Ilina and elephant were nearly the same. Somehow it slipped from the Therian lexicon to the human."

"So the original saying really was 'an Ilina never forgets.'" He laughed, then gripped the back of her head and kissed her thoroughly once more.

But thought of the past had opened more doors, allowing memories to pour through. She pulled away, laying her cheek on Fox's shoulder. He cupped her head, caressing her, comforting her, and they lay there for a long time.

"You've turned pensive," he murmured. "Are you remembering?"

With a sigh, she nodded. "More than you can imagine."

"Can you share with me . . . anything? Were you in love with Castin?"

"No. But I thought we were friends. We'd been lovers

for nearly a year. He was one of the cheetah clan chieftain's lieutenants. I met him when I attended one of the war-council meetings with my queen, Rayas."

He stilled beneath her, his breath catching, his palm freezing on her head. "Mel . . . *how long ago was this*?"

She lifted up, peering down into his shocked face. "Five thousand years. In the weeks after the Sacrifice."

He stared at her as if she'd grown a second head.

Melisande scowled. "Are you horrified that you just made love to an ancient?"

Slowly, he shook his head. "Awed. You were there at the time of the Sacrifice, in the time of the Daemons."

"I was. And for almost a thousand years before. I'm quite old, Feral." She started to push off him, and he lifted her, setting her beside him. Together, they rose and donned their clothing, boots, and weapons.

As she began to plait her hair, Fox strolled to the cave's mouth and peered through. "The snow is piling up. We're going to have trouble getting out."

"They have no intention of letting us out. And where will we go if they do?"

Fox turned back and placed another couple of logs on the fire. The smoke rose instead of filling the cave, telling her there must be an opening high in the ceiling they couldn't see.

As Fox knelt to stoke the fire, he glanced at her, his eyes deep wells of compassion and curiosity. "Will you tell me more? About the past? About you?"

The barriers she'd erected were all gone now, burned away in the warmth of her newfound love. No longer did she feel the need to hide the past. Instead, with this male, she longed to share everything.

Fox knew he wasn't going to like what Melisande had to say. The thought of anyone hurting her had his hands shaking with the need to rip off heads. But there was so much turmoil inside her, so much torment. He needed to understand what was going on if he ever wished to help her. And he wanted to help her, desperately.

As he stoked the fire, Melisande took a long, shuddering breath, her fingers plaiting her hair with quick, tense efficiency. "The Daemons were newly defeated, the Sacrifice but weeks old."

Everyone knew the story, that both the Therians—all of whom were shape-shifters back in that time—and the Mage had pooled their great power to defeat the Daemons and lock them in the enchanted Daemon Blade. They didn't call it *the Sacrifice* until years later, once they'd realized the horrible truth—that little of that power would ever return.

"I knew that the shifters were having trouble accessing their animals, but I didn't know the extent of it," she told him. "None of us did. When Castin extended an invitation to the cheetah clan's celebration at the end of the war, I gladly accepted. He asked me to bring seven friends, and while requesting eight Ilinas to attend their event, and only eight, was odd, I didn't question it. Most Ilinas can sing quite well and are born dancers and courtesans. We were highly sought out at such gatherings, as you can probably imagine. Highly prized. Requesting all that wished to attend, I would have understood. But he asked for eight."

She looked away, a ripping sadness in her eyes that made him want to smash something. "I brought my seven best friends with me that night."

Castin was going to die ten thousand deaths. Fox joined her, sitting beside her on the hard-packed dirt, where he could at once see her face and the cave's entrance beyond the fire. He gave her knee a gentle squeeze.

Melisande continued. "At the end of one of our dances, the chieftain ordered his guards to bestow a gift upon each of us, a silver bracelet set with what appeared to be lumps of tar. He claimed it was a cheetah tradition to honor beloved guests with such, and he stood beside me as his warriors placed a bracelet around each of our wrists, Castin giving me mine. I didn't realize it at the time, but the tar hid the red moonstones that stole an Ilina's ability to mist. As soon as they got the moonstones around our wrists, they turned on us, knocking us out. They moved us miles from their caves and warded the new caves so that our sisters and queen would never find us. And they never did."

"Why?" He'd tried to remain quiet while she spoke, but he couldn't. "Why would they do such a thing?"

Melisande turned her delicate face to him, the anguish in those eyes slaying him. "Because the chieftain believed that Ilina power might be able to restore their animals if only he found the right way to access it." Her braid complete, she tossed it over her shoulder and looked down, drawing a thin line in the dirt with her fingernail. "And because I was a Ceraph."

Fox frowned. "A Ceraph?"

She looked up. "It's hard to explain. Most Ilinas are born through magic and ritual, as I was. But every dozen millennia or so, an Ilina is born who is something more. It's said I was touched by divinity, by the goddess herself. And they call Ilinas like me Ceraphs." She shrugged. "Angels."

He stared at her.

A smile pulled at her mouth, but her eyes were sad. "Most of the Feral Warriors would have a laugh at that, wouldn't they?" She shrugged. "My gift . . . to ease the torment of others . . . was considered the gift of grace from the goddess herself. It was that power the cheetah chieftain believed might heal his clan and restore their animals."

"He couldn't simply have asked?" Fox growled. "Why hurt you?"

She sighed. "You have to understand, we'd all endured over a century of war with the Daemons—a war in which our enemy, over and over, had demonstrated the ability of torture to access deep power. I believe it's part of the Daemon nature, or the way they access their own power. Castin and I had been lovers for months, and in those weeks after the Sacrifice, I'd been trying and trying to heal his animal. To no avail. They decided to find out if torture would access the power they needed. And death."

Fox's heart clenched.

Melisande resumed drawing in the dirt. "Castin handed me over to them, a lamb for the slaughter. And with me, the women closest to my heart." Her voice turned bitter. "I was so naive. I could not conceive of anyone's intentionally trying to harm me, especially one with whom I'd shared so much laughter, so much pleasure."

Fox felt a stab of jealousy among the fury, even as he ached to pull her into his arms. But she needed to get this out, and he needed to hear it. Instead, he clasped her knee and held on, hoping his touch might ease the awful truth of her words.

"When I awoke . . ." She pressed her lips together, digging deeper with her finger as if she would dig herself a hole in which to escape the past. "I found myself staked to the ground." Her words caught. His chest ached. "The chieftain was the first to rape me, torturing me as he did so, but he was far from the last. I lost count and lost track, but the brutality went on hour after hour, day after day, for weeks. Perhaps months."

It wasn't until her hand slid over the one he'd curled around her knee that he realized how tightly he was gripping her.

"Sorry," he murmured.

"You don't want to hear this."

"I . . . do. But no, I don't, because I *hate* what they did. I'm going to flay the skin from Castin's bones before you kill him." He lifted her hand, pressing a kiss to her knuckles. "Don't stop, Mel. I need to know the rest, angel." He snorted softly. "You really are one, aren't you?"

"Was. Not anymore." When he released her hand, she returned to her digging in the dirt. "Castin never found the guts to face me again after his betrayal. I'm certain he was first in line with my sisters, instead. I'd been isolated from the rest of the Ilinas and could neither see them, nor communicate with them. But for days I heard them scream. And, one by one, I felt them die."

Without warning, she leaped to her feet as if unable to stand the misery of her tale. But as she paced the small cave, she continued. "The first two were killed within hours of our captivity." She whirled on him, horror in her eyes. "They cut out their hearts and ate them, Fox. They *ate* them. Then they told me all about it, and I prayed they'd do the same to me because at least it would put an end to the pain."

Crossing her arms, she stared at the fire, rigid. "I

don't know how long it took the others to die. Days, weeks perhaps. All I know is that my screams echoed long after theirs went silent. And then mine went silent, too, because they left me. I think they believed I'd died. Even an immortal body can only take so much, and I knew I was close to the end. I believe I tipped over, turning gray. I may even have remained like that for some time. Most Ilinas will never return from that ashen state, but I was not most Ilinas. I was a Ceraph.

"With the last of the Ilinas believed dead, they left. But I wasn't dead, and they'd left me staked in the dark, bound by moonstones and a warding that made it impossible for my queen or sisters to find me."

Fox stared at her with horror. *"How long?"*

She looked up slowly, blinking as if she'd been back in that cave. "Three years."

His jaw dropped. His gut cramped.

"My need for sustenance became a torture in itself, but eventually even that left me. Slowly, everything inside me died but a hatred so cold that it turned my heart to ice. The Ceraph was gone. Everything I'd been was gone—all the goodness, all the gentleness, all the love. All gone."

Fox held out his hand for her, unable to watch her standing so alone. "Come here."

She blinked, her rigid stance softening as she went to him. He pulled her down onto his lap, wrapping his arms around her, pulling her close to his heart. The scent of wild heather wafted over him, a sweet scent, her natural scent. And he tried to imagine the sweet, graceful *angel* that she'd been. Abused. Tortured. Left staked to the ground for *three years*.

Skinning wasn't good enough for Castin. He'd shift into his animal and chew off the male's limbs first.

He rubbed his chin against her silken hair. "How did you get free, pet?"

She pressed her cheek against his shoulder blade, tucking her head against his neck, accepting the comfort he needed to offer. "A couple of human kids found me. Their father freed me, draped me with his cloak, and carried me out of the cave. The sunshine on my face after so much dark woke me from my comatose slumber. I tore at the cuffs, tossing the moonstones aside, and misted away." She grunted. "I've never stopped to wonder what he must have thought when the woman in his arms disappeared."

"It's a wonder you survived with your mind intact."

She snorted. "Some might argue that I didn't. I'd think you'd agree."

Pressing his mouth to her head, he kissed her hair. "What I think is that your strength of mind and will is remarkable, Melisande." He held her tighter. "After you escaped, you got your revenge?"

"I returned to my queen and demanded vengeance, and she granted it. Truthfully, I think she was afraid of me, afraid of what I'd become. It took me five years to find the cheetahs—they'd moved in the interim, probably afraid they'd eventually face Ilina retribution. And I cut them down, one after another, digging their hearts out of their chests with my blades."

"Except for Castin's."

"He wasn't with them, and no one knew where he'd gone. I never found him."

"He dies."

She pulled back far enough to meet his gaze, her own flint. "But not at your hand. He's mine, Feral. Mine alone."

Fox cupped her face in his hands and kissed her lightly on the mouth before pulling back. "I'll give you the killing blow. If you want me to, I'll even let him heal first before you take him on. But he's going to feel my wrath, angel. Allow me that. I need to make him suffer for what he did to you."

She watched him with fathomless eyes. "Why?"

Tracing her lovely eyebrow with his thumb, he told her as much as he understood. "Because . . . you've become important to me. Precious to me." And, goddess, it was true. He'd never wanted to care too deeply for another, having always known that caring . . . *loving* . . . only led to heartache. But he was absolutely falling in love with Melisande.

She turned and pressed her cheek to his shoulder again, a sadness in the move that made him hurt. "I've done some terrible things, Fox."

He stroked her head. "Nothing you didn't feel you had to do. Or that you hadn't been driven to do."

"Perhaps, but you don't understand. When I was . . . dead inside . . . when I was the woman you first met, I couldn't feel remorse. I couldn't feel guilt, grief, love, joy, any of it. Just anger. And hatred. And duty. After a thousand years, I knew right from wrong, but the end justified the means. I wreaked my vengeance on the cheetahs. And when the world believed us extinct, I eliminated the threats to my race so thoroughly, so thoughtlessly, that I left a nine-year-old orphaned."

Fox stroked her back, aching for her. "We all do things we regret."

She pulled away from him, standing. "The thing is, I want to go back to being that person."

He stared at her. *"Why?"*

"Because I can't live like this, Fox. I *feel* . . . And I'm tired of feeling. I *won't* live like this."

"What are you saying?"

Sadness and determination drenched her eyes. "I'm saying that when this is over, when Castin's dead, and we're home again, I'm going away until I stop feeling again, until I've reclaimed that coldness for good."

And he'd likely never see her again.

Chapter
Fifteen

Fox stared into the fire, thinking about Melisande's words. When this was over, and they were free of the labyrinth, she meant to leave him, meant to turn herself back into that cold, unfeeling warrior.

Anger built inside of him until he thought he was going to have to awaken her to help pull him back down. It was well past midnight, he suspected. Outside, he heard the wind howling and knew the storm had yet to abate. Inside it was warm, now, Melisande curled into a ball beside him, asleep as he remained on watch. Protecting her.

She was his, dammit.

He shook his head at the thought. He didn't want her

to be his . . . did he? He ran his hands over his face. Goddess, he didn't know what he wanted.

Melisande. He wanted Melisande.

Deep inside, his fox made a low, rumbling sound of agreement. Then growled, as if it didn't know what it wanted any better than he did.

What she was suffering was his fault, the fault of the connection between them that had somehow made her feel again. If he'd never come into her life, she'd be stronger.

That was all he wanted for her, to be strong and whole. To never suffer as his sister had. The thought of her like Sheenagh, in too much pain to live, killed something inside him. As did the thought of living without her, but there was no help for it. He was going to have to let her go, as hard as that was to accept. All he could do was hurt her. In a different way, perhaps, but just as surely as so many shifter males had before.

How could Castin have betrayed her like that?

He hadn't known the male long—they'd worked together for a handful of months about 130 years ago in the north of England. And he hadn't known him well. His memory of Castin was of a serious and focused warrior not interested in the pranks Fox and some of the others had enjoyed playing on one another. He supposed he could imagine the male so focused on reclaiming his animal, back in that dark time, that he'd willingly tortured helpless females. Damn him to hell.

His time to pay for that crime had come. And once Melisande's vengeance was complete? It wouldn't change anything. He knew, both from Sheenagh's experience and from watching other revenge killings over the years, that vengeance never solved anything.

Still, Castin had to pay for his crime. A man who would visit such torture on a woman was not a man an animal spirit would willingly choose. Castin wasn't the one meant to be chosen. The worst, not the best.

His brothers wouldn't be happy that he'd taken matters into his own hands. They'd just have to get over it.

The more immediate concern was that they were, for all practical purposes, trapped in this cave. He was torn between staying where they were, letting the fight come to them, and leaving the cave come sunup. If he could figure out when the sun was up. If they could even dig their way out through the snow.

It was cold out there, and while he could shift into his fox and probably be fine, Melisande would be miserable. The worst of it was, there was no place to go. Unless he was mistaken, the labyrinth would not spit them out of this world until they'd sprung whatever trap it had set for them. Would walking away be the equivalent of springing it? Or would it only delay the inevitable while Melisande froze?

He glanced at her, the firelight dancing over her soft, sleeping features. His heart tightened, so full that he thought it might burst. On some level, he'd known she was meant to be his the very first time he saw her standing beside Ariana at Feral House. She'd been so full of spit and anger, but some part of him had recognized her as his mate. He knew that now. Even if he didn't want a mate. Even if she needed to get away from him for her own survival.

When she was gone from his life, he was going to suffer.

As he gazed at her, she began to move fitfully, her head shaking back and forth.

"No!" The word tore from her lungs, low and tormented. "So many dead. *So many dead.*"

The anguish in her words clawed at him, drawing blood. He'd thought he'd heard misery in her tone as she'd told him about the brutality of the cheetahs, but she'd not told him everything, he knew that now. So many dead? Who? Her sisters? She'd said seven. Or the cheetahs she'd killed in vengeance. He'd sensed no great guilt in her over that.

As he watched, she curled into herself as if the pain were too great to bear, and he couldn't stand it any longer. He reached for her and stroked her head with a featherlight touch. "Angel, it's over. It's just a dream."

She calmed slowly, her eyes trying to flutter open and failing. "Fox?"

"Go back to sleep, pet." He stroked her arm, all the way to her hand, squeezing it gently. "I'm here."

She nodded ever so slightly and settled back into

sleep, but he remained at her side, stroking her hair for a long, long time.

Until the flashback hit him with all the delicacy of a cleaver to the skull. He doubled over, gripping his head as his vision turned black, then bright with lamplight, revealing a room he didn't recognize. A room in bright color, not sepia tones. The Cub's flashback, then, not Sly's.

The vision flickered and disappeared, then returned only to flicker out again. Deep inside, he felt the desperation of his animal, as if it tried to reach him. As if it were trying to show him something. The flashback? Was it his animal who'd been sending them to him?

A snarling sounded in his mind. *Two* snarlings. As if there were two fox spirits in his head about to duke it out. *What the feck?*

Was this the reason he sometimes thought his fox hated Melisande and other times adored her? Two animal spirits. Or perhaps not. He'd seen people infected with dark spirit before. Both Grizz and Lepard had struggled to fight past the darkness, to act as they willed, not as the darkness wanted. What if *this* was the result of whatever Inir did to his fox spirit after he separated it from Sly? What if this darkness was trying to subjugate the good animal spirit?

The vision reappeared, solid this time, and he saw a woman, a pretty redhead in a slinky green dress, cruelty in her copper-ringed Mage eyes.

"Why, Zaphene?" the Cub asked, his youthful voice rich with betrayal.

The woman moved to him, sliding her hand up his chest. Fox sensed the Cub's muscles bunching in a desire to push the bitch away, but he couldn't move. Mage enchantment?

"Because the trigger Inir placed within your animal spirit didn't work," the Mage witch said.

"What trigger?"

The woman smiled, pure evil. "Inir separated your predecessor from his animal, then attached a dark enchantment to the animal that should have controlled you both. But it didn't work. It's lain dormant for two years while every attempt Inir has made to trigger it has failed. So I came to trigger it for him."

"I thought you loved me," the youth said.

The witch laughed at him silently. "You're too young to recognize true love." She shrugged. "The enchantment didn't work even when triggered. All it's been able to do is affect your natural gift, sending you false intuition."

"False? But . . ." The Cub tensed. "The shivers. My intuitions never made me shiver before." He looked at her with disbelief and rising fury. "My animal spirit's working against me?"

"Not enough. The spirit fights the darkness. Which is why Inir decided more drastic action had to be taken."

The Cub scowled. "What action?"

"Inir is going to cut out your soul, young Feral. Once he's done so, the dark enchantment will have full control of both you and your animal. The beauty is, you won't know it. You'll be the boy you've always been."

"I'm not a boy," he growled.

The witch ignored him. "The darkness will control your actions now, leading you to compromise the Ferals and free the Daemons."

"I'll never hurt the Ferals!"

"You'll have no choice."

Fox could feel the young man's anguish, his fury.

The flashback shorted out with a burst of pain, leaving Fox reeling even as his mind spun from all he'd learned.

The shivers, the Cub had called them. And with a slam of understanding, he knew the same thing had happened to him. Always before, he'd felt goose bumps lift on his forearms seconds before his gut delivered him a truth. He'd thought the sudden shivers were merely a change in his gift thanks to his becoming a Feral. Now, he knew better.

He wished he remembered which of his intuitions had been preceded by shivers. But he knew, didn't he? The ones that had led him, or tried to lead him, into traps. And almost certainly the one that had led him into the warding with Melisande and Phylicia behind him. *Bloody hell.*

And, unless he was mistaken, the flashbacks were

the doing of the fox spirit, the good one who struggled against the dark enchantment. It was his way of warning Fox, of teaching him what had gone before. And the flickering and shorting out? The darkness trying to stop him.

All this time, he'd thought himself lucky that he hadn't been marked by one of the infected seventeen animal spirits. Now, it seemed, his own animal wasn't just a carrier of dark infection, but in a battle of its own.

Just a few days ago, the Shaman had checked him for dark infection and found nothing. But perhaps the Shaman hadn't been able to sense the darkness in the animal spirit. Fortunately, his animal didn't have any real control over him. The darkness could only send him false signals from his gut. Signals he'd already learned to ignore.

The animal spirit should not be able to harm him any longer.

But goose bumps broke out over his arms, presaging a true moment of intuitive insight. One word.

Wrong.

Kara woke to find Polaris striding through the doorway of her small cell. She pushed herself up, her hand going to her damp forehead. Yeah, still not feeling good.

"Come, Kara. There's another new Feral to be brought into his animal."

Oh, hell. And now she felt a hundred times worse. "Ewan," she began, using his real name, praying the good man was still in there somewhere. "Help me get out of here. You know how evil Inir is. And I know you're a good man."

As if to refute her claim, he grabbed her roughly by the arm and hauled her to her feet. "I am Polaris," he said coldly. "Inir is my master until Satanan rises. Until the High Daemon rules us all."

His grip on her arm too tight, he led her out of the prison block, down the long hallways, and up the stairs to the main castle. Inir's stronghold was simply, but richly, decorated with high ceilings, wood paneling, and an abundance of leather and dark woods. Servants scurried through the castle as if they feared for their lives, while Mage sentinels walked with the cold-eyed calm of the soulless.

Ahead, Inir stood talking to half a dozen of his soldiers, his voice ringing clearly through the great hall. "Four more have breached the warding. You will bring them to me once they are caught."

Kara's pulse sped. New Ferals? Or *her* Ferals? While she prayed it was the latter, the thought terrified her, too. The more new Ferals she brought into their animals, the less the good Ferals' chances of defeating Inir and his evil army. How could she live knowing she'd helped turn the tide against those she loved? How would she ever survive without Lyon?

Inir looked up and saw her, then turned and headed for the back door. Polaris steered her after him. Together, they followed Inir down to the large rock where she'd performed the last Renascense, and found five men waiting—Croc, Witt, and Lynks, along with the wolverine and a man she'd never seen before, one who had the dark good looks of a Spaniard.

The sound of a child's moan had Kara's gaze flying to a rocky ledge off to the side. As she stared at the little girl Inir had cut earlier, she sickened. The child lay on the rock in nothing but her panties, her abdomen stitched with a hundred stitches. The girl watched them with eyes dark with pain and bright with fear. Kara lurched and only remained upright thanks to Polaris's too tight hold.

"Refuse this time, Radiant, and I'll take off her ears, one at a time, then her nose, then her lips."

The little girl began to cry with panicked, gulping sobs.

Shaking with horror, Kara jerked her arm free of Polaris's grasp. "I won't refuse." *Lyon, forgive me.* He would understand.

As she went radiant, Polaris told the new man, "Stay back, Estevan." Minutes later, the ritual complete, Estevan, stood on the rock, a black bear.

A wave of sick pain rushed over Kara, making her tremble and sway as her flesh suddenly felt cold and bruised, her knees too weak to stand. Her vision narrowed to nothing. And she went down.

Sometime later, perhaps an hour later, Fox shivered. The prelude to a false intuition. He tensed, waiting. Wondering. Moments later, his "gut" told him they had company waiting for them outside. To remain hidden.

Which meant, contrarily, that there was no one outside and the safest thing for them to do was to leave the cave. Now.

"Melisande," he called quietly. She woke instantly at the sound of her name and, three seconds later, was on her feet, her hand on her sword hilt, her eyes only slightly hazed with sleep and confusion.

"Are they here?"

"No. I don't think so. We're leaving now, while we have a chance."

"Are you sure that's . . . ?" Her words cut off as the ground beneath them began to shake, violently. A large slab of rock crashed to the cave floor right in front of the entrance, blocking their escape.

Goose bumps rose on his arms at the same time that he shivered. And then his gut was shouting at him. *Run! Climb onto that rock slab. No! Run to the back of the cave!*

Bloody hell. What did it want him to do?

Loose rocks and chunks of ceiling rained down upon them. He grabbed Melisande close, shielding her from the falling debris as he lunged toward the door, determined to push the slab away from the cave's mouth.

A rock struck his shoulder, another his foot. Behind him, the back wall began to crumble, and he glanced back just in time to watch it crack open like an egg, falling away. Sunshine and frigid air poured in on a cloud thick with dust and debris.

"Onto the rock slab!" He knew, now, which intuition to listen to. But he'd figured it out too late. The floor beneath his feet began to give way. "Leap, Mel!"

But they weren't close enough. They were going down.

Chapter Sixteen

Fox pushed himself out of the rubble, gasping at the stab of pain in his side. A broken rib? "Mel!"

"Here. I'm fine. I just lost my boot."

Relief weakened his knees. He could see little through the dust cloud released with the cave's collapse, but he soon became aware of a rock face rising on all sides. They'd fallen into some kind of hole. A big one, to be sure, but a hole all the same. The best he could judge through the haze, escape was a good twenty feet above them on all sides.

The damned labyrinth had caught them at last.

As the haze cleared, he caught sight of a man clinging to the high edge on the other side of the huge hole.

The male struggled, digging his boot into the rock face as he levered himself up and out of the pit. So someone else had been caught by the landslide. Or the trap. Someone who'd been lucky enough to keep from going all the way down.

As the male turned, Fox caught sight of his face. *Castin.* His dark hair was cut shorter than Fox remembered—military short. And like Fox, he was sporting a several-days' growth of beard. But Fox would know him anywhere. Hatred burned in his gut as he stared at the man who'd betrayed Melisande. Deep inside, his fox growled. They were of like mind, each ready to rip the bastard's heart out.

Castin caught sight of him, recognition and surprise flaring in dark eyes. Fox shuttered his own expression, hoping Castin hadn't recognized Melisande. He glanced back to where she was retrieving her lost boot, her blond head bent, and decided he hadn't. Without a word of greeting, Castin circled the pit, unfastened a long length of rope he had strapped to his belt, and unfurled it across from where Fox stood. Castin had never been much of a talker.

Fox turned to Melisande, gripping her shoulder, grimacing from the pain that shot through his side as he lifted his arm. "Don't move."

She froze, her gaze flicking to his, warrior still.

"We have a way out of here . . . if he doesn't recognize you."

He knew the moment she put two and two together. A sound of fury hissed between her teeth. "Castin."

"I'm going up first. Keep your head down, Mel, I'm begging you. Let's get out of this pit safely." And if Castin recognized her, there was no telling what he might do.

"All right." The words were a low growl between clenched teeth.

Fox crossed the rubble slowly, to where the rope hung. But as he reached for it, he felt the magic rush over him as if he'd called on his animal form. What the *feck*? He fought the shift, battling it back. A fox wasn't going to be able to climb the rope out of this pit.

And that was the plan, he realized. That evil within his animal spirit wanted him to stay right where he was, trapped and waiting for the Mage sentinels who were sure to come.

Again, the magic rushed over him and again, he fought it back, frustration lunging. His jaw clamped hard. If he got most of the way up that rope and shifted, he was going to be one aching puppy when he fell. Taking a deep breath, which hurt like hell, he grabbed the rope and began hauling himself up, fast and hard.

Castin would get him out of here if he could. Ironically, he trusted the male to do that. The one whose actions he didn't trust was Melisande, and how could he? For five *thousand* years she'd sought vengeance against this male. Keeping her head down and staying silent was going to take every ounce of control the woman possessed.

Finally, he reached the snowy lip of the wide pit, and Castin hauled him out. Fox bit down on the groan of pain.

"What are you doing here, Kieran?" Castin's words were laced with surprise, his accent ancient British. "I heard you were marked."

"I was. I'm the new fox shifter. What are *you* doing here?" He took stock of their surroundings. From what he could tell, the rocky outcropping was something of a spine running down the center of the plain. The back of the outcropping had dropped away, leaving this crater between the rocks and the snowy plain at the back. And the snow was deep, nearly to his knees.

Castin's brows drew low. "Are you not going to free your woman?"

"In a moment. What the *feck* are you doing here, Castin?" He struggled not to act on the hatred that seethed inside of him as he stared at the man.

The male watched him with quiet curiosity. "It's a bit of a tale. I heard a rumor that the Ferals aren't trusting the newly marked."

Damn. And how had that gotten out already?

"So you thought you'd offer your services to Inir instead?" Fox's tone sounded acidic even to his own ears.

Castin's eyes narrowed only slightly. "I came to kill him."

Fox blinked, not sure what to do with that. Perhaps the male wasn't a villain through and through. Fox had known him once and had thought him an honorable male. But men changed. And men lied.

"There's dark magic involved, Castin. You're infected with it."

"I feared as much. It's the pull of it I'm following. Are you infected as well?"

Fox cleared his throat, struggling to mask his anger. "No." At least . . . hell. He wasn't sure of anything anymore. "Inir has our Radiant. We were hunting her and fell into the labyrinth."

Castin snorted. "I've been wandering the thing for days."

"As have we. Keep an eye out for the Mage, will you, while I pull my companion out?"

With a nod, Castin turned away.

"Angel," Fox called softly.

Melisande grabbed the rope and climbed with a grace and ease he envied. He reached for her as she neared the top, and pulled her out, though she could have done it easily enough without his assist.

Castin turned around, then did a double take. *"Melisande?"* A bright, disbelieving smile lit the usually taciturn warrior's face, as if he were genuinely delighted to see her. As if he had no recollection of betraying her.

Fury flayed Fox, jealousy beating at him. They'd been lovers.

But Melisande's face turned dark with hatred, her hand grasping the hilt of her sword.

Out of the corner of his eye, Fox saw movement in the rocks. *Mage.* "We have company," he warned. Mage sentinels were beginning to crawl out from the rocks like a plague of rats, half of them mounted on horses.

Castin frowned at Melisande even as he pulled his sword to fight. Melisande threw Castin a hate-filled promise of a battle to come when this one was over. Fox pulled his knives, grimacing against the pain that told him he still hadn't healed. And the Mage just kept coming.

Melisande was shaking, choking on her hatred as she turned from Castin to face the attacking Mage. How dare he act as if she were a long-lost girlfriend he was delighted to see. As if nothing had happened. As if killing and/or torturing eight innocent Ilinas was nothing!

"Let's pull this battle away from the pit," Fox said, coming up beside her. "Give no quarter. Every one of these feckers stands between us and Kara." He stayed close to her side as they raced out onto the snowy plain, as if he didn't entirely trust her not to attack Castin instead of the Mage.

Truth to tell, it was a near thing. Seeing Castin again had brought it all back as if that first, horrible night had happened hours ago and not five millennia—the torches set at intervals around the glade, gleaming on the flowers that had been cast onto the pond. Blankets had been laid out, laden with food and overflowing casks of wine. The summer air had been thick with the scent of flowers, forest, hot bodies, and the perfume of Ilina mating scents.

But there had been a tension in the air that night that she hadn't understood. When she'd asked Castin about it, he'd admitted only that they were worried about their inability to call their animals. But the celebration would take their minds off it. The beauty of the Ilinas would turn their thoughts to more joyous pursuits. And she'd believed him.

Fool.

She jerked her mind back to the present and counted more than a dozen Mage, half of them on horseback. As she and the two shifters pushed through the powdery snow, the mounted sentinels circled them, cutting them off.

The cave leaped into her mind as she'd first seen it that night, after fighting her way back to consciousness. Flickering torches, the smell of mildew and damp fur. The cheetah chieftain standing over her with eyes awash in an unholy light. Her arms were tied above her head as they would remain for *three years*. But her legs were free.

She'd tried to kick out at him as he'd knelt as her feet, but he'd grabbed her ankles in one hand, his shifter strength far greater than her own. Lifting her feet into the air, her hips off the ground, he'd driven two stakes into her lower back, one after the other, then dropped her, mounted her, and raped her as she'd screamed. Then he'd left her and returned with half a dozen of his warriors.

Shaking her head, focusing on the present, she watched the Mage leader draw his sword, his sentinels following.

"Back-to-back," Fox ordered, and the three formed a tight circle, shoulder to shoulder, as they prepared to take on the enemy. As the leader of the Mage battalion gave the order to advance, the three sprang forward as one.

Melisande struck out at the nearest Mage, one on foot, channeling her raging fury. She dove, spun, sliced through his hamstring, then his back as she leaped to her feet behind him. How she wished it was Castin's flesh beneath her blade. As the Mage fell to one knee, unable to stand, Melisande spun, sword out, and lopped off his head.

As the blood spurted up from his neck, another memory slammed into her, watching the blood spurt from the chest of a young cheetah, a male only a handful of years past his maturity, as she held his warm heart in her hand. He'd begged her for mercy, terror in his youthful eyes, but she'd given him none. Just as he'd ignored her screams as he'd driven into her in that cave.

"Mel!" Fox's voice pulled her back to the present, and she ducked, barely in time to avoid being stabbed through the skull by one of the mounted sentinels. Instinct and long experience took over, and she leaped onto the horse behind him, stood on the animal's haunches, and drove her sword straight through the rider's skull. Yanking her blade free, she swung, lopping off his head, too.

Pushing the headless rider from the horse, she stood on the animal's back, surveying the dying Mage on the ground around her. In her mind's eye, they weren't Mage, but Ilinas. Not dead, not yet, but writhing in pain and madness, crazed from the poison the Mage potion master had infected them with.

So many dead.

Screams echoed in her mind, escaping the box she'd tried to lock them in. Her body turned to ice.

Ninety-six Ilinas dead.

Castin's fault. It was all Castin's fault. He had to die. She had to make it right.

Melisande half fell, half leaped off the horse. Out of the corner of her eye, she saw Fox yelling something, but couldn't hear what he said. All she could hear were the echoes of those ancient screams.

It was starting to rain. Just fucking great, Grizz thought as he strode across the open field on the slope of the mountain. Finding a lone woman in the fucking Rocky Mountains was worse than searching for a needle in a haystack.

After talking to Brinlin last night, he and Lepard had rented a motel room, then set out at daybreak. They'd found the lockbox easily enough, in the middle of the woods, in the middle of fucking nowhere, just as Brinlin had warned. There were no trails leading away from it. No roads or trails of any kind in any direction. At least none that they'd been able to find. They'd even shifted into their animals and tried to track scents, though neither of them had much experience with it. And they'd been wholly unsuccessful. Then again, if Sabine only came down here once a month, and the last time was nearly four weeks ago, they weren't likely to find any kind of trail, scent or otherwise.

Finally, they'd decided to split up, afraid if they didn't, they'd be at this for days. The woman could be anywhere.

Grizz was just cresting the next rise when a loping bear cub caught his attention not ten yards to his right. Cute little guy, and a grizzly, if he wasn't mistaken. The incredible nature of seeing a real grizzly wasn't lost on him. Nor was the fact that he was in very real danger.

Because where there was a cub, there was almost certainly a mother.

A quick look left confirmed his suspicion. The mother, all right. The very pissed-off mother if the ears lying flat to her head were anything to go by.

Hell. This wasn't what he needed right now. He hesitated two seconds before tossing his backpack to the ground and yanking off his boots. But as he shucked off his pants, the sow began charging and he didn't have time to divest himself of his shirt, jacket, or briefs. And there'd be no seeing them again. He wasn't one of the lucky ones who could hang on to his clothes through a shift.

Pulling on the magic that lived within him now, channeled by the golden grizzly-head armband that curled around one upper arm, he shifted into his animal in a spray of colored lights.

Mama grizzly pulled up short. But her confusion didn't last long or change anything. He was still standing between her and her cub, and that was the only thing that mattered.

Grizz was far larger than she was, but he had no desire to hurt her, so he took off running, lumbering over the open grass, getting the hell away from that cub. Finally, he glanced back and found her turning back to her baby. But the moment he slowed, she turned toward him, snarling, slapping the ground, making it clear he wasn't nearly far enough.

I'm going, I'm going, he thought to himself. But, shit, now he was going to have to wait until they left, then circle back to retrieve his jeans, boots, and pack. Fucking hell.

A scent tickled his far more sensitive bear's nose. A sweet scent. Human? Glancing back at the mom and cub, who'd moved off slightly, but not nearly far enough, yet, he decided to follow the scent for a ways, see where it led. Maybe he'd gotten lucky at last even if he had lost his favorite leather jacket.

And that's when he saw her. A woman of perhaps thirty, she was walking across the grassy embankment below, a shotgun slung over one shoulder, her stride long and confident. Tall and slender, her auburn hair curling in a ponytail down her back, she was striking to watch even dressed in jeans and a flannel shirt.

Sabine?

As if possessing a sixth sense, she turned and saw him, then turned away and continued, as if the sight of a grizzly bothered her not at all. And maybe it didn't.

But he'd be damned if he was going to lose her now. He started after her, lumbering down the hillside, for a moment forgetting just exactly what he looked like.

She turned, suddenly, raising her shotgun.

Oh hell. He pulled up fast.

Wait, Sabine. I just want to talk to you.

Her head jerked back, her eyes widening, then narrowing as she took aim and fired.

Pain exploded in his shoulder. *What the fuck did you do that for?* Maybe she wasn't Sabine. Maybe she was human and thought he was some kind of devil.

"Go away!" she shouted at him, and shot him again, hitting him in the neck.

He swayed, shifting back to human without meaning to. Christ, he was still bleeding. Not stopping. Why wasn't he healing? His vision began to narrow.

"You're a Feral Warrior!" she called.

Okay, so she was Sabine. And she'd still attacked him. He didn't bother to answer her. Slowly, he lifted his hand to his neck and felt the stickiness.

Gun aimed at his heart, she stalked toward him, her eyes flashing green fire. A beauty. Two beauties. Now four.

His world began to tilt. Why had she shot him when she knew what he was?

But then he realized he knew. Sabine could see into a man's soul. Apparently she'd done just that and found his to be as black as his hair. But he knew that. He'd been afraid he was the worst of the grizzly line. Now she'd just confirmed it.

He hadn't even realized he'd gone down until he felt the mud sinking into his wounded shoulder.

Another face swam in his vision. Blond, pale, lovely. A visage long departed from this world. Had she come to welcome him to the afterlife?

"I tried, Hildy. I tried." Then his vision went black.

"**M**el, behind you!"

Almost too late, Melisande turned and attacked the Mage. Fox could swear she hadn't even heard his shout. As he lunged at the nearest rider, knocking his sword arm up with one hand, cutting it off with his other, he kept an eye on Melisande. She was shaken by Castin, he could see it in her eyes, in everything about her.

Fox grabbed the bloody stump of his opponent, pulled him off his horse, and beheaded him. The wind, already furious, kicked up another notch, blowing with stinging force, clouds blotting out the sun as Mother Nature fumed over the deaths of her Mage.

A shiver stole over him. *To your right!* He almost listened, though he knew better, almost saw the Mage swinging at him from the left too late. Fox barely missed being skewered by the sword, though he wound up taking a deep cut across his left biceps. Grabbing his assailant's wrist, he yanked him close and cut off his head, too. Usually, the Therians avoided killing the Mage whenever possible, if only because the Earth took their deaths so poorly. But not today.

He began to shiver in earnest, the false intuitions bombarding him until he could barely hear himself think. *To the right! Left! Behind you!*

Fox shut down his mind, focusing on his senses, his warrior's instincts. Only those. He killed another horseman and turned to find Castin battling two foot soldiers, Melisande fighting another.

As the battle raged, Mage deaths piling up, the weather turning increasingly foul. The remaining foot soldiers rushed them, two running straight for Melisande with orders, no doubt, to kill the Ilina. His heart in his throat, Fox called on the magic to shift . . . and nothing happened.

His scalp prickled with disbelief. The darkness within his animal spirit apparently thought he'd be more effective in his animal and didn't want him to reach it. So Fox lunged for them in human form, taking on both of them until Melisande dispatched the sentinel she'd been fighting and took on one of his.

Side by side, they fought. Blood flew, heads rolled, Mage died, and the ground shook from the fury of the Earth. Black clouds blotted out all but the faintest trace of sunlight until they fought in near dark.

And, finally, the battle against the Mage, the first battle, was over.

It was the battle to come, the one with Castin, that Fox dreaded. Because, without a doubt, Castin had just saved their asses. And now Fox was going to have to kill the bastard. Or, worse, stand by and let Melisande do it.

Melisande whirled on Castin with a snarl, her bloody sword tight in her hand.

The whoreson stared at her with confusion. "Melisande, wait. Talk to me."

"Talk to you?" she cried. "You traitorous, lying bastard. What in the *hell* do you think I have to say to you?"

Castin gaped at her. "You think I had something to do with that night."

"You betrayed me in the most heinous of ways."

"No. Never." He lifted his free hand in a motion of surrender even as his right hand remained firmly clamped around the hilt of his sword. "I had nothing to do with what happened that night, Ceraph. I don't even *know* what happened. As my chieftain knocked you out, I was tackled to the ground and trussed up before I could fight my way free."

"Liar!" Melisande advanced on him slowly, the screams ringing in her head, the need to kill him, *to end this,* a writhing, living thing breathing fire down her neck. All around her, the bodies lay, bloody, lifeless.

So many dead.

Castin took a step back for every one she took forward. "I was sold to wolverine slavers, Melisande, without explanation, without cause. It was five years before I escaped and returned to my clan lands, but my clan was gone. Rumor had it they'd been destroyed, slaughtered by another clan."

Melisande snarled. "They were slaughtered by *me*. For what they'd done to me. And for killing my sisters."

Castin blanched. "Those fucking blackguards. They must have used me to lure you, then disposed of me before I could try to stop whatever they had planned."

He was speaking. Some part of her brain was hearing him. But mostly she heard only the screams in her head. Enough talk.

She lifted her sword and ran at him, attacking him. Castin lifted his own blade and parried her blows. Time ceased to exist. Hatred burned until all she could see was light and red and blood.

"Mel. *Angel.*"

She was trapped in a berserker's haze, needing blood, needing to kill, *needing to end this.*

A second attacker joined the fray and she struck at him, too, her blade finally sinking through flesh.

Fox's stunned, pained eyes penetrated the haze. A red stripe bloomed across his chest. *Blood.* It was Fox she'd struck, Fox's flesh her sword had pierced. *And he wasn't healing.*

She stumbled back, staring with him at horror. "No. Not you, too. Not you, too." The screams rose and rose as if they wanted to rip out her eardrums and crush her mind. "I'm sorry. I didn't mean to. I never meant for anyone to die. My fault, my fault."

She covered her ears with hands coated in the blood of the dead. *So much blood.*

"Goddess help me, *it was all my fault.*"

Fox lunged for her, grimacing at the pain searing his chest. She'd sliced him from shoulder to shoulder, but her blade hadn't gone deep, thank the goddess, or he'd be a dead man. He grabbed the blade from her hand before she skewered him again, then gathered her against him as she sank to the pavement.

While she'd pressed Castin, the landscape around them had made another of its abrupt changes, the labyrinth propelling the three of them into the next stop along the gauntlet. They stood in the middle of a deserted street, now, in the middle of a deserted town that looked like it hadn't been inhabited since the 1960s. An old rusted-out station wagon sat parked against one curb, an equally decrepit truck against another. The street was lined with shops—a diner, a druggist's, a tailor's—but the windows were all broken, the proprietors long gone.

"Easy, pet." He cradled her against him, sinking to the ground with her where he could keep an eye on Castin. The male had turned pale at her accusations and appeared honestly shaken. In his arms, Melisande quaked, her skin like ice where it touched his own.

"My fault," she whispered over and over. "My fault."

"Mel." He kissed her forehead, stroking her head, her shoulder, her back. "It's okay, pet. It's over. You're safe."

But she shook her head, looking up slowly to meet

his gaze, her eyes twin pools of agony. "I killed them. Ninety-six sisters. *I killed them*."

"No, luv. The Mage killed them. They poisoned all of you."

Tears began to run down her cheeks in a hot, bitter torrent. "I was the one who sought out the Mage potion master. My hatred for shifters was so great that I couldn't bear the thought of Ariana marrying one. I was certain she would never be happy with Kougar. I told myself I was protecting her, that I was protecting all of us, when I sought a potion that would keep their mating bond from fully forming."

Fox's gut cramped, the rest of the story so clear, now. "He took advantage of you."

"Yes. He was not only the potions master but the poison master. The potion he sold me was designed to wipe out my race. The Mage didn't want an Ilina-Feral alliance any more than I did. They died"—she choked on a sob—" because of me. Two-thirds of my race dead because of me. *I killed them*."

Fox held her close, her sobs tearing at his heart. And he thought he finally understood why she'd been so desperate to return to that unfeeling state in which she'd lived for so long. It wasn't the trauma of the cheetah attack she couldn't live with. It was her guilt over the deaths of her sisters.

"Shh, luv. It wasn't your fault." He stroked her hair, kissed her temple. "It wasn't your fault. You never meant for them to die. You were just doing, as you've always done, what you thought best."

Slowly, her tears subsided. With a shuddering breath, she wiped the moisture from her face, then looked at his chest, her mouth tightening. "I did that to you."

"It's shallow. And healing." He cupped her cheek. "It was an accident, Mel. You must learn how to forgive yourself."

She looked at him with deep, shattered eyes. "You forgive me?"

Fox smiled at her tenderly. "Of course." He kissed her softly, then set her on her feet and rose beside her.

Melisande turned to Castin, her arms crossed protectively. Never had she looked so fragile. "You really didn't know what your chieftain meant to do to us?"

Castin shook his head, misery in his eyes. "I would never have allowed you to be hurt, Melisande. I cared for you far too much."

Fox's animal growled with displeasure, Fox barely managing to keep from doing the same.

"I always wondered what became of you," Castin continued. "I had nightmares for centuries, you calling out for help and me unable to answer. But I never again crossed paths with an Ilina, and I had no way to find out if you were all right." His eyes narrowed with pain. "What they did to you . . . it must have been terrible."

"Yes."

Fox gripped Melisande's shoulders, pulling her back

against his chest. "That's a story for another day. Right now we need to find the key, and Kara, and get out of here."

Castin nodded, his expression slowly returning to its usual warrior stillness. Beneath Fox's hands, he felt Melisande straighten. She stepped away from him, taking a deep breath. And when she turned to him, the strength was back in her eyes.

"Better?" he asked.

For a moment, she said nothing. But she nodded briefly, telling him she was still hurting, of course she was. But she was too strong and too stubborn to let it keep her down for long.

"Let's have a look around." But as he reached for Melisande's hand, the shifting magic tore over him without warning and he shifted into his fox. *Feck*. He tried to shift back, could feel his animal fighting to help him, and failed.

"Did you do that on purpose?" Melisande asked.

No. His gut told him they were going the wrong way. Which made no sense considering they weren't going either way. But in his animal form, he'd gotten neither shivers nor goose bumps and couldn't tell if the intuition was true or false. A moment later, another intuition hit him. *Look up.* He did and saw nothing. *Sniff the sidewalk to your right. Lift your left hind leg. Lie down and go to sleep.*

The intuitions were flooding his head until he could

barely think through them. *Stop it!* he shouted. His fox
let out a pained whimper.

"Fox?"

He felt Melisande's hand in his fur, felt his animal
leap with pleasure at the warmth of her healing gift.
And all of a sudden he could shift again. In a spray of
colored lights, he was once more standing on two feet.

She gazed at him worriedly. "What happened?"

But before he could answer her, he heard a shout.

Fox's head jerked up at the sound of the familiar
voice. *"Kara."*

A moment later, Kara came racing around the street
corner half a block up, barefoot and unkempt, her ponytail akimbo, but looking no worse for wear.

"Kara!" He ran toward her.

She flung herself into his arms. "Oh, thank God."
Trembling and pale, she looked up at him with eyes
wild with fear. "I escaped. But they're after me."

"They're not going to touch you again," he vowed.
Setting her on her feet and pulling her against his side,
he turned to where Castin and Melisande stood watching them. He met Castin's gaze. "Our Radiant, Kara."

Castin offered her a shallow bow. "Radiant."

Kara looked up at Fox. "I know which way to go."
She pulled away, started forward, motioning them to
follow. "Come on. We need to run. They'll be here any
minute, and there are too many of them to fight."

Fox waited for Melisande, relieved to see the battle

fire back in her eyes. Side by side, they followed Kara and Castin, throwing glances behind, but Fox saw no sign of the Mage.

Shivers tore through him, goose bumps rising on his arms. *Kill Melisande. Don't trust Kara. You're going the wrong way.*

Bloody fecking *lying* intuition!

"This way!" Kara called and made a hard left into a narrow alley lined with the rotting corpses of ancient motorcycles. But halfway down the alley, she began to slow. Tears started running down her cheeks. "I'm too tired. They're going to kill us!"

"Kara . . ."

But as Fox approached her, she lifted her hands as if to ward him off. "Don't touch me!"

He stared at her. Those bastards had done a real number on her. "Let me carry you, Radiant."

"No!" She backed away, against the side wall, knocking over one of the motorcycle husks. "Don't touch me. I don't want anyone to touch me!"

Fox felt a hard fist of dread. Had they raped her? He frowned. She'd leaped into his arms when she first saw him.

"If the Mage are really coming, we need to keep moving," Castin said behind him.

Fox heard the rumble a heartbeat before the steel caging shot up out of the ground like twin walls, one in front of them, the other behind, running the entire width of the alley. High above, another piece formed the cage roof, snapping shut with an ominous clang.

Fox met Melisande's shocked gaze. Caught . . . *again*.

With a massive creak, the cage walls began to move ever-so-slightly inward.

"They're going to crush us!" Kara cried.

Fox reached for Melisande's hand.

Castin shook his head. "Not crush us. They'll pin us close to the bars, where they can easily reach us."

"Hell," Fox muttered. Because a single touch by a Mage's hand and they'd be enthralled, puppets who would follow their Mage captors without a fight, right to their own doom. Or to the doom of the Feral Warriors.

Chapter Seventeen

As one, Fox and Castin leaped for opposite sides of the cage that spanned the narrow alley in this latest world along the Mage's labyrinthine gauntlet. Fox gripped the iron bars, throwing all of his weight, all of his strength into stopping the cage from collapsing inward, either crushing them or pinning them so they would be easily enthralled when the Mage came for them. He struggled until the sweat ran down his temples and soaked his back, until his muscles ached from the strain, but the cage wall just kept moving.

Behind him, Kara wailed, "They're going to kill us!" He was tempted to knock her out just to quiet her screeching.

The thought stopped him cold. He hadn't known Kara long, or well, but if there was one thing he did know, she was no coward. The Kara he knew would never screech.

His scalp crawled with memory. What had Melisande said? The key could be anything—animal, mineral, or vegetable.

Or Kara?

Holy shite.

Destroy the key, and I destroy the magic.

His scalp went ice-cold. And if he was wrong? If this was the true Kara? The thought that he might accidentally kill his Radiant, Lyon's mate, had his flesh creeping with horror.

"You okay?" Melisande asked at his elbow.

As the contracting cage forced him back another step, he leaned close to Melisande's ear. "I don't think she's Kara."

Melisande looked at him with surprise, her gaze turning thoughtful. "I think you might be right. I never felt like slapping the real one, not even when I hated all Therians. In fact, I kind of admired her." She frowned, then mouthed, "The key?"

"What if we're wrong?"

"What if we're not?" Melisande stroked his back, pleasing him utterly. "Is there a way to test your theory?"

Goose bumps rose on his arm, and he shivered. *Feck.*

He was about to get another mishmash of intuitions. *She's the real Kara. She's the key. Lie down and go to sleep.*

Damned useless intuition.

Taking a deep breath, he attempted to calm his mind. He'd been at Feral House such a short time, he didn't have the history with Kara that might have afforded him information the Mage might not have. And perhaps there wasn't anything the Mage didn't know since they had access to the real Kara and, possibly, her memories.

But would the soulless Mage remember what it was to love a mate? And, goddess help him, he was beginning to think he did.

He turned away from the caging and his futile struggle to keep it from moving. Striding to Kara, he grabbed the screeching woman's arm roughly. "Lyon's furious with you for running away from Feral House, you bitch."

She gasped, cowered. "It wasn't my fault! They took me against my will."

No, this woman was not Kara. Lyon worshipped the air his mate breathed, and his mate knew it. The real Kara wouldn't believe, even for a second, that Lyon was angry with her.

Goddess help me if I'm wrong. He pulled his blade and, with one vicious swipe, cut off her head.

"Fox!" Castin lunged at him, then stopped abruptly

as the woman, the cage, and the town disappeared, leaving them once more standing among the trees on the mountainside where they'd started.

Castin stared at him, the shock of Fox's action still in his eyes. "How did you know?"

"Once you meet our Radiant, you'll understand."

"Look," Melisande said.

Fox turned to find a fortress sitting high on the mountainside not more than a quarter of a mile away. His jaw dropped, a smile lifting his mouth. "Inir's stronghold."

He held out his hand for Melisande, and together, the three started toward it. But they'd traveled no more than a dozen yards when shouts echoed in the distance as dozens of Mage sentinels began to flow out of the fortress's main gates.

The three of them exchanged glances.

"We broke their toy," Fox murmured.

Melisande grunted. "So much for the element of surprise."

This was not a battle for a Feral who wasn't healing, an Ilina who couldn't mist, and a shifter who couldn't shift. If he could be certain that the temporal cage had been disabled for good, he might try to find Lyon and the others before breaching the fortress. But the labyrinth could reset at any time, the other Ferals could be anywhere, and the real Kara needed them. Now.

"Any plan on how to get in there?" Castin asked.

Fox was about to shake his head no, when something about the rocky terrain far below the fortress caught his eye. A tree formation he'd seen before. And suddenly he remembered. The flashback he'd had on the beach, the one where he'd entered a tunnel through the rock. Sly had stolen into some place he shouldn't have been, desperate to reach a woman he'd been in love with. A woman, he'd realized too late, who had already had her soul stolen. Fox had felt Sly's heart cave at the realization, and been privy to his thoughts as he'd chosen to go forward anyway, to steal her away and try to help her reclaim her soul. A task at which he'd obviously failed.

But this was the fortress Sly had breached. And whether or not they could do the same, and not get caught, was anyone's guess.

There was only one way to find out.

"I can get us in there."

Castin glanced at him curiously.

Melisande, too. "You've seen it in one of your flashbacks."

"Aye. I know of a hidden entrance in the rock far below the castle. If it's still there, and still open, I can find it. What I don't know is if the Mage have it guarded."

Castin shrugged. "I don't have a better plan."

"Me, either," Melisande said, glancing at Castin. Fox watched her look at the other male, saw the way her brows dipped, confusion in her eyes where before there had only been raw hatred.

Now that she knew the truth, and Fox believed Castin had told it, would she have feelings for the male again? Was it possible to hate someone for so long, even mistakenly, then begin to care for them again? He didn't know and was pretty sure he didn't want to find out.

Ignoring the twist of jealousy as he did the pain of the cut on his chest that still hadn't fully healed, he started forward, Melisande falling into step beside him, Castin beside her. He took Melisande's hand, relieved when she grasped his tightly, and together the three made their way toward the mountain and their one chance at reaching Kara.

Halfway to their destination, the magic swept through him without warning and he shifted into his fox. *Dammit.* Worse, he lay down on a pile of dead leaves and pine needles and, struggle as he might, could not force himself to stand.

Panic flew through his head. Deep inside, he felt his animal spirit cry out. The darkness was getting too strong.

"**W**ulfe! To your left!" Lyon's voice rang across the beach, over the shouts of the half-naked painted warriors bearing down on them in growing numbers.

They'd battled more than a dozen of them already, but they just kept coming.

Wulfe pulled his sword from the neck of the dead warrior at his feet and turned, ready to take on more. The stuff this mind-fucking world threw at them just kept getting weirder and weirder. Kougar assured them the savages weren't real. Or shouldn't be real, at any rate, which was of little comfort when they were trying to dig the Ferals' hearts out of their chests.

Knees soft, swords gripped tight, Wulfe prepared to take on the leading edge of the enemy. Suddenly they were gone. In the blink of an eye, the savages, the sand, the beach were all gone and the four Ferals were once more standing in the woods, on the mountain. Back in West Virginia, by the looks of it.

"What the fuck just happened?" Jag demanded. "Not that I'm complaining."

Kougar sheathed his sword. "If I had to guess, Fox found the key and disabled the magic."

"Go Foxylocks," Jag cheered.

A structure of some sort, far in the distance, caught Wulfe's eye, and he started up the hill to get a better look at it. As he cleared the trees, he saw what had caught his attention and whistled low. "Come see this."

Far in the distance, high atop a rocky cliff, sat a mammoth stone mansion.

"Inir's stronghold?" Jag asked, coming up beside him.

"Probably," Wulfe replied.

Lyon wasted no time. Shucking his jeans and sword,

he shifted into his lion and took off at a run, his mane flying back from his ferocious, determined face. Kougar lunged for Lyon's jeans. As he shoved them in the backpack Wulfe and Jag stripped and tossed him their pants as well. Kougar strapped their swords on his back, then, as one, the three shifted into their animals in a spray of colored lights and took off after their chief.

In his head, Wulfe heard Lyon call to both Kara and Fox. He heard no answer, but they were still several miles from the stronghold.

They'd traveled less than half a mile when Wulfe did begin to hear voices. Voices he'd heard before.

I've collected more than four dozen humans for your consumption, my lord. Will that be enough?

Adequate, yes. My horde will disperse the moment they're free.

The voices faded. Wulfe's scalp went cold. His horde. *Satanan.* It wasn't Inir and a minion he'd been hearing, but Inir and Satanan? Holy. Shit. And suddenly the earlier discussion he'd overheard made a terrible kind of logic. Chills snaked down his spine, turning his blood ice-cold.

I sense one of mine.

That's not possible. The Ferals killed them all.

Not one of those. This is different. Blood calls to blood.

Wulfe swallowed, his stomach twisting in on itself,

forming a lump the size of his fist. No one needed to know. But for the next mile, his conscience flayed him. He *had* to tell them.

I've been hearing the voices again, he told his friends. *Just now. And earlier. I think one of them is Satanan's.*

Three large animal faces swung to stare at him.

He's been freed? Jag exclaimed.

I don't know, but his horde hasn't. He said they'll disperse the moment they are.

Kougar joined in. *Satanan isn't free, then. At least not physically. I've suspected for a while that the essence that infected Inir was stronger than most. And Inir, or Satanan through Inir, has been working to strengthen it. It's not unreasonable to think that Satanan is now fully conscious within Inir.*

How are you hearing them, Wulfe? Lyon asked quietly.

And that was the real question. The one he didn't want to answer. He hesitated as the lump in his stomach slowly turned to lead. He was the only one who could see the warding. Warding that was made of Daemon magic, Kougar had said. He was the only one who could hear the High Daemon speak.

Blood calls to blood.

Perhaps the goddess had known what she was doing when she gave him these scars all those years ago. Perhaps his outside matched his inside more than he'd ever believed.

There's a legend, he told them, *that the wolf clan, at least my branch of it, was descended from the mating of a female wolf shifter and a Daemon. I never believed it before. Now I think it might be true.*

Fuck, Wulfe, Jag said. *You're part* Daemon?

Wulfe's head began to pound.

Melisande knelt at the huge fox's side, stroking him, burying her hand in his fur. He'd shifted without warning and lay down, not moving.

"What's happening, Fox?"

My animal has been compromised.

"What do you mean?"

The flashbacks. I haven't told you about all of them. Inir infected my animal spirit with darkness after he cut it out of Sly, one of my predecessors. It's not the same as the seventeen—I'm not infected—just the animal spirit. But he's starting to be able to control my shifting . . . and my actions. He won't let me move.

"That's what happened last time, isn't it? My easing you helped you regain control."

Yes. The fox spirit seems to be strengthened by your touch.

Taking a deep breath, she pressed her hand to the top of Fox's furry head, closed her eyes, and called on her gift. But though she felt her hands warm, Fox didn't move.

"I'm not helping you."

You are. But the darkness is growing stronger.

Melisande refused to give up. She dug deeper, pulled harder, until sweat broke out on her brow. Finally, she felt him shifting beneath her palm. Snatching her hand away, she sat back on her heels, catching her breath, as he turned back into a man.

He kissed her softly. "Thank you."

"You're welcome."

He rose to his feet, pulling her up with him, and they were off again.

Keeping to the trees, hiding, dodging the sentinels' more rigid paths they avoided Inir's troops, who were scouring the area. But as they reached an open space between the forest's trees and those hugging the rocks, three Mage sentinels approached.

Melisande and the two Ferals ducked behind the nearest trees. Her heart thudded in her chest, the tree bark biting into her back as she listened for any indication they'd been spotted, and heard none. The sentinels' footsteps didn't change tempo at all.

The flash of sparkling shifter lights drew her gaze to where Fox once more shifted into his animal, but this time he downsized quickly and did not appear to be in distress.

Did you do that on purpose? she asked him mentally.

Aye. We're going to have to silence these three, I'm afraid. The weather will turn on us, but just knocking them out is too risky. They could come to at the wrong moment.

Like just as they were attempting to escape with Kara. Assuming they ever reached Kara. At the thought of killing one of the Mage, the memory of the bodies they'd left in the snow came back to her, blending once more with the memory of her sisters writhing in their death throes.

As if he heard her thoughts, the small fox turned to her. *Pet, I don't want you using your sword unless it's for self-defense. Not yet. Promise me.*

The thought of sitting by while her companions fought disgusted the warrior in her. But she was still badly shaken by her emotional implosion, and the last thing any of them needed was a repeat of that event.

All right, she told him. And she was relieved because that old, old part of her, the Ceraph, recoiled from the thought of killing.

Are you still a dead aim with your knives, Castin? Fox asked.

I am, but I only have one.

Keep an eye on me, then. Take out the third when I go after the second. Then, without further talk, the small fox trotted across the clearing, diving into the bushes not far from where the Mage approached. Two of the sentinels walked side by side, but a third trailed them by several yards.

As Melisande watched, Fox shifted directly behind the trailing man, covered his mouth, and yanked him into the bushes. Moments later, the small fox trotted out of the bushes, following the remaining pair. A bolt of lightning tore across the clear blue sky.

Out of the corner of her eye, Melisande saw Castin twirling his knife between his fingers. She was still reeling from his words, his claim that he'd never betrayed her, that he hadn't even known what happened to her. All the years of her captivity, he'd been a slave to the wolverines.

And she believed him. Not once had she seen him in all the time she was a captive though she'd cursed his name often and loudly. So much hatred. Wasted. If there was a good side to all of this, at least she'd found him when she couldn't mist and couldn't easily kill him. Because, apparently, he'd never deserved to die.

Deep inside, something eased, righting itself. For so long, she'd castigated herself for being duped, for believing him a good man. Perhaps she hadn't been wrong at all.

As she watched, Fox suddenly shifted and took one of the Mage from behind. At that exact instant, Castin threw his knife, burying it in the other sentinel's chest.

Castin turned to her, motioned with his head for her to join him. Together, they ran to Fox, and as dark clouds rolled in overhead and began spilling rain, pulled the two dead Mage into the bushes, where they wouldn't be spotted by their brethren. The sudden deluge ensured that any trace of blood would soon be washed away.

Melisande rubbed her chest, right over her heart

where it was beginning to ache. She'd thought killing Castin, completing her vengeance, would return her to her cold, unfeeling state. Now she knew that refuge was lost to her. There was no way to go back. Only forward. But to what?

Who was she if not the emotionless warrior or the kind Ceraph? As both of those women, she'd had a place, a purpose. She had neither of those anymore, not as long as her Ceraph self balked at the need to kill.

Fox curved his hand around the back of her neck, a protective, tender gesture that melted something inside her and reminded her how much she'd missed when she couldn't feel. No, she didn't want to go back to that, not really. What she wanted was to be able to continue to do her job as Ariana's second. And she wanted . . . Fox.

He glanced at her, a wealth of affection and caring in his eyes. Love for him welled up until she feared it would overflow. Yes, she wanted to be with Fox, for as long as he wanted her in return.

Assuming they made it off this mountain alive.

Once the bodies were hidden, Fox began to lead the way between the brush and the rock, disappearing suddenly. A moment later, Melisande knew why. He'd found the tunnel.

As the three ducked inside, Fox turned to her, stroking her cheek. "Wait here. Hide, Mel. Don't try to defend the entrance, just hide."

She scowled at him. "I'm not helpless, Feral. Besides,

you need me. What if you get stuck in your animal again?"

"I don't want you in danger."

In his eyes she saw a softness, a caring, that stirred the feelings for him that had been growing within her until she thought they would burst from her chest, too big to contain. She would protect him as he sought to protect her. Because if his animal spirit shut him down inside Inir's stronghold, he was a dead man.

She used his worry for her against him. "Do you really think I'm safer out here? *Alone?*"

She knew the moment she had him. With a sigh of resignation, he nodded. "All right."

The three of them started into the tunnel together. As Fox led the way, Castin pulled a slim flashlight out of the pocket of his pants and turned it on. His other hand retrieved his knife and he began weaving it, twirling it, between his fingers, faster and faster, the muscles in his arms tensing.

Melisande's trouble radar leaped. The Castin she'd once known had always been calm and reserved.

"Fox?"

The name had barely left her lips when Castin lifted his knife and aimed it for Fox's back, for his heart.

*Chapter
Eighteen*

Fox heard the alarm in Melisande's voice and whirled, turning just as Castin swayed, grasping the wall, his knife falling from his hand.

"I can't . . ." the new Feral gasped. "The pull . . ." Bending down, he snatched up his knife, turned, and strode swiftly back to the cave's entrance. Standing in the rain, he arched his back, taking deep pulls of air.

Fox followed him, Melisande close on his heels. "What in the hell just happened?" His gaze went to Melisande but it was Castin who answered.

"I almost attacked you. It was as if something inside me took over."

"The darkness," Fox muttered. "It's trying to claim you." *Bloody hell.* If Castin turned on them, they were sunk.

"I felt it building as I walked into the tunnel, like steam rising inside of me, about to explode.

Fox eyed him intently. "And how do you feel now?"

"Fine. The pressure's gone."

Which gave Fox two choices. Leave the male here and hope to hell he didn't lead the sentinels into the tunnel after them. Or kill him.

The thought sickened him. He really thought it likely that Castin was the best of his line, the one meant to be chosen. From the story he'd told of the night of Melisande's capture, he'd been the only one the chieftain had disposed of, the only one of the cheetahs who would have fought to save the Ilinas instead of torture them. Then again, a lot of cheetahs had been born since then. And those who'd tortured the Ilinas had died at Melisande's hand a long time ago.

Castin might be the best of his line or he might be a hell of a fine liar. Fox couldn't be sure.

But he couldn't take the man's life. Especially not now, not when Melisande was still absorbing the probability that Castin had never betrayed her at all.

"Stay here and wait for us," he told the male who might one day become the cheetah Feral. As Castin handed his flashlight to Fox, Fox nodded his thanks. Then together, he and Melisande headed back into the tunnel. As she slipped her hand in his, as his fingers closed tight around hers, his animal sighed with relief. He flicked on the flashlight and, following Sly's memories, led the way into the narrow passage through the rock, a passage barely wide enough for them to walk side by side.

"Do you still have feelings for him?" he asked her, unable to hold back the question any longer.

Melisande snorted softly. "I have no idea what I feel for him anymore. It may take me weeks, or even years, to sort it out. Would it bother you if I did?"

"Aye."

She cut him a look that was almost coy. A coy Melisande. Who'd have thought it possible?

"I have feelings for you, too, Feral. In fact, I can honestly say that what I feel for you is a hundred times stronger than anything I ever felt for Castin."

The pressure eased inside him. "I'm glad." He grinned, delighted when she smiled back. Pulling her close, he kissed her hair. "I don't want you to leave when this is over. I never want you to leave."

She sighed, melting against him just a fraction. "I don't think I could, Feral. You're becoming annoyingly important to me."

He kissed her hair again, grinning. "I'm glad."

They came to a long, stone staircase rising into the dark. As they started up, he released her hand. "I'm going to try to find Kara." He shifted into his fox, then, climbing on four paws, called to Kara, opening his mind so that Melisande would hear as well.

Kara? If she was in the fortress, she should be close enough to hear. If she wasn't . . .

Yes? Kara replied excitedly. *Who is this?*

Fox sent a prayer of thanksgiving winging to the goddess. *Fox.*

Fox! You're here?

Aye. Hidden. Where are you, sweetheart?

In a jail cell deep beneath the castle. Lyon's not with you. It wasn't a question. If Lyon were within communication distance, he'd have already spoken to her, they both knew that. *Is he okay?*

Last I saw him, he was fine. Physically.

Thank God.

He's with Kougar and Wulfe. I have Melisande with me. One of the new Ferals, Castin, is waiting for us outside. We had a hell of a time reaching this stronghold, but we're inside now.

He remained in his animal, engaging his keener fox senses as he listened for sound of Mage. Melisande stroked his fur as she climbed beside him, pleasing him immensely. At the top of the stairs, they followed the passage, side by side, as it wound through the rock. The scent of the air changed, growing more damp and smelling of mildew. Far in the distance, he could make out the faint rumble of voices. They were at least a couple of levels away. Nothing close.

Finally, ahead, he saw a faint glow of light and knew they'd found the entrance into the underground prisons where Sly had come out. He'd seen that much in the vision though little more. Hopefully, the Mage never knew how Sly had gotten inside their stronghold. With any luck, they hadn't barred the passage from the inside any more than they had the outside.

Following the path to the light, Fox sniffed, scenting no one close. In a spray of lights, he shifted back to human, then bent low and peered through the decorative grillwork that hid the passage, confirming with his eyes what his animal senses had already told him.

Another flashback hit him out of nowhere, hard and fast, his animal helping him once more as he showed him Sly being led through a passage, seeing the grillwork through which he'd stolen into the castle as he was led past it and down two more passages to a bank of cells. Sly had watched it all through the eyes of the enchanted, his will no longer his own.

Fox came back to himself to the feel of Melisande's soft hand against his cheek, his animal spirit leaping with joy at her touch, loving her. In another part of his mind, he heard the snarl, but knew it for the darkness it was. He grabbed her against him, kissing her soundly.

"Are you okay?" she whispered.

"Another flashback. My animal's trying to help us. I think I know how to reach Kara." But he needed to know something first. Releasing Melisande, he shifted back into his animal.

Kara, is there anyone there with you? Any Mage in the vicinity at all?

I'm not sure, Fox, but I don't think so. My cell door is locked. I don't know where they keep the key.

We'll free you, Radiant. Never fear.

Fox . . . I'm not well. I've brought two more new Ferals into their animals, and it's taken so much out of me that I can barely stand.

Have they hurt you? He growled low.

No, not really. It's just the ritual that drains me so badly. I may need help.

I have strong arms, Kara.

He shifted back to human, then turned to Melisande, reaching for her hand.

She shook her head, as if reading his mind. "Don't even think about asking me to stay here. We're safer together, and you know it."

"Unless we get caught."

Her eyes flashed. "We're in this together, Feral."

He grinned at her suddenly and pulled her close for a quick kiss. "Is that a promise?"

To his surprise, the look she gave him was as deep as the sea and filled with an emotion he hardly dared credit. She reached up, stroking his jaw with her palm. His breath caught as he waited for her words, but all she said was, "Let's get Kara."

Carefully, silently, he removed the grill and slipped into the empty corridor, then motioned for her to follow. Replacing the grill, he led the way to the right. If he shifted, he could probably follow Kara's scent, but he couldn't risk the darkness in his animal barring him from shifting back, not out in the open like this.

Sweat broke out on his brow. Somewhere above sat Inir, the most dangerous immortal alive. A bastard who, if they couldn't stop him, would free the most vicious immortal who'd ever lived, Satanan, turning the Earth into a living hell.

Hand in hand, Fox and Melisande made their way through the corridors, following the path his animal spirit had shown him. But as they approached an intersection with a second corridor, the magic swept through him yet again, forcing him into his fox, forcing him onto his belly on the cold stone floor.

Frustration and fury roared through his muscles, the fox spirit crying out inside his head, but he couldn't move. He'd been shut down. Again.

Melisande fell to her knees beside him, sliding both hands into his fur, calling up the warmth. And while his animal leaped at the healing gift, Fox felt no easing of the invisible chains this time. Just as the darkness had grown stronger in Castin as he'd breached the stronghold's walls, so, too, had the darkness within himself.

The sound of voices and footsteps heading toward

them from the cross corridor had him whimpering with fury, frantic to shift back.

Go, pet! Someone's coming. Go back to the tunnel, back to Castin, and get out of here!

By the sound of the voices, he guessed he had a minute, maybe two, before the pair—and he was fairly certain there were only two—reached the intersection of the corridors and saw him.

"No," she whispered, pressing her hands more firmly against his back and head. *I'm not leaving you.*

Melisande's warming gift ran through his body, his animal spirit leaping up to accept it, but the darkness refused to let him go.

As the voices grew louder, closer, he became crazed with the need to save her. *Mel, go. Please go.*

She shook her head, her eyes gleaming with determination. *I can take them.*

Mel . . .

Her eyes filled with an emotion that could only be love, and she kissed his head. *I'd give my life for you, Feral.*

He prayed she wasn't about to do just that.

Melisande rose from beside Fox, pulled her knives, and moved to the corner, pressing her back against the wall where she would stay hidden from the approaching Mage until the last moment. Her heart pounded in her chest, perspiration rolled in rivulets down her back as she eyed Fox, lying on the floor, a giant fox trapped by the darkness that had infected his animal spirit. If she failed, he'd die. Or worse.

She eyed his location, deciding he was far enough out of the line of sight that she could wait until she saw the sentinels out of the corner of her eye before she attacked.

Her gaze met the animal's, Fox's, the intensity of emotion in his eyes leaping at her, wrapping around her, filling her with strength.

Deep inside, her old self trembled at the thought of killing again, then sighed, giving up the fight . . . no, *joining* it. Because there was no way in hell that *any* part of her would let Fox die when she might be able to save him. When she loved him.

She would never kill someone who didn't need to die. Not now, at least. Her heart clenched at what she'd done to Julianne. She'd acted so coldly, but the danger to the Ilina race if word of their existence had leaked had been extreme. When it did finally leak, thanks to Kougar, the Mage poison master had attacked immediately and nearly killed them all. Their survival had been a near thing, and only due to Kougar's help. Killing Julianne's parents had been cold, yes, but not wrong.

The hardest thing to live with had always been the deaths of her ninety-six sisters, and for that she would forever feel the deepest remorse. But as Fox had said, she'd never meant for it to happen. She'd been wrong to go to the Mage for help, but she'd had no reason to think he'd turn on her. She couldn't possibly have conceived of it.

As the terrible guilt lifted some of its debilitating weight from her shoulders, her world righted itself a little bit more. Deep inside, she felt a sigh as the battle she'd been waging against herself drained away. Ceraph and warrior joined together as one.

As the footsteps drew near, Melisande tensed for battle, her hand tight around the hilt of her sword. Taking a deep, slow breath, she calmed her mind, drawing on millennia of experience. Her mind clear of the fury, her compassion once more in good working order, she saw battle for what it was. A necessity. In this moment, it was the only way to save the man she loved.

Out of the corner of her eye, the Mage came into view and turned her way. There would be no attacking them from behind, as she'd hoped, but for one instant, she had the element of surprise and she took it.

Calling on her warrior's instincts and experience, she attacked with everything she had. By the time the Mage saw her, she was already swinging. One head rolled and she spun toward the other. The second Mage was strong and skilled and dodged her blows, spinning to catch her in the thigh. But she refused to go down. Fox's life depended on her winning this fight, and she wasn't about to lose. Instead, she rolled, chopped off one of his hands, then launched herself on his back, grabbing his forehead, pulling his head back, and slicing her blade across his throat once, twice . . . his head came off in her hands.

As the second sentinel collapsed, she leaped free with a shuddering breath and a surge of triumph. Dropping the head, she ran to Fox.

Nice job, pet. But the eyes that watched her held worry.

She shoved her bloody hands into his fur, determined to free him from the chains of the darkness this time. As Fox watched her, as she pulled on the energy of her gift, she smiled at him.

"I've had a little practice," she murmured, then smiled. "Five thousand years."

Love shone in his eyes. *You're okay.*

"Better than okay. I feel . . . purged. Free. And I'll feel a hundred times better when I have you on your feet again."

Me, too.

All of a sudden, her healing gift leaped into her hands, twice as powerful as before. And a moment later, Fox shifted back into a man. Bounding to his feet, he hauled her into his arms and kissed her soundly, tenderly.

"You're incredible."

She grinned at him. "You're not so bad yourself, gorgeous."

He returned her grin, then grabbed her hand and started down the hallway. Several minutes later, they were standing before a heavy wooden door, banded with iron, a small barred window at the top.

"Kara," Fox breathed, peering into that window.

"Fox!" the Radiant cried softly.

He turned to Melisande. "We need a key."

Melisande nodded, then searched, but found no sign of one. Returning to Fox she shook her head.

"Roll close to the wall and cover your face, Kara. I'm going to have to break down the door."

Which the Mage would surely hear, but there was no help for it.

"Ready?" Fox called softly.

"Yes," came the muffled reply.

As Melisande moved out of his way, Fox backed up, lifted one powerful leg, and kicked the door in with a monstrous crack of splitting timbers.

They had only minutes, if that, before the Mage swarmed them. Fox leaped through the opening, scooping up Kara.

The Radiant threw her arms around his neck, tears in her eyes. "Thank you, Fox." Her gaze caught Melisande's, a sweet smile of thanks lifting Melisande's heart and bringing tears to her own eyes. "Thank you, both."

"Thank us when we've got you safely back in Lyon's arms," Fox murmured.

Melisande's hand curved around the hilt of her sword. Together, they would return Kara to her mate. Or die trying.

Melisande led the way, backtracking through the passages as Fox brought up the rear, Kara in his arms. In the distance, Fox heard voices and the sound of footsteps. More than a couple this time. And he did not want them to have to fight their way out. Not with Kara so vulnerable. Not with Melisande at risk if they were badly outnumbered.

"Run, Mel," he urged. They needed to get back to the tunnel before they were seen. As she took off, he followed. They passed the two dead Mage and kept going.

Just as they reached the passage that led to the tunnel, a shout went up in the distance. They'd either found the bodies or Kara's open cell. Either way, the Mage knew they had intruders. The good news was, it was clear the Mage had no idea there was any way in or out of the dungeons except by the stairs above, or they'd have had guards posted down here.

Reaching the tunnel, Melisande pulled off the grill and stood back as he ducked in. For one moment, their gazes met, and he saw the steel in her sapphire eyes and knew she was solid.

Melisande replaced the grill and followed him into the tunnel. Behind, he heard the pounding of booted feet and more shouts.

"The Radiant's gone! Find her!"

Melisande carried the flashlight, leading the way back to Castin, who appeared to be collecting dead Mage, by the stack of bodies piled just inside the cave's mouth.

Outside, rain slashed, the wind howling. Thunder crashed in the sky.

Castin motioned with his head. "The coast is clear at the moment. Come on."

Together, they crossed the clearing through the deluge, ducking into the woods without a single shout going up. For the first time, Fox allowed himself a deep breath. If they stayed to this wooded path, straight out from the castle, they might be able to get away without being seen.

When Melisande motioned for Fox to pass her, he shook his head. "You first." He didn't want her out of his sight.

But she threw him a grin, loving him with those warrior eyes. "You're carrying the precious cargo. I'm covering your flank." She laughed, low. "Move your gorgeous ass, Feral."

He threw her a grin that promised all kinds of carnal fun . . . if they got out of here alive . . . and let her bring up the rear. It was damned hard not to try to protect her, but she'd been a warrior for more than a dozen times as long as he'd been alive. And apparently she was one once more, though with her heart and conscience and smile fully intact this time.

They traveled quickly and quietly, hidden by the trees. About a mile from the castle, Fox began to think they just might make a clean getaway. But moments later, Melisande's voice came from behind him.

"We have four Mage on our tail."

"More in front," Castin said. And Fox could see them—eight more appearing over the rise not twenty yards ahead.

Mage sentinels on every side.

Chapter
Nineteen

They were surrounded by Mage, an even dozen of them as they stood in the blinding rain. They'd taken on this many and won once before, but not with an injured woman in their midst. Fox set Kara on the ground, and the three of them quickly surrounded her.

Fox looked at Melisande, and she met his gaze with that same blue steel in her eyes. He nodded, trying to toss her a grin and failing. There was too damned much at stake. He'd been in tighter spots in his life, but never had a battle meant so much to him personally. Because never had the woman he loved been fighting at his side.

"Anyone have an extra knife?" Kara asked.

Castin handed her one, approval in his eyes, before turning to face their attackers.

"And just where do you think you're taking our Radiant?" one of the Mage asked, a smirk on his face as the sentinels slowly closed the circle. That Mage would be the first to die.

Fox shifted, upsizing as far as he could, until the Mage sentinels in front of him took several steps back, eyes wide, faces paling. Damn, he was the size of a pony.

"They're here," Kara said quietly.

And before he could ask what she meant, he heard the low snarls and growls of large, predatory animals and his pulse leaped with thanksgiving. A quick glance behind and he saw them—a lion, jaguar, wolf and cougar coming over the rise behind the Mage and slowly circling until the four made up the outer, and by far the most vicious circle.

Jag's voice slid into his head. *I'm glad to see you and the misses made it, Foxy-woxy.*

Fox grinned. *Damn am I glad to see your sorry furry face, boyo.*

In his mind he heard the sound of Jag's laughter. Then Lyon's stern command. *Protect her.*

Aye. Fox shifted backward, placing Kara between his front legs, where she fit easily. Anyone coming for her was going to have to get past his teeth.

The moment Lyon caught sight of his mate, his beloved Kara, sitting weakly on the ground between the giant fox's forelegs, his control shattered. His logical mind urged him to keep quiet for fear of alerting the rest of the Mage. To attack rationally with cool self-control.

Fuck. That.

The deep, massive roar barreled out of his lion's chest and throat as he leaped for the nearest Mage, the fury and frustration and anguish of the past hours, the past days, fueling his actions until he was caught in a berserker's rage, ripping apart his enemies.

Limbs flew, heads rolled. A blade slashed through his fur and flesh, but he couldn't feel it through the righteous wrath blazing through his mind and muscles. The bastards had taken his Kara!

Thunder crashed around them, hail pelted them from the skies, but still he fought and clawed and destroyed his enemies. With a single swipe of his paw, he tore off the head of his opponent, then turned to attack the next. But there were no more. It was over, the Ferals standing, the Mage all dead.

His gaze flew to Kara, where she stared at him, loving him, tears running down her cheeks. Desperation to feel her in his arms fueled his muscles as he lunged for her, shifting into human form even as Fox

stepped back. And then he was sweeping her into hi
arms, feeling her slender arms tight around his neck
her tear-streaked cheek pressed to his as he held he
against him so tightly, he feared he was crushing her.

His arms shook, his eyes burned as he inhaled he
sweet scent, as he felt her beloved heart beat fast and
strong against his.

"I love you, Lyon." Her words thickened with tears
"I've missed you so much."

"I've been lost without you, little one. They took my
heart when they stole you from me." He pulled away
studying her, touching her face, her hair. "You're pale."
He growled. "They hurt you."

Her mouth tipped up in the sweetest of smiles, the
tears still running down her cheeks. "You're here. I'm
perfect, now."

Her sweet words fell like healing rain onto his
parched soul.

The battle was over.

As Lyon swept Kara into his arms, Fox shifted back
into a man and swept Melisande into his. Holding her
tight, he kissed her soundly, then tucked her against his
side as he turned toward the others. Wulfe's arm was
bleeding, he noticed. And bleeding. With a frown, he
looked at the others and found a cut on Lyon's shoulder
that didn't appear to be healing, and another on Kou-

gar's thigh. So it wasn't just him. And what did that mean?

As Jag sauntered over to them, Melisande grinned at him. "Hello, Jag."

Jag stopped abruptly. "What did you do with Miss . . ah . . . ?"

"Miss Bitch?" she asked saucily. "You'll be happy to know, she's gone. I think. Unless you start making Fox genuinely angry, then you'll see her again in all her bitchy glory."

A smile began to curl at the edges of Jag's mouth. "Well, I'll be damned."

"Let's go." Lyon's voice carried to them, low and urgent.

"We going after Inir?" Wulfe asked.

Lyon shook his head. "Feral House. Priority number one is getting our Radiant safe and secure. If we get ambushed before we escape this mountain, it could take every one of us to protect her. We're not splitting up. Besides . . ." He glanced at his shoulder. "We're not healing, and I want to know why. The Shaman should be able to tell us."

"There are hundreds of sentinels within that fortress," Kara said softly.

Lyon continued, "I'm aware that we may have trouble reaching the stronghold a second time. Inir may move his forces altogether though I think that's unlikely.

But we have an advantage they may not be aware of Wulfe."

At Fox's curious expression, Jag elaborated. "Th Wulfe-man has Daemon blood. He can see the warding.

Holy shite.

"Roar, I'd be happy to . . ." Kougar began.

Lyon shook his head. "No discussion. We're return ing to Feral House to regroup. All of us. We *will* keep Inir and his evil army from freeing Satanan and hi Daemon horde. But not today. Now let's find that ward ing and get out of here."

Wulfe motioned with his head. "The warding is clos est this way." He turned and started running up the hill veering from their original path on a forty-five-degree angle.

Fox grabbed Melisande's hand, and together the ran after him, the warriors surrounding their chief and their Radiant as the rain and hail pummeled them and lightning tore across the sky.

Fox squeezed Melisande's hand. "You fought bril liantly, pet."

She looked up at him with eyes shining with battle lust, and love. "I had no trouble," she said wonderingly "It helped that they were soulless, Daemon-raising scum. But inside, I'm all right, I think. The Ceraph and the warrior are coming to terms. It's still going to take some time to process all that's happened and to work through the guilt issues. But I feel . . . good." Her eyes oftened. "Better than good." But a second later, she bit her lip, worry creasing her brow. "Or I will once we get through that warding."

Feck. The warding. He squeezed her hand tightly. "I've gotten you through it twice, now. I'll do it again. I won't let anything happen to you, Mel. I swear it."

She smiled. "I believe you."

"Fox?" Lyon called.

Fox steered Melisande to Lyon's side. As they ran abreast with the Chief of the Ferals, Lyon gave them both a nod, his gaze meeting Fox's and holding. "I have no words to express my gratitude. To both of you. You honor all of us by being one of us, Fox. The animal spirit chose well."

Lyon's gaze shifted to Melisande. "Did I hear you say you're a Ceraph, Melisande?"

"You're an *angel*?" Jag crowed. There was no speaking too low for Feral hearing, not in this tight group.

But Melisande only smiled, a serene smile flashing with steel. "I was, millennia ago. Soon after the Sacrifice, I was captured by shifters trying to get their animals back. I lost that part of me and everything soft in the months they tortured me. I lost my heart. But Fox has helped me to reclaim it."

Lyon nodded. "A mated pair?"

Fox looked at her, meeting her gaze, and realized he had no doubt it was what he wanted. None. "Yes. If he'll have me."

A sweet, loving smile crossed her lovely face "There's nothing I want more."

Fox grinned, then let out a laugh, his joy uncontainable. Melisande's sweet laughter melded with his.

"The transformative power of love never ceases to amaze me." Lyon smiled. "Welcome, Melisande. I have to admit, I much prefer calling you friend than enemy."

Kara cocked her head. "I'm thinking 'sister' fits you better. The Feral sisterhood always has room for one more if you don't have too many sisters already."

Fox felt Melisande's hand tighten in his. Tears began to shine in her eyes. "I happen to be missing some sisters, as a matter of fact. I would be honored to be considered one of yours, Kara."

Kara grinned. "Done."

They'd traveled another mile when Wulfe said. "There it is."

For once, Fox's gut kicked in when he needed it with a rise of goose bumps on his arms and Wulfe's name in his head.

He turned to Melisande, meeting her worried eyes "Wulfe can help you through safely."

A short distance away, Wulfe pulled up, turned to Melisande, and held out his hand. "You'll come through with me." His gaze met Fox's. "Shift, but stay close just in case."

"You can count on it."

Fox pulled on the power of his animal and followed close behind Wulfe and Melisande. He felt the power slipping along his fur and watched with relief as Melisande walked beside Wulfe without being affected by the warding at all. Daemon blood. Unbelievable.

When they'd fully cleared the warding and put some distance between it and them, Fox shifted back into human form and pulled Melisande tight against him. In the distance, he saw Ilinas materializing. Kougar must have called his mate for transport within seconds of their freedom.

"I can mist again," Melisande said, bone-deep relief in her voice. "I can feel it. Are you ready?"

"Wait a minute." As the small band went to join the newly-arrived Ilinas, Fox turned to Melisande, stroking her precious cheek.

Sapphire eyes turned to his, soft as a summer rain.

"Lyon put you on the spot back there, I'm afraid, but I meant what I said, Mel. I love you. Completely, utterly, madly. I want you to be my mate. But if you need time, or simply want to be lovers, that's all right, too. I will take as much or as little as you'll give me."

Her smile bloomed slowly, stealing his breath. So beautiful. Her eyes overflowed with love. "You were always meant to be mine, Feral. I felt it the first time I saw you. The most beautiful male ever to walk this Earth. And the sweetest. I adore you. I love you. And there is nothing I want more than to be yours, and for you to be mine, for all eternity."

"Aye?" Relief weakened his knees, and he gave a shout, unable to contain his euphoria. He picked her up, swinging her around, loving the sound of her laughter. Loving everything about her.

He'd fallen in love with an angel.

Epilogue

In the cavelike ritual room deep beneath Feral House, firelight flickering over the dark-paneled room, Fox drove into his mate high atop the altar, sealing their mating bond. Nearby, Kougar intoned the ancient rite, dribbling the combined blood of the Ferals on the floor around them. The ritual was as primitive as any Fox had witnessed, dating back far into the mists of time, and somehow incredibly fitting for a man who was half-animal and a woman who'd been alive since the days of the cavemen.

Though all of his Feral brothers circled the altar, Melisande's Ilina sisters stood closest, their backs to the mating couple, acting as a living privacy curtain.

Not that either Melisande or he cared. *Modesty* was not a word in either the Ilinas' or shifters' lexicon.

Fox stared into the beautiful sapphire eyes of his mate as they joined in this most primal of ways, slowly, lovingly, opening hearts, souls, and minds to the power that would bind them for eternity.

The chanting ended. Out of the corner of his eye, between the heads of two Ilina maidens, Fox saw Kougar pour the last of the blood into one of the ritual fires. Power roared through him without warning. He and Melisande came as one in a burst of fireworks and pure joy as the mating bond inside him—inside them both—formed, brilliant in color and strong as steel. Nothing would ever separate them again.

As they stared into one another's eyes, breathless with passion and love, Melisande's eyes grew thoughtful. Perhaps a little sad.

"What is it?" he asked, slain.

"I'd thought the power of the mating bond might make me the Ceraph again."

"And you want that."

She smiled softly. "I want you. Just that."

"You're perfect the way you are, Mel. Everything I've been looking for, even if I didn't know it. And so much more."

She lifted her hands and pressed them to his cheeks, startling him with the sudden blast of healing heat. Deep in his mind, he heard a snarl, then another, a vicious battle erupting inside him. An animal battle. His fox against the darkness?

"What are you doing, pet?" His mate. Goddess, *his mate*. He loved the sound of that.

Her eyes shone with joy. "Healing you as you healed me. My gift is strong through the mating bond, Fox. Give me a minute."

He pressed his hips up, driving himself even deeper inside of her. If they stayed here much longer, he was going to be ready to take her again. "You can have all the minutes of my life, luv."

As his animal brushed his mind, a hazy image appeared in his head of smoke in the form of a fox. The darkness. Battling it was another fox, a red one, smaller and bloody and injured. At first, the smaller fox's attacks made no impact, the smoke re-formed, the darkness remaining whole.

Fox tensed. This was real.

All of a sudden, warm energy began to flow through his body, similar to radiance, but different. Softer. *Love*. He felt so much love. Deep inside, his animal responded, leaping with joy and gratitude, growing larger, stronger.

"Help him, Fox," Melisande urged. "Concentrate. Between the three of us, we'll destroy that darkness in your spirit right now. I can do this."

Fox did as she asked, focusing on the smoke's demise as Melisande's heat rushed into him, as the red fox grew

larger, and larger, until he towered over the smoke fox
And then he attacked, ripping away chunks of darkness that no longer re-formed, again and again until the
darkness was no more.

The red fox turned to him, grinning, love and gratitude in his eyes. Then turned to Melisande with a look
of utter adoration.

Inside, he felt whole, his animal's tension draining
away. Fox blinked. "It's done."

Melisande laughed. "It's done."

With a sound kiss, he pulled out of her. When they'd
straightened their clothing, he swung his new bride, in
her diaphanous ruby mating gown, off the altar.

A moment later, Ariana was throwing her arms
around Melisande, hugging her tight, both women
laughing, crying. Then one by one, the others stepped
forward, Ferals with their mates, and the Ilinas, in a
flurry of hugs and congratulations. Melisande's musi-
cal laughter rang through the ritual room, her beauty
incandescent, her golden hair falling to the small
of her back, the ruby gown clinging lovingly to her
curves.

He swallowed as he watched her, marveling that this
wonderful, exciting, darling woman was his. Goddess,
he loved her.

Olivia enfolded Melisande in a big hug. "Welcome
to the family."

Jag placed a kiss on Melisande's cheek, then shook

his head with a grin. "No offense, sister, but you are the *last* female I ever expected to do that to."

Olivia rolled her eyes.

Melisande reached up and kissed Jag's cheek in return. "No offense taken, Jag. I'm glad we're friends."

"Me, too . . ." His voice trailed off as he cocked his head. "I'm short on female angel names. But never fear, Blondie, I'll come up with something to call you."

Melisande laughed. "You could call me by my name."

"And break tradition?" He grinned. "Hell no, I'll come up with something."

Kara gave them both a hug from the safety of Lyon's arms. The chief of the Ferals had barely let go of her since they'd arrived back at Feral House, and Fox couldn't blame him one bit. His heart utterly stolen by another, he didn't know how the male had survived the abduction of his mate.

Kara was still weak and, according to the Shaman, would get no stronger until she was able to undo the damage the evil Ferals had done to her. The only thing he believed would help was bringing a good Feral into his or her animal. And while three new Ferals currently resided in the prison beneath the house, no one was willing to stake her life on any of the three being the best of his line, not even Castin. Because if they guessed wrong, if Kara brought one more evil Feral into his animal, she would die. The Shaman was quite certain of that.

Fox hated that Castin now languished in the prison along with Rikkert and a third newly marked Feral who'd arrived while they were stuck in the labyrinth. Though his gut had been silent on the issue, his instincts told him that Castin was an honorable male. But his certainty was far from one hundred percent. And while he detested that Castin's life might be on the line, there was far too much at stake to set him free. The fate of the world might well depend on the decisions they made about the new Ferals. All they could do was hope they found a way to tell the good Ferals from the bad. And soon.

Kougar and Ariana joined them, and Kougar bent to give Melisande a kiss on the cheek. Her eyes widened with surprise. As he pulled back, she watched him, bemused.

"Does this mean you've forgiven me?" she asked quietly.

Fox suspected she was asking about what she'd done to his and Ariana's mating bond a thousand years ago. The poison had forced Ariana to sever the mating bond for fear of killing Kougar. And while, thanks to Melisande's machinations, the incomplete bond was severable, Kougar had thought Ariana dead, and had mourned her for a thousand years.

Kougar's eyes turned thoughtful. "If you were then as you are now, would you have tried to sabotage our mating bond?"

Melisande didn't answer immediately, but when she did, it was with a sigh. "I was so filled with bitterness, Kougar. My hatred for the shifters knew no bounds, and I genuinely believed Ariana would rue the day she wed you. I honestly believed I was saving her that pain by keeping the mating bond from fully forming. That way she'd be able to walk away from you, unharmed." She shook her head. "I will always do what I think must be done to protect her and the rest of my sisters." Her eyes cut to Fox, softening, filling with love as she met his gaze. "And to protect my mate, his brothers, and their wives."

Slowly, she turned back to Kougar. "But I no longer see the world through bitterness and hatred alone. My compassion has returned, and my wisdom, I would like to think. So, no, I would not do it all over again. I have seen, for a while now, the truth I was too blind to see then—that you're perfect together. You're stronger, we're all stronger, for the love you two share."

Kougar nodded once, slowly. "I forgive you, Melisande. I regret those years as I regret what you endured at the hands of the shifters. The past cannot be undone. But the future is ours." He turned to Fox, extending his arm. "You did a hell of a job, Fox. A hell of a job. Both of you."

Fox nodded his thanks. Ever since their return, the others had been treating him like a conquering hero. It felt good to contribute, especially something that mat-

tered so much in so many ways. It was his animal spirit
that was the real hero, sending him the flashbacks that
told him what he needed to know to find Kara. And it
was Melisande, of course, who'd saved them both.

An hour later, as they shared champagne and wedding cake in the dining room, Hawke came to stand
behind Melisande, a hand on her shoulder.

"They're back," he said.

Melisande nodded, then turned to Fox, trepidation in
those beautiful eyes of hers.

He took her hand. "Are you ready for this?"

Her mouth set with determination. "As ready as I'll
ever be." Hand in hand, they walked to the foyer where
Zeeland and Julianne were just entering the house.
Hawke had told them the pair had returned to the Alexandria enclave just that morning to replenish clothes
and toiletries and would be back later that afternoon.
Fox was just as glad that Zee and his bride had missed
the teams' homecoming and the quickly performed
mating ceremony.

As Julianne strolled into the foyer ahead of Zeeland
she glanced at Melisande, then jerked with disbelief.
Zeeland joined his mate a second later, his arm going
around her waist, hauling her back against him as he
stared with surprise and uncertainty.

"Melisande?" Zeeland asked, his tone half question,
half snarl.

Melisande stepped forward, releasing Fox's hand.

and he let her go. Now that she could mist again, he knew she was in no real danger. But he would take no chances. "She's my mate," he told his old friend. "As of an hour ago."

Zeeland's eyes registered shock as his gaze returned to Melisande. "You've changed."

His angel nodded with serene grace, so unlike the spitfire she'd been such a short while ago. "I have. In more ways than you can possibly know." She stopped half a dozen feet in front of them and told the pair her story. "When I took your parents, Julianne, I did what I felt had to be done, but it was cold, callous, and cruel beyond measure. I don't know what other choice I might have had, or might have chosen had my conscience still been intact, had I been able to *feel*, but I should have found something that wouldn't take the lives of two good people and leave their daughter an orphan. I'm sorry. From the bottom of my heart, I apologize."

To Fox's surprise and consternation, Melisande pulled a knife he hadn't realized she'd strapped to her thigh, and handed it, hilt first, to Julianne. "I will accept any retribution you see fit to inflict, now or in the future, short of death. I'll not have my mate suffer."

Zeeland's gaze met Fox's, acknowledging the Feral's silent warning . . . if either of them hurt Melisande, they'd be lucky to leave Feral House alive.

Julianne pulled Zeeland's protective arm from around her waist and stepped forward. Fox tensed, but Julianne reached for Melisande's free hand, not the knife. Gripping Melisande's hand in hers, she said, "I'm sorry for all you endured. I'm sorry for all you lost."

Melisande nodded. "I hope someday you'll be able to forgive me, Julianne. I have a lot of regrets, and it will be a long time before I'm ever able to fully forgive myself." She put her knife away, took both of Julianne's hands, and they stood there in that way women sometimes did when they had too much to say and no words were adequate, two women of grace, strength, and compassion.

Finally, Julianne pulled her hands from Melisande's and returned to Zeeland's side. Melisande faced the male. "My apologies, Zeeland."

Zee nodded, still wary, and more than a little confused. Fox doubted the male would let his guard down entirely with her anytime soon. But unless she attacked Julianne, he'd never hurt her. Not after Fox had taken her as his mate.

That evening, alone in his bedroom, Fox took his beloved into his arms. "I adore you, do you know that?"

She grinned at him. "Not as much as I adore you."

He kissed her soundly. "Do you want me to show you how much I adore you?" He began to slide the ritual gown from her shoulder.

"Show me, my beautiful shifter."

And he did.

At Avon Books, we know your passion for romance—once you finish one of our novels, you find yourself wanting more.

May we tempt you with . . .

- **Excerpts** from our upcoming releases.

- Entertaining **extras**, including authors' personal photo albums and book lists.

- Behind-the-scenes **scoop** on your favorite characters and series.

- **Sweepstakes** for the chance to win free books, romantic getaways, and other fun prizes.

- Writing **tips** from our authors and editors.

- **Blog** with our authors and find out why they love to write romance.

- **Exclusive content** that's not contained within the pages of our novels.

Join us at
www.avonbooks.com